VAMPIRE HUNTERS

AN INCOMPLETE RECORD OF PERSONAL ACCOUNTS

Speculation Publications

ISBN-13: 979-8-9918553-4-1
Ebook : 979-8-9918553-6-5

Original Illustrations:
Pg 84 Skull Potion by Sarah Doebereiner
Pg 128 by Caolán Mac An Aircinn
Pgs 45, 97,146,200,222 - L Allingham
Photos from Vampa Museum
Used with permission from Ed Crimi - Pgs 210 & 272
Other Modified Photos from Vecteezy and Envato
Public Domain Images:
Tablet Supposed to Contain a Mention of the Babylonian Garden of Eden - University of
Toronto Libraries
"The Right Hand of God Protecting the Faithful against the Demons" - The Metropolitan
Museum
Modified from "Dante and Virgil entering the area devoted to simoniacs and magicians"
from The Divine Comedy
"Battles prophesied" from The Holkham Bible Picture Book
"The Nobleman" By Hans Holbein
Modifed from "The Subject and His Skeleton" from Magic: Stage Illusions and Scientific
Diversions, including Trick Photography
"Ephialtes" by Louis le Breton
"But, for many minutes, the heart beat on with a muffled sound" by Harry Clarke
"Civil War Amputation Being Performed in Front of a Hospital Tent, Gettysburg, July
1863" from US National Library of Medicine
Modified "Frozen Russian soldiers melting away before the Japanese army (the Rising
Sun)" By Kobayashi Kiyochika
Modified from "Skeleton of a Human Being (Heroic)" by Cornelis van Dyk
"Greetings from Florida, (the Sunshine State)"
Modified from "Different Stages of a Diseased Tongue with Yellow Fever" by Charles
Philibert de Lasteyrie
"And a Large Bird, Descending From the Sky, Hurls Itself Against the Topmost Point
of Her Hair" by Odilon Redon
"The Bite" by Edvard Munch.
* "Be Careful What you Wish for" is a retelling of "The Legend of Sleepy Hollow" by
Washington Irving

Cover Art and book layout: LCW Allingham
Copyright © 2025 Speculation Publications LLC
Published by Speculation Publications

No part of this book was created by AI

For More Information go to www.speculationpub.com

Content Warning

The stories are gory af.

Infanticide, suicide, homicide, animal harm,
racism, sexism, homophobia, suggestion of
sexual assault, body horror, psychological
horror, starvation, war, despair and graphic
depictions of torture.

Please proceed with care for yourself.

For a specific list according to story go to

www.speculationpub.com/vampire_hunters

Vampire Hunters

AN INCOMPLETE RECORD OF PERSONAL ACCOUNTS

Edited by LCW Allingham and River Eno

Table of Contents

An Incomplete Record of Personal Accounts

Part 1

Sir Charles Titus Hawthorne
44 Prospect Park West
Brooklyn, NY 11215

September 13, 1890

Miss Cynthia Bledsoe
Valley Union College for Young Ladies
7916 Williamson Road
Roanoke, VA 24020

To my beloved niece, Cynthia,

My child, it grieves me to leave you with this
burden. These records I have spent my life collecting.
Forgive the state of them. I always thought I had
more time to organize them. Make them make sense.
I have asked my secretary to type them up,
especially the translations, so at least you may be
able to read them.

You will understand more as you go through it
all, but here is the heart of the matter.

Vampires are real, my girl. They come in many
different forms, but all of them feed on men.

However, there are also those who protect us, who
hunt them.

I have done my little part in collecting their
accounts. Now I pass this task onto you.

You were always the most clever of your siblings.
Your brothers, no matter how your mother doted on
them, were great dolts compared to my little scholar.

You may already suspect, it was I who paid for your university even when your great fool of a father objected and tried to marry you to that awful solicitor. Though I always knew you would be my heir, I have never been more sure than when you turned him down for education.

I hope my assets will ease the discomfort of this task.

I only wish I had more time to teach you, but I am sure you will succeed, even where I failed.

With great affection and admiration,

Sir Charles Titus Hawthorne

An Incomplete Record of Personal Accounts

In 1875, an archaeological dig in northwest Anatolia uncovered a small tomb. Inside were fragments of clay tablets. They provide a Mycenaean soldier's firsthand account of his encounters with a strix, or vampire, during the siege of Troy. After a lengthy process of authentication, these translations, from the original Linear B script, are published here for the first time.

1. THE STRIX - George K. Angelou

Lunation 3, year 12 of the reign of Agamemnon (c. March 1194BC)

Fragment 1

We put the ships to sea again today, but didn't get far. Why won't the winds blow? Does Artemis truly oppose us, as Achilles' Myrmidons claim?

The only good that comes of this delay is the time spent with Broteas, the precious hours trying to best each-other in training, or retelling old tales by the campfire, while drinking too much honeyed wine. The years since we were last together, back on Samothrace, seem to have melted away.

I've heard a priestess has been sent for. Perhaps she'll placate Artemis, so Broteas and I can at last stop playing at being heroes, and fight side by side in a real battle.

Fragment 2

I almost failed to recognize the priestess as she came ashore, until I saw Broteas' broad grin. It is Iphigenia, daughter of Agamemnon, who was with us there on Samothrace, as we partook in the Bacchic mysteries. I don't know whether to be happy for Broteas, or sad for myself, as I doubt I'll see much of him once Iphigenia has finished preparing for the ritual.

Fragment 3

They killed her. They killed Iphigenia. In the end, she consented to it, but I know it's only because she didn't have a choice. Even when she had stopped pleading, her eyes still begged her father for mercy. They sacrificed Iphigenia, under the light of the full moon, so Artemis would release the winds.

Afterwards, Agamemnon approached Broteas. "It's a good omen that you're here with us today, you who bear my ancestor's name, and share my family's curse," said the Archon. "Tomorrow will bring the wind, and then a victory just as swift."

I thought Broteas might vomit right there and then, at the great king's feet, but he held off long enough to be invited to his tent.

"I hear your friend is a man of letters," Agamemnon added, as if I wasn't there. "Bring him with you too, I need someone to chronicle our glories."

Inside the tent he offered us wine, but it did not taste of honey. I know not what it was mixed with, but Broteas looked sick once more as he took a sip.

I had meant to send these papyrus parchments to you on the first ship back to Argolis, but I can't risk anyone seeing them now. I will have to hide them until my return.

Lunation 6, year 12 of the reign of Agamemnon (c. June 1194BC)

Fragment 4

We arrived on Trojan shores at last today, but our joy was short-lived. Priam's sons awaited us on the beach. Hundreds of our men must have perished, as their arrows forced us back into the sea. It seemed the war was lost before it had even begun, until the Myrmidons arrived. Upon the prow of their lead vessel stood Achilles, bright as the sun, as he began launching one spear after another at the enemy, each tip laced with certain death. As the Trojans fell back, we were able to make landfall at last and rout them!

When they were gone we combed the beach for fallen treasures. I found the snapped off tip of one of Achilles' spears and couldn't resist taking it, though it has no real worth. I will fasten it to my linothorax, as a good luck charm.

I hope Broteas won't mock me too much for my superstitious keepsake.

Fragment 5

After the battle on the beach, I found Broteas surrounded by Agamemnon's honor guard, an arrow protruding from his side. Four days have passed since then, and he has become ever paler, his brow ever hotter. Agamemnon has called for the healer Machaon, but I fear that even he lacks the skill to mend such a wound. Poor Broteas, he dreamed for three years of finding glory here on Trojan shore, yet it lasted but a moment.

Fragment 6

Broteas' condition continues to worsen. Tomorrow I will take part in a raid, and I fear he may have already passed by the time I return.

Fragment 7

When I returned to camp last night, I was shocked to find Broteas out of his tent and supping with some of Agamemnon's guards. His fever has broken at last, though he's still horribly pale. I couldn't help but throw my arms around him, and I think it embarrassed him, because he stood stiff and awkward.

Agamemnon claims the credit. He says that Broteas' recovery is proof his familial curse has been lifted by his sacrifice. Let him say as he pleases. Today, I can feel only joy.

Lunation 8, year 12 of the reign of Agamemnon (c. August 1194BC)

Fragment 8

Broteas and I went on our first raid together today. In training I had been able to hold my own against Broteas, even best him on occasion, but in the heat of battle I have never seen a warrior as fierce as him, save for Achilles. He still appears pale and gaunt following his sickness, so I can only imagine the heights he'll reach when he's fully recovered.

In the camp the spoils of war are beginning to pile high. Bronze armour, precious stones, and slave girls. Fear not though, I have not eyes for them.

Lunation 1, year 13 of the reign of Agamemnon (c. January 1195BC)

Fragment 9

The war goes well, with many battles won, but strange happenings have begun to plague the camp. Our captives, mostly the women, keep going missing. At first Agamemnon suspected a traitor was helping them to escape, but then we began to find body parts in the scrublands outside the camp. Only the Myrmidons have been spared; all of Achille's women are safe and accounted for.

Lunation 4, year 13 of the reign of Agamemnon (c. April 1195BC)

Fragment 10

The disappearances are becoming more and more frequent. Some of the men claim to have seen a strix prowling around the camp. I know such talk is superstitious nonsense, and yet each night, I dream of being enveloped by dark wings.

Fragment 11

Last night, as I patrolled the camp, I heard a woman calling out from one of the tents. At first I gave it a wide berth, mistaking her cries for moans of pleasure, but they soon became anguished screams. I drew my sword and cut my way in through the back of the tent, hoping to catch her attacker by surprise. The girl, not more than eighteen years old, was lying still and naked on the floor. Kneeling over her was something like a man, its skin a strange shade of grey, its jaws still locked around her neck.

I shouted something, and it turned towards me, gaunt, ghoulish, yet unmistakable; the strix, and all at once Broteas too. He gave a shriek, more terrible than his victim's, and rushed from the tent.

Fragment 12

No one will listen to me. I reported the attack to Agamemnon's guards, but they were only interested in disposing of the body, and pretending all was well. Agamemnon and Achilles have been at each other's throats again, arguing over treasures and tactics. Nothing but this rivalry seems to trouble the Archon. If I'm going to stop Broteas, I'll have to do it myself.

Lunation 5, year 13 of the rule of Agamemnon (c. May 1195BC)

Fragment 13

The Trojans raided us today, slaughtering our cattle, and threatening the camp itself. I was part of a hastily assembled force sent to repel them, as was Broteas. He fought like a demon, and only became fiercer as the battle went on.

There was a moment of confusion as Trojan reinforcements appeared at our flank, and suddenly Broteas and I found ourselves cut off from the other men. He had his back to me, and I had my sword in hand. I could have struck him down there and then, and no one would have ever known, but I became frozen, and the moment passed. If another girl is taken tonight, her blood will be on my hands.

Fragment 14

Every day; more Trojan raids. Every night; more girls dragged off by Broteas. I can bear this no longer.

Lunation 7, year 13 of the rule of Agamemnon (c. July 1195BC)

Fragment 15

I asked Broteas to ride out with me this morning, so we could talk. I thought he'd find an excuse not to come, but responded with a solemn nod. We went along the coast, for miles and miles, without a word, until we reached a small cove. Neither of us wanted to stop, yet we both knew we must, and that this was as good a place as any. I really did want to talk to him, to beg him to stop what he was doing. I wanted to reassure him we'd find a healer, or an oracle, to instruct us on how to reverse the curse of Iphigenia's blood. In the end though, it took but a glance for him to know my thoughts, and to reject them.

We dismounted from our horses and drew our swords. We stood silently with them by our sides for a while, until I summoned up the memory of the girl in the tent, and Broteas' lips upon her throat. "No more," I cried, to myself as much as to him. "No more girls gone missing, no more bones buried in the sand." Still Broteas did not move, so I swung for him.

Now he moved, with inhuman speed and grace. He evaded my slash with ease, and then responded with a volley of his own. I desperately blocked and dodged and parried, while he barely broke a sweat. I knew I couldn't hold him off for long, so I tried to surprise him with a sudden lunge, aimed at his heart. I succeeded only in losing my sword, as he batted it away.

He dived at me with his own blade held high, and I realised, too late, that this was but a feint. Instead of bringing it down, he grabbed my throat with his free hand and wrestled me to the floor. His teeth grew sharp and his flesh became grey as he held me in place, eying my throat.

I groped desperately around me, though I knew both my sword and his were out of reach. As his lips neared my flesh, and I felt his breath upon my neck, at last my hand brushed upon something other than sand.

From where it had hung since that first day upon Trojan shores, I pulled free my lucky charm, and this time I did not hesitate. I thrust the tip of Achille's broken spear into the strix's heart. For just a moment, it looked like Broteas once more.

Fragment 16

I returned to camp leading Broteas' horse, his body lying limp across its back. I told Agamemnon that we had been attacked by Trojans, and that Broteas had died a hero, saving me. That night we made a pyre for him, and placed his ashes in a bronze goblet. The next, I was at last able to weep for him, as I etched his name upon his tomb, high on a hill facing out west to Achaean shores. I wished then that I could leave for those shores, just take a boat and go, but there were three men in the great king's tent on the night of Iphigenia's death, three who drank the cursed wine. Does the Archon understand what he has done? Does he know what Broteas was, and what we will both become? Perhaps it would be better if none of us returned home.

Fragment 17

The next morning I visited Broteas' tomb again. I spent hours there, talking to him as if he sat beside me. Later, as I headed back to camp, I was confronted by Agamemnon and his guards. They had searched my tent and found my parchments. The Archon condemned me for treason. I tried to run, but they knocked me to the ground. I tried to warn them that what I had written was true, but the great king's only response was to pierce my side with his spear, while the others held me down. They dragged me back up the hill to Broteas' tomb, and rolled aside the boulder with which it had been sealed. They cast me in, along with my parchments, and the clay tablets upon which I was supposed to record Agamemnon's exploits.

A fever came over me as I lay there, soaked in blood and sweat. I don't know how long has passed since that day, only that sometime later, I awoke again, changed, and yet the same. I wonder sometimes if my flesh has become pallid grey, as Broteas' had been, but I have no way to tell. Within the tomb there is no light, no day or night, no sun, no moon. My only companion is Broteas, his silent ashes watching over me.

I must accept now that it will be long years before this tomb is opened, and that I will probably never see you again. I must accept, too, that you will likely never even read these words. I can only hope that whatever lie you were told about my fate, it was a comforting one.

All that's left for me is to finish my work, as best I can. Aided by the unnatural sight, and unnatural life, bestowed by Iphigenia's blood, I have painstakingly transferred my words from papyrus to clay, that they might withstand the test of time. I have told Agamemnon's story, as he once commanded me to, though not the version he'd choose. I failed to stop him here at Troy, and now I can only hope my words will one day reach someone who can. To them I say; beware the twice cursed line of the Atreides. Hunt them, until they are erased from the earth.

For my part, I know what I must do. As I engrave these final words, the broken tip of Achilles spear lies close to me. It's time for me to rest at last, with Broteas by my side.

EVS INAOVTORIVM MEV INENOE ONE AO AOIV

```
Though considered by many to be a myth,
the legend of Robin Hood has persevered
in English folklore for centuries. The
recently discovered 'Sherwood Papers'
however, suggest that the story may be
darker and stranger than any of the
previous tellings.
```

2. THE SHERWOOD PAPERS - Dale Parnell

3 November, 1191

I did not believe it, but it is true. The devil has come to England.

King Richard left, running half-way across the known world to fight his holy crusade. Seeking God's glory rather than defending his own people. And in his absence his brother, John Lackland — the Count of Mortain, has returned from France seeking power and influence; a snake intent on filling his own pockets, taxing good, honest yeomen of the land. Those who stand against him find themselves imprisoned in the Tower of London. There are rumours that he courts an alliance with France, and the cities run with whispers of treason and war.

I had thought this the extent of his evil. I was wrong.

I do not know why I write these pages. The things I have witnessed are not of this world and fall so far from God's grace that I fear the country is lost. Yet whilst I have strength, I will fight. I must.

7 November, 1191

We have made camp at the Major Oak, deep in the Kingswood. Will and Little John say the game is scarce, and I don't yet have the heart to tell them why. Sherwood was once a vast and teeming forest preserve, fit for the very finest hunts. Now the trees stand silent, stoic. You feel it all about you, a darkness and a sadness also. Death layered upon death layered upon death. It bleeds into the ground, hangs cold and angry in the air.

I pray that we have not come too late.

9 November, 1191

We found our first encampment early this morning, four or five crude huts fashioned from sticks and sod, damp with fresh rain so the constant drip-drip-drip played all about us. There were few belongings scattered around, torn rags, and spoiled bread crushed into the bare soil. We set to searching the area, following tracks that led through the waist-high bracken, and gradually, one by one, we found the bodies.

A man hardens to almost any situation; labour, imprisonment, even death. I had seen victims before, it is what led me on this path, but they had been soldiers. Stout men who had long-since become numb to the horrors of the world and showed no fear at the end of things.

But this was different. This camp contained families; young men and women barely grown with children of their own, some with babes still in their arms. Innocents who by rights should have had God's protection, whose only crime was their poverty. They were nothing more than cattle to the monsters who hunted them, stalked them in the cold, dark nights and who fell upon them as frenzied demons, ripping the life from them and leaving their twisted, terrified corpses to rot in the open air.

I heard Will Scarlet cry out, and arrived at the same time as Little John. We found him weeping on his knees, cradling the body of a young girl of maybe twelve, the headless corpse of an infant clasped in her arms.

We gathered the bodies and the Friar gave last rites before we buried them. And as the moon rose high above the bare branches over our heads, I told the men what we faced.

John Lackland is more than a usurper, more than a count of the French courts seeking the English throne. He is a man cursed, a demon. He is vampyre, a creature of death and blood. And he has brought his unholy plague to England's shores.

15 December, 1191

We have captured a warden of the forest, a sickly weasel of a man who fashioned his own grand title of High Sheriff of Nottinghamshire, a position which must have been ratified by John the Usurper to serve his own needs. This so-called sheriff should have been minding the wildlife; managing the deer and boar populations for hunting parties, monitoring grouse and pheasant stocks and tending the land. But there is a sickness in this man's mind that reduces his opinion of his fellow man to that of a lowly beast. He is without empathy or pity, and seeks only his own reward. He claims a familial bond with Count John, and on more than one occasion during our interrogation of him, referred to the man as his master. My men had hoped to extract information from him with righteous force, but the man is such a coward that we had barely asked a question before he was spilling his guts. He showed no remorse or guilt during his confession, even grinning at his recollections. It took all my strength not to strike him down then and there in the mud.

His role, these past months, had been to ensure the Kingswood held a steady population of peasants; impoverished families with nowhere else to turn and who would not dare question the Sheriff's supposed authority. They were to be the new game of the forest, cattle for the nobility to feed upon.

It sickened me to speak with the man, to suffer his existence made the world less bright, less good. But our torment bore fruit.

We have learned that a hunt has been planned, and that the Usurper himself is to host a party from France. King Phillip and his courtiers, along with John's own inner council, will be in Sherwood in three days' time.

I do not know how far the count's plague has travelled, or how many of the English and French courts have been cursed. But I do know that it began with him, and I pray that by striking this serpent's head from its body, it may yet save their souls.

17 December, 1191

Our plan is simple. We know the location of the planned hunt—a new settlement in the south of the forest, and for two days we have learned the lay of the land. Every tree, shrub and pasture. We dug traps, re-strung our bows and sharpened our swords. A plain, fire-hardened arrow to the heart will stop the creatures, but they are just as easily killed by decapitation. Any other wounds only seem to enrage them, and I made this point as clear as I could to the men.

Little John has taken to carrying an executioner's axe, and to see his towering frame welding it is a sight of pure terror. I worry the damage I have wrought on these men, Little John especially. He is a rock when I find myself wavering, and in all the years I have known him I have never seen his good humour fail. But since coming to Sherwood he is changed. I know there is nothing I could say to make him abandon me or my cause, and for that I love him as if he were my brother. But in that same breath I see that I have opened his eyes to an evil that no man should bear. I think maybe I was too afraid to face it alone, but a horror shared is not a horror halved. God may yet forgive me, however I don't know that I can ever forgive myself.

18 December, 1191

We are lost.

The plan was solid, and as a full, pale moon stared down on us we heard the hunting party approach. They made no attempt to hide themselves, and the attitude of wealth and privilege sat rank upon them all. The lead coach bore Count John's emblem, and for one brief moment I caught sight of the man, his pinched face staring out into the forest, hungry eyes gleaming in silver moonlight. I was ready to give the order when I saw her, heard her high, excited voice. She appeared at the coach window, howling and laughing like a banshee, her once-gentle features twisted into something primal and wicked.

Marion.

I had thought her dead, I had mourned her these past three years. I still remember the heat of the fire, the sounds as her father's house collapsed into flaming rubble. I knew of her family's connection to Count John, but he was in France at the time, he had been forbidden by King Richard from entering London. Little John recognised her, and I saw in his face that he knew. He knew I could not proceed. He signalled the men to stand down, and the hunting party passed us, disappearing into the dark of the forest.

The men have questions, but I have no answers.

I have nothing.

My Marion. He was there that night. He may even have set the fire that destroyed your father's home, that took the life of your parents, your sisters. How long had he coveted you, I wonder?

And when did he curse you? When did he turn you into the thing I saw tonight?

25 December, 1191

I went alone to the settlement.

I found the bodies and dug a grave for each one. Their blank, dead eyes stared up at me and a dozen silent voices asked me why I had left them to die.

I found Marion's necklace; a gold-set ruby I had given her as a declaration of my love, grasped in the tiny, bloodstained hands of a young boy. He couldn't have been older than four years. I lost myself for a while after that, and came to my senses stood in a freezing stream, miles from the settlement, my hands dripping red into the running water, washing away the last of my madness.

I did not know of your fate, Marion, and for that I am truly sorry. I cannot make amends for what you have become, for what you have done, but I can release you from damnation.

And by God, I can punish the man who did this to you.

17 February, 1192

The mist sits heavy between the trees this morning, blurring the edges of our camp which has grown five-fold these past weeks. We do all we can, seeking out the camps and huddled settlements that have been brought to the forest, and where we can convince them of the danger, we bring them back to the Major Oak. The men have built barricades, setting traps and tripwires at the perimeter that might help warn us of any approaching evil. But not all believe our tale, and not every group will come with us. We leave them what weapons we can spare, along with instructions of how to find us. I pray they will change their minds, but too often we have heard screams carried across the night sky. I mark them all, and I swear the count will answer for every life he has taken.

20 February, 1192

Little John claims to have spied will-o'-wisps again last night, out beyond the boundaries. He fears we are haunted, whereas the Friar laughs them away as one of God's own mysteries.

I do not know what they are, though I believe I have come to recognise the pattern of their appearance, for every morning following their sighting we discover a camp raided, the bodies bloodied and lifeless. They are a warning, whether from God or some unknown force, the message is clear enough. The Usurper and his unholy flock are near.

27 February, 1192

We have sent the Sheriff away. His presence in the camp had become unbearable, and twisted though he is, I could not bear to kill the man. He is possessed by his master's will and has forgotten his own humanity. I could no more strike down a sick mongrel than I could him. And he may yet serve our needs. I have sent him back to his master with a message—Sherwood and its people are protected.

3 March,1192

I made a mistake.
I had hoped to warn the count away from the forest. Instead I have enraged him.

They attacked last night, encircling the camp with some twenty or thirty of their kind. They moved silently, falling upon us from all directions with blood-chilling screams. I never saw the count himself, nor Marion thank God, but many of their host I did recognise, including the King of France himself.

We fought as best we could, but these creatures move with unnatural speed, seeming to slip in and out of the darkness as if they were shadows themselves, and falling upon their prey with claws and fangs gleaming white. Many of the men, women and children we had sworn to protect fled into the forest, so few have returned this morning.

I will muster the men, and we will search the area for survivors, though after that I fear I have no idea how to keep them safe.

4 March, 1192

Will Scarlet is dead.

We found him some two miles from the camp late yesterday afternoon, and though his wounds were severe he clung to life. Little John carried him back, I have never witnessed such tenderness in him, and the good Friar attended Will as best he could. But by evening a fever had overcome him, and he began speaking such dark riddles and blasphemy.

This then was the truth of the count's methods. Whatever evil lies in the count's heart, its poison is passed in the creatures' bite. As the fever took him, Will became more deranged, screaming and writhing on the ground as if his very soul were being tortured. And then near the end there came a brief lucid moment of clarity, and as Will's eyes met mine, he was able to speak one last prayer—

"Kill me, that I might still be embraced by God in Heaven."

My brother died by my hand, and I am damned for that. But the count will answer for his death also, I swear it.

15 May, 1192

We have a hope, small though it is.

We have learned that the count is to host a gathering at the castle in Nottingham. Reports from France say that Phillip and his entire court are to be in attendance, and there is a good chance that any English nobility invited will be vampyre also.

I have spoken with the men and put my plan to them. I had hoped to have at least half stand with me, but in fact they have all agreed. Will Scarlet's death was not the last—the enemy's raids on our camp have continued, and we have lost many friends and brothers, and the good people of this land live in fear and poverty. We are losing the fight, and as our numbers decline the count brings more and more under his control. If we do not act now, their kind will wash over this country as a flood, and England shall drown in spilled blood.

28 May, 1192

We have trained and prepared. Most of the women of the camp have taken the children and left. I would not let them tell any of us where, for if we are captured we could be made to give up their location. Some of the women made a case that they should be allowed to fight alongside the men, and I could not refuse them. Their skill and their spirit are just as strong, as is their right to fight for their families, their land. We stand together before this darkness, and I will use every blade and arrow I can muster.

I had ordered the good Friar to leave with the others, but he refused. I think it is the first and only time we have ever had cross words. In the end, he simply told me that he did not fear death and that it was God's plan that had crossed our paths.

It is strange to hear the camp so quiet, to see everything so still and empty. Only Little John seems to have any life about him, sharpening swords and singing in his soft, low voice a ballad of a lone knight riding to face down a fierce dragon. The dragon is old and wicked, and the knight is young, untested. Yet he is brave and good, and his heart is strong.

And sometimes that is enough.

1 June, 1192

We have watched parties arrive at the castle all day, black carriages with the windows all barred by thick velvet curtains.

As the sun set, the evening air cooled, and a blood-red moon rose steadily in the black sky, hanging over the castle like a great, eyeless face.

The men and women are in place, and the last of the carriages has arrived. I do not know what will happen this night, or even if we have a chance at all.

But where there is a hope, and good, strong hearts, then anything is possible.

Testimony of Friar Tuck. 4 June, 1192.

We waited for two days as our friends lay siege to the castle, and the evil that lay within. On the third day, hearing no sounds coming from within for several hours, we entered. It had always been Robin's plan to hold a group back, whether to act as a second wave of attack or provide reinforcements. I do not know what happened within the castle, only that we found many dead from both sides.

Little John was found alive, though barely. I do not know if he will survive the night, but he is strong and stubborn, and he may yet surprise even the Good Lord Himself.

Our other brothers and sisters were found and identified one by one, and we have put them to rest.

Of the count, no sign could be found. I fear he has slipped our grasp, escaping the castle unseen during the fighting. The grim work of matching severed heads to noble bodies continues, and it may be several more days before we know the extent of our success or failure in our fight against this unholy evil.

It was Robin's body that we found last of all. He was discovered in one of the high towers, cradled arm in arm with Marion, both their hearts pierced with arrows.

We buried them side by side at the base of the Major Oak, leaving no other marker than the great tree itself.

As per his final instruction to me, I have gathered up all Robin's papers, and I leave in the morning for the Holy Land. I will find King Richard, and I will tell him what has happened to England in his absence. I will demand his return as our protector, and I will see him rid these lands of the evil that threatens to destroy us all.

I do this in God's name, but moreover I do this for my fallen friends.

May Heaven keep them.

* King Richard I died in France in April 1199, whilst at war with King Phillip II of France. He was succeeded as King of England by his brother John, the Count of Mortain, who remained King until his death in October 1216 at Newark Castle, Nottinghamshire.

Records of the whereabouts of Little John and Friar Tuck at this time remain inconclusive.

These pages were found preserved in a cave in the Vosges Mountain during a mining excavation. It is believed they were torn from a larger journal kept by a Knight Templar, although who he was has never been identified.

3. SAINT ORIANNE - LCW Allingham

12th of October, 1222, Anno Domini

I am three days in the mountains and have come across the most grisly of sights. The trees were hung with the bones of Frankish soldiers. Were it not for the ravens I may have missed it altogether. Likely a Hohenstaufen scouting team sent from Alsace. There was flesh on the bones, but no blood on the ground beneath them.

Something drained them dry before hanging them high in the ash trees, like an offering to a bloodthirsty pagan god. I cut them down and gave them the proper Christian burial they deserved.

I am on the right track.

3rd of November, 1222, Anno Domini

The villages here have no knowledge of the unholy demon I have tracked. They are simple folk, isolated in their villages, nearly untouched by the wars that have ravaged the lands around them.

Do they know of the missing armies? Though they say they've hosted soldiers from France, Alsace, Bavaria, Swabia, and Switzerland, on their way from the crusades to Phillip's war with England, the further they are from the many mountain passes the less often they have entertained my most honorable brothers in arms. They do, however, enjoy my stories of the noble soldiers of the Knights Templar, the great heroes of the crusades and of King Fredrick's Imperial armies. Some of the women swoon when I speak of the sacrifice and heroism of even the lowest foot soldier, and there may be some young men that take a vow of protection to the cross come spring.

They think I am confused about the demon. They claim many outsiders do not understand the mountains. That God has blessed them with peace, abundance, and protection. No evil molests them.

In three villages now I have heard mention of a Saint Orianne, who, I am sure is in no record the church keeps. Instead she seems to be a folk saint, likely from their rustic lore. The women say she protects them when they are caught out in the forest at night.

I asked how and was told she hides the girls in trees, away from wolves.

It did make me think of the bodies I saw in the ash trees, but a demon cannot be confused with a saint, no matter how simple the peasant. I have sent a message to the Bishop of Strasbourg with news of my slow progress. If he wants me to continue my search, I may best find a place to stay for the coming winter.

13th of December, 1222, Anno Domini

While I regret missing advent with my brotherhood in Jerusalem, I have found myself in the warmest of company in the village of Siècle, not far from the summit. I stopped here on my way to Mont Sainte-Odile, where I intended to offer my services to the nuns and winter down amongst their archives to see what I could learn, but an early frost, and generous hospitality I've received at the inn, has kept me.

The church here is old, but well tended by Pere Guidi and the brothers. I am unfamiliar with their order but they adorn their otherwise humble altar with a cross that belonged to Charlemagne himself.

The people too are warm, vintners, foresters, swineherds and weavers. They gather each night at the inn where I have been granted a comfortable room, and beg me to tell them stories of the crusades, the Knights Templar, and Rome.

I must confess, I am always eager to share the exploits of the knights and soldiers I have served with over the years. I hold military men, from recruit to veteran, in the highest regard. The bravery, wisdom they share, the sacrifice they undertake for God and country, make them the finest sort.

The people share their Yuletide celebrations with me. Their devotion to God and Church is without reproach, but when prayer is finished, their celebrations and wine is second only to King Frederick himself.

They have welcomed me most graciously, and I think after many years fighting holy causes, it will be good to rest.

I am beginning to suspect my hunt for the demon took a wrong turn, and I ended up instead in this place most beloved by God. I will take up my search again in the spring.

His Excellency has urged me to use all my skills as a Poor Fellow-Soldiers of Christ. I suspect he is under a considerable amount of pressure from the king to account for the slain and missing soldiers.

After I am rejuvenated, I will avenge those good men who serve the church and king.

16nd of January, 1223, Anno Domini

It was a delightful advent, and I am just now recovering from many days and nights of celebration, starting with the Midwinter Festival.

The people here celebrate the old Yule tradition of staying up until sunrise, eating, drinking, dancing and telling tales. I shared more stories of Jerusalem, but I was intrigued with the histories of the mountains and village that the elders shared. Their stories go back to the Roman times, before the church illuminated our paths to heaven.

Again, there were tales of Saint Orianne, but this time, I pressed for the whole account. It chilled me to the bone for it alludes to my quarry and suggests he has been lurking about these mountains so much longer than the bishop realizes.

Here is the story:

A soldier in Charlemagne's army retired to the mountains after the war. Orianne was his only daughter. All was well for many years, and they became a part of the community, but then war broke out again, and their small village was ravaged. The villagers abandoned God in their despair and turned to their old pagan ways. They performed black magic to raise a demon deity. They wanted Orianne to be wed to this demon in

34

exchange for its power. Orianne, even on threat of death, refused to denounce God or to take part in their wickedness.

They imprisoned her in the mountain for six moons to get her to agree, but when they brought her out again, she escaped to the summit, near this very village. The demon gave chase, right to the edge of a cliff. Orianne prayed to the Blessed Virgin, and instead of plummeting to her death, she flew off the side of the cliff and into God's eternal glory.

The demon, denied his bride, devoured the village, and all were lost to oblivion, except for Saint Orianne. Now, when danger threatens the villages, it is said that Orianne's protection hides the people from the evil eye.

Mademoiselle Marie Pampielle told me about young women and children who have found themselves outside the village at night and stalked by wolves and other wild animals. They claim hands, as soft and light as a dove, lift them up and hide them in the trees.

One woman, a grandmother who swears she was so saved in her youth, said a woman's voice whispered to her, "Close your eyes, and be still until morning."

I have written all this in a letter to the bishop, that I will send as soon as the paths thaw. I do not know what to think about this local saint of theirs, and her supposed miracles. I am inclined to think it simple folly, but I have seen stranger things first hand than the power of local saints. Once in Jerusalem, an entire battlefield was consumed in holy light, and all soldiers, Christian and Muslim alike, lost their will to fight and laid down their arms.

I do wonder if this devil of the old gods now dwells in the forests, butchering good soldiers who march through.

13th of March, 1223 Anno Domini

I have received word from His Excellency that I am to depart from Siècle and move south to pursue my quarry. There are reports that an entire brigade went missing in a pastoral pass. But first, I intend to complete my visit to Mont Sainte-Odile. With the first thaw, the trails will be clear and it should be no more than two days walk. I was reluctant to leave my new friends behind so I asked one of the village's huntsmen, Charles DuLac, if he would act as my guide through the pass. Our excursion became a pilgrimage when Marie and Madam Bouleitte asked if they could join us, along with a small hoard of excited children. Finally Pere Guidi requested to join our party, having need of certain tomes kept at Hohenburg Abbey.

I confess I am glad for such fine company, watching this beautiful part of the mountains come to bloom. I shall consider it a few more days of rest before I return to The Order of Solomon's Temple.

21st of March
    The things I have seen
    I cannot.

23rd of March

I cannot seem to rouse myself. I was supposed to leave for the south two days ago.

9th of April

I have tried and failed to commit this account to writing. Even now, I can only compel myself with the pretense that I am merely transcribing a folk story, rather than documenting the events of our ill turned journey.

I will start with the facts as removed from passions as I can manage.

On the morning of the fifteenth of March, shortly after we broke our fast, Pere Guidi, Charles, Madam Bouleitte and young Mademoiselle Marie Pampielle led a procession of seven children ages nine to fourteen on a short pilgrimage to the old Benedictine nunnery along the east trails to the peak of Mont Sainte-Odile. The day was warmer than we expected, and the paths were clear and easy to walk.

We encountered tradesmen along the way. One such fellow warned us that Ottrott, where we intended to stay for the night, was under quarantine, having lost thirteen souls to the flux in the last month. Charles suggested we could make our shelter in a hunting encampment he'd used many times before. It seemed a fine plan and a more direct route to Mont Sainte-Odile.

Moods were high and conversation was jovial. Perhaps we all had caught a spring fever from the sun and fresh air, but we didn't realize we were off the trail until we'd been off it for some time.

Even so, with the hunter to guide us, we were not alarmed, and he found the trail just after dusk. We were so relieved we didn't consider caution. That was our mistake.

My mistake.

I had lived the winter as if it were a dream. After years of warfare in the noble but rough company of my brotherhood, my time in Siècle was so gentle that I lost sight of the very reason I was here.

We came upon the encampment at twilight, tired but boisterous after our long day's walk, eager for the supper we'd packed.

We didn't see the soldiers until we were nearly on top of them. I realize now they must have smothered their fire when they heard us approaching.

The captain gave me a start when he stepped forward, but I was glad to see him. He wore the black and gold surcoats of King Fredrick's Imperial guard, so I assumed he was on important business.

I told him with enthusiasm that we were on a short pilgrimage. That I too was a soldier, but of the highest calling, of The Order of Solomon's Temple.

While I blathered on, Pere Guidi and Charles must have seen what I did not. They stepped in front of the women, who were gathering in the children.

I was a fool. I realize now that I, having been amongst soldiers and mercenaries, the worst and best in the world, assumed that the Holy Roman Emperor himself would employ captains of honor to represent him through all of Europe, especially when faced with a man of the cloth and a Knight Templar.

I did not understand the way the captain's eyes shifted to his men or notice their chuckles, or the way they slid around me through the shadows. I was simply eager to be in the company of soldiers again.

Everything happened quickly.

Little Oda shrieked. I turned to see one of the soldiers had tossed her over his shoulder, laughing as the other children reached for her, crying. Another grabbed two of the boys, and a third seized Marie around her waist. They had swords at the backs of Charles and Pere Guidi and I turned back to the captain only to find a sword at my throat.

I demanded, "What is the meaning of this? We are pilgrims!"

He explained that his troop was caught outside of Ottrott for two long months, all the paths snowed in, while the flux moved through the village. They were hungry and lonely.

And I, the fool I was, had thought it vulgar and unnecessary to bring my sword on a pilgrimage.

They knocked poor Charles out and bound Pere Guidi to a tree. When they started tearing at poor Marie's clothes and taunting the children, the priest condemned all their souls to hell. I stood still, waiting for the captain to drop his guard so I could grab his sword. I thought I would be able to fight my way out, but I had to be tactical now. I had never conceived such darkness could malign the hearts of soldiers, but I could not allow any more harm to come to my friends.

Before I had my chance to move, the crickets, and the night birds suddenly stilled. The soldiers stopped their assault as the air seemed to thicken around us. Then there was a sound, like the wind over a bottle, followed by a hollow thump.

One of the soldiers screamed. The captain turned, and I snatched the sword from his hand and plunged it through his chest. Blood gurgled from his mouth like water from a Roman fountain.

Marie screamed, so terrified it nearly froze my heart in my chest. I spun about, searching to fight off her assailants, but she was gone. The two men who had been groping her were running. I charged after them, but a white hand reached out of the darkness and pulled them away.

There was a wet crack, and one of them fell at my feet, his head twisted on his neck like a berry not yet ripe enough to pluck.

There was so much screaming, but it was from the soldiers. I lunged one way and another looking for the women and children, but there were only soldiers, frantically swinging at air until the invisible foe sliced the limbs from their bodies and lopped their heads off their shoulders.

Something grabbed my ankle, and I looked down to see a soldier dragging himself across the dirt, his jaw hanging off his face like a door falling from its hinge.

I have never been so useless. I ran in circles, unsure who the enemy was. The soldiers who would have killed us and raped our wards, or whatever dismembered them from the shadows.

Another failing of mine, I didn't guess that it could be the very demon I hunted until the screaming stopped, and she stepped out of the shadows. A tall, lean woman, pale as the moon, slick with blood, her eyes glowing like hot coals in the night. I raised my sword ready to fight. I spoke my prayers, ready to die.

I do not know what happened next.

I awoke the next morning, tucked in my bedroll between Pere Guidi and Charles. Charles was still asleep, a nasty gash at his temple, but breathing evenly.

"What happened? Where are the children? Where are the women?" I rambled to Pere Guidi, panicked.

Pere Guidi put his finger to his lips and pointed to where Marie and Madam Bouleitte were helping children down from the trees.

"Saint Orianne," he said.

Of the soldiers, there was no trace. Pere Guidi claims he saw nothing from where he was tied to the tree, and merely woke up to find himself untied and unscathed. I don't quite believe him.

We had to build a litter for poor Charles. He vomited every time he tried to stand, but I got everyone to the abbey by late afternoon, and the sisters were able to attend to him and ease his headache.

I gave my confession, or a semblance of one. I must admit that I am unsure what I confessed, for my mind was plagued with guilt and fury.

I only know I intended to complete my task. For the last five years I had been given the charge of hunting and killing demons and other foul creatures that offend the church. It was a mission given to me by the Most Holy Father, himself.

If I could not trust the sacred brotherhood of soldiers, I at least maintained my faith in the righteous truth of the Holy Roman Catholic Church.

The abbess found me a sword and a few other items, and I set out a few hours before nightfall.

I came across one body, just a league into my excursion. It was hung high in an ash tree, stripped of all his gold and black finery. I still recognized it as the captain. I did not linger there. I didn't think she would return to that spot.

I was much quicker on foot without my party. It wasn't long after nightfall that I reached the summit near Siècle.

I am not sure what drew me to the place where Saint Orianne flew into God's grace, but it was there that I found her, sitting on the flat stone overlooking the Andlau river valley. The sky was brilliant with stars, and the moon hung fat and golden on the horizon, casting her in an ethereal glow. I drew a sword in one hand and the abbess's own rosary in the other, but she didn't bother to turn around.

"When they made me, this rock was sacred," she said. She spoke Latin perfectly, her voice rich golden, but there was an archaic lilt to it, I had only ever heard in elders.

I found myself, again, frozen. I could neither speak nor move.

"I have protected these people for almost four hundred years. Since I submitted myself to be their guardian. Since I made the pact."

I forced myself to speak. "They are God-fearing people now. You are a demon of the old world. You have no place here."

She turned back to look at me, and I saw that her face was young. Now cleansed of blood and filth, she was a mere mountain girl. A narrow nose and wide dark eyes. She looked a woman of twenty, just starting her life of fat babies and sweet husbands and fussing over lace at the market.

Then I saw the burning coals in her eyes, and she said to me, "But I do still have a place. Do you think these villages would thrive if I were not here to divert the soldiers always marching through? If I were to leave the girls and children on the ground when the wolves catch them out after dark?"

I raised my sword and then lowered it.

"But you are a demon, who drinks the blood of men."

"I am," she said. "And so you must slay me. It is the only way I am freed from this pact I made. The people have forgotten their part of it. That their great great grandparents revered me, fed me, loved me as I loved them. Your god changed them. Turned them away from the ways of the mountain. The magic and the shadows and the gods who protected them. First they attacked me, reviled me, hated me, then they forgot me."

"They didn't forget you. They call you a saint. A gross profanity of the truth."

"I agree. I loathe to be one of your sterile glass idols. But I remember my pact in blood at the foot of the Allfadir. I cannot forsake my people. Death is the only end to it."

She swept her black hair over her shoulder and leaned her head forward, exposing her thin white neck. She closed her eyes. I lifted my sword. I would bring her head back to His Excellency. He would give me a holding on the route to the holy land. I could retire my sword. I would live in wealth, take a pretty young wife, have my own fat babies, and be beloved of God.

I thought of the women in the trees. I thought of the dark hunger in the soldiers' eyes.

How often did men forget their honor when there was no one to watch them?

How easy would the people of Siècle laugh and love and celebrate with strangers when the demon no longer hunted?

I lowered my sword and then dropped it. I walked to the edge of the cliff where Saint Orianne supposedly flew away. What had truly happened that night to the young woman who she had been? She said she had made a pact, a vow similar to my own, to protect her people.

From my people.

When I turned around, she was gone. Maybe she had flown, but from good Christian folk, who had forgotten the life she'd sacrificed to protect them.

13th of April, 1223, Anno Domini

I have decided to stay in the mountains, at least until the Knights Templar call me back to the holy lands. The bishop is not pleased, but he has agreed.

I will ensure there is order here, that any travelers who do not obey the laws of land and church are punished for their crimes. I will make sure these people are protected.

All of them.

God forgive me.

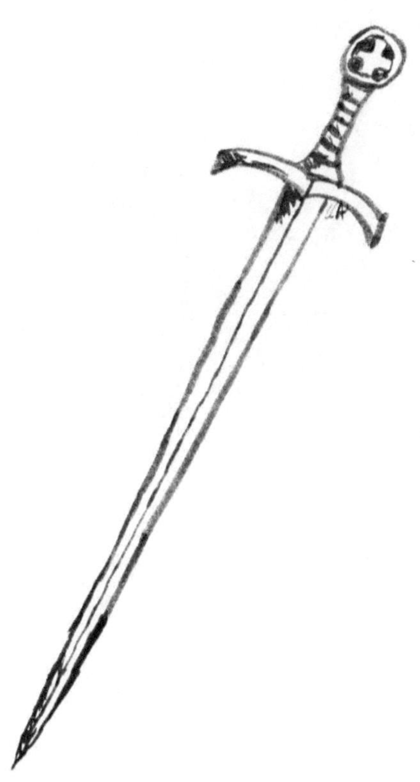

4. THE <u>APPROPRIATED</u> JOURNAL OF BARON VON HERBERSTEIN – River Eno

29 Lulius, year of our Lord, 1512

I have arrived at the easternmost fortress at Smolensk. The vibration of war is in the air. Lithuanian and Polacy arrive daily, along with men from my native German Nation under the Holy Roman Empire. They flock to join the forces of the Grand Duchy of Lithuania and the Crown of Poland: promised bread, shoes, clothing and a weapon. The Grand Duchy is vastly outnumbered yet does not fear the mighty Muscovite army. I am not convinced their boldness will deliver a victory; however, I worry little. Being who I am, a baron, an academic and chronicler blessed and charged with a holy task by the Pontificus, God's might is on my side.

I have seen up close many campaigns during my work as historian. I can handle the rabble and will not be swayed from my duty.

The beast is here. Of this, I am sure. Though I have slain his acolytes and progeny over the last three winters, he has eluded me. This area, dense with squalid population and the coming war, will provide proper concealment for his proclivities.

I admit, I am bolstered by the warrior's exuberance and am sure I will be able to slay him this time. Two structures, both many miles downriver, have caught my eye as his possible daytime resting place.

The innkeep is accommodating and has acquiesced to bring wine and meals to my small room each day. Once my hunger is sated, I will take to the streets to find evidence of his presence.

—Baron Sigismund von Herberstein

3 Augustus, year of our Lord 1512

Difficult as it is with the thickness of populace and fog-covered darkness, I saw him the second night. A cloaked figure, tall, a bit hunched and bustling through the unwashed bodies that linger restless and slumbering in the streets.

Last afternoon I walked about six miles along the river's edge to the closest edifice, an abandoned military outpost. The inside was destroyed by the river water flowing into its lower chambers. Irritably, I found no evidence of the beast. An assumption on my part; a wish, a mere desire for him to be there, as the other building, a derelict castle, is so much farther. Tired, I returned to my room. The castle is a much longer walk for a different day.

—Baron Sigismund von Herberstein

7 Augustus, year of our Lord 1512

Just after dawn, two men were found dead, clumped near decaying food rubbish in a dank alley near the water. From their blue eyes and square jaws, they appeared to possibly be of my own German Nation, and approximately twenty summers in age.

The town "doctor," a self-important heretic, suspects starvation or consumption, but I have seen the beast's victims firsthand and know starvation is the look of his fatalities, freed of their blood down to the last drop. I did not mention it. These people are simple and would be terrified to know what I know.

Fearing the beast's strategies for his own legion—and I will confess, brokenhearted at my failure to dispatch him before he stole two more lives of my own people—I concealed my face and crept into the charnel house, searching through the fetid stench. I found them in the back with the consumptive dead. I adorned their bodies with plain silver crosses and stuffed their mouths with old garlic. Using a heavy rock as a hammer, I split the younger lad's heart with a wooden stake. A disconcerting black ooze spewed over his filthy tunic. He was altering already; such signs were not usually visible outside of seven days. They had been dead longer ago than anyone realized. Unusually flustered, I moved to the next, the older by only a year or two. His face gave me pause. Handsome. Large blue eyes stared up vacantly. I do not know why this bothered me. Perhaps it was the innocence lost, or the putrid stench of my surroundings. I felt I would retch and struggled to control myself. My discomfit cost me precious moments, and I heard the charnel door open, and the voices of the undertaker and his men.

Fearing I would be seen, I hurriedly, and quietly, used my weight to push the stake into the lad's chest. When I felt his bones crack, I pulled the stake free and concealed myself under the damp, rotting, wooden pallets until they left, at which time, I fled.

I could not be caught idling amongst the dead and lose the confidence of the town folk. Many have assumed I am clergy, and although I have not lied outright, I have allowed them their assumptions, as I am a servant of the Pontificus, and of God, in good standing.

—Baron Sigismund von Herberstein

13 Augustus, year of our Lord 1512

Six days since the incident in the charnel house, and I have been unable to get to the abandoned castle down river. At least one body is found each day, from consumption, starvation or the beast, I cannot know. There is much chaos! Being only one of a handful of truly godly men, I am asked to help the dead to peace and to comfort the living.

I have caught two glimpses of the beast in the eve. His cloak flowing as he hurries in the opposite direction. As if he's taunting me, luring me to follow, knowing I am too fatigued from the day's activities. I am confident that cannot be. I have done well to conceal myself. Surely, if he knew who I was and why I was here, he would have tried to dispatch me already.

My rooms are impenetrable with holy might: crosses, holy water, and over ripe garlic. I am safe. Yet I wake each morning drained of energy, knowing I will be informed of more deaths and then asked to comfort the living, all while quietly searching for my deadly quarry.

—Baron Sigismund von Herberstein

18 Augustus, year of our Lord 1512

Nothing. It has been days since the last sighting of the beast. I do not have the energy for the long walk down river. I will admit, the memory of the older boy's vacant stare and waxen skin in the charnel house has vanquished me. I have nightmares. Perhaps because he was similar in age, and even appearance, to my dear sister's son? Though I have not seen him nor his mother since he was a boy, and I do not think my nephew old enough to travel so far from Lützelburg. However, the resemblance created a gloom and paranoia that creeps into my mind as I sleep. I wake not rested but depleted. He was someone's child, someone's treasure and namesake, and I failed to save him.

Last eve I drank a bit more with dinner to relax my nerves and then left before full dark to search the streets once more. Just as the sky turned dusk, I stumbled upon what I thought was a lost young woman. Her dress was dirty with street muck, and in my weakened state, she befuddled me, bade me to follow her into a dark recess between two small edifices down from the corner where we had met.

It was then her evil took me over. She groped me, her disgustingly knowledgeable fingers, caressing parts of my body no woman had the right to touch on a man that was not her husband and certainly not a Godly man. She smiled her darkened toothed smile as she stroked the uncontrolled ache of my manhood. Her devilry paralyzed me, leaving me gasping and groping at her bosom on full display.

When her dark magic released its hold over me, I pushed her filth away like the vulgar harlot she was. I threw two coins into the gutter fearing the riffraff with which she surrounds herself would make a scene.

I hastened from the dark and made my way to the church in the town square. Before Midnight Mass, I made confession to the priest and felt sure the ill-begotten girl's black magic was excised from my soul. It would seem the beast's devilry is spreading, but I cannot succumb. I will not!

A few hours before the sun broke, I made my way back to my small room, head pounding, fatigued and defeated, again unable to use the day to search the castle ruins.

—Baron Sigismund von Herberstein

23 Augustus, year of our Lord 1512

I am vexed! I wake burdened by dreams of the horrors I cannot prevent. Bodies are found in every part of the town, and I am too exhausted to complete tasks. And now, I fear I am being watched! After my noon meal, I noticed my desk was in a strange disarray. I cannot say I am a tidy man, but the arrangements of the papers seemed...wrong. If someone was here, it was not the beast. The room has been consecrated. Crosses hang at the window, door and over my bed. It cannot be him!

This evening, I saw something—not the quarry I have pursued for so long. A face in the crowd, a face I knew. Only, it cannot be. I am sure, it cannot be. My dinner had turned in my belly soon after I had eaten, so it must have been a hallucination caused by spoiled food.

I hurried back to my room. The items on the desk seemed the same as I had left them. I believe I was overtired earlier to think someone had been here. I will make an effort to steady my thoughts and not give way to paranoia.

—Baron Sigismund von Herberstein

29 Augustus, year of our Lord 1512

I saw it again! There is something about this place. The horde of men waiting for their war, arguing and rutting on corners and alleys. The death, the sadness and the fervor of impending combat has stuck to me like a foul smell. It is making me see things.

Two nights ago, a traveling sideshow entertained the men in the square. In the crowd, I saw him. But no, it is but demons haunting me!

—Baron Sigismund von Herberstein

9 September, year of our Lord 1512

Yesterday, at dawn, the war with the Muscovites began. The carnage is ghastly. Even with my experience, I have never seen slaughter like this. The dead and dismembered cover the streets. Even had I the energy, I could not have gotten to the water, past the swarms of bodies, where I knew the beast would be, slaking his hunger on the unknowing soldier—a feast concealed in the middle of the carnage.

I helped the injured and moved the dead to one of the many piles outside the overflowing charnel house. The pang of stale blood still fills my nostrils. It was during this time I felt the beast close to me...like someone breathing down the back of my neck. I cannot fully explain it. Where before I was concealed, now I feel exposed. But if he knows who I am and what I am here to do...I am undone. In all the miles I have traveled to hunt him, I do not know how the tables could have turned when I have been so careful and diligent to be seen only as a humble man working for the church.

Adding insult, I am in the second week of my autumn rose fever. The innkeeper brings me wine each day, but my head is pounding, and I cannot eat. Sleep eludes me.

—Baron S. von Herberstein

5 September, year of our Lord 1512

Perhaps it is the depth of this conflict, but I am at my lowest. When I leave the inn, I feel his eyes on me no matter where I go. I keep to the shadows, returning back to my room within the hour only to fall into a fitful, nightmare-filled sleep.

I am weak. I cannot eat but small bits of bread lest I retch.

Baron S. von Herberstein

17 Sept, our Lord 1512

I have learnt who is following me! Rather, he showed himself. It was late, and my body sore from the cough I cannot seem to rid myself. I ventured out, keeping to the shadows, hiding from the madman, hoping to gain surprise and then rounding a bend, I nearly knocked someone over. A young man. Though dark of night, his clear blue eyes were obvious. The same stare, only this time fixed on me. It is the elder boy from the charnel house! I have not been imagining him! That day, it would appear, I did not, in fact, set his soul free.

In shock, I fell back to the wall. He said nothing, but his expression conveyed a haunting sadness deep within. I could not speak. I had failed him twice, and now he was hunting me as the beast's progeny!

To my shock, he backed away. I was too distraught to follow. I do not know why he let me see it was him, or why he let me live, but now I have two duties. Slay him and his master. This burden is too difficult to bear. The weight of my failure may crush me.

Baron S v Herberstein

19 Sept, 1512

Beyond my physical illness, I am now sick with grief. I have failed this mission every possible way. I drink, but cannot put food to mouth, the stench of the dead is so strong, and the streets are overrun with vermin jumping from puddle to puddle of stagnate bodily fluids. I am near my limit of toleration.

Combat has stalled, and I will force myself to leave this room come morning. I will stuff my frock's inner pockets with silver crosses, holy water and garlic, and I will carry a sack of wooden stakes and venture to the abandoned castle down along the water's edge. The beast and his progeny must be there, for where else?! I will, once and for all, end this monster that consumes my thoughts and weakens my countenance.

Though brutally depleted, I have roused myself with one thought—God. I am here on a mission from the church and God. My skills are needed, and He is on my side. With thoughts of His goodness and His might, success is imminent. I cannot fail. Not with Him beside me. I will not fail!

Baron S von H.

26 September, year of our Lord 1512

Baron Sigismund von Herberstein is dead.

Your baron did indeed make it to the abandoned castle along the river, arriving malnourished and sick. Whether too strong-headed or too slow-witted to admit it, I do believe he had contracted the consumption disease, and without sufficient food or water, he collapsed after his long walk, awakening only when I roused him after nightfall. My maker was, for a long time, amused by the baron's persistence and ignorance, but grew bored of him. It would appear he is a capricious enemy.

Baron von Herberstein is of the true death. He was not given the choice I was—to live as the beast lives or die by his hand. I know this because I participated in his end. He did not suffer. He was afraid before his head was removed, but it was taken cleanly, and his blood devoured, of which, having no more particular feelings of shame, I partook.

My maker says the syndrome he bestowed upon me is altering, for although I, like him, cannot tolerate the rays of the sunlight, I have rummaged the baron's room three times without the slightest feelings of unease, pain or sickness by his crosses or consecration. I, now, infiltrate his blessed journal to write to you, Pontifex Maximus.

Unpredictable enemy and volatile creator, my maker has since abandoned me. The baron was correct, I am from Lützelburg, from military and clergy families of the German Nation, and I do not know what exactly I am to do. I arrived with my cousin to this battle for Orsha, to my mother's dismay and my father's behest.

But I find myself bearing the weight of profound grief at the loss of my beloved cousin and a more overwhelming anger at your baron's ineptitude and then still more rage at my maker's savagery. A noble death is what I expected. To live, a bonus. To live as an abomination, a disgrace.

For your clarity, in his haste, your baron managed only to crack my rib cage. A fact upon waking to this new life brought much distress, along with a mouthful of rotting garlic and learning what I had to consume to survive.

So...a courtesy for an attempted courtesy. To his credit, thinking I a stranger, your baron tried to save me from a life of damnation. I will resume his quest and do what he could not, kill the merciless monster scouring the lands and damning the unknowing to Hell.

My hope is that this journal reaches the Pontifex intact and with an understanding: I expect to be left alone. I am young and strong and have been forever torn from my family, having now done things they would be unable to forgive, things I would not forgive. I will destroy the one who has subverted your world and ripped me from mine. You must trust I will not prey on the innocent nor be like him in any way.

Do not send anyone to hunt or slaughter me, or my good graces will fall to an end, and I will make my way back to Rome with you, Pontifex, as my first victim.

In good faith,

Esteemed nephew of Baron Sigismund von Herberstein,

—Karl von Ahn

The following letters were collected by
Giovanni Manassi in October 1597 after
the disappearance of Aldus Manutius,
grandson of the famed Venetian printer
and vampire hunter of the same name. He
believed they constituted a body of
evidence significant enough to
necessitate a state-sponsored vampire
hunt, but his theories were discredited
due to the impeccable reputation of the
accused.

5.   BLOOD STAINS TRUE -
Nico Martinez Nocito

Aldus Manutius of the Aldine Press
2343 Calle della Chiesa, San Polo
Campo Sant'Agostin, Venice
13 January 1597

Gentile Signore Giovanni Manassi:

I write today with a most peculiar quandary, one
which necessitates the consultation of a vampiric
scholar as preeminent as yourself. You will recall, I
hope, my father, Paulus, as he always spoke of you in
the most elevated terms. He liked to say that you were
a second son to my grandfather; while he preserved the

printing business, you carried on the Manutius family tradition of vampire hunting.

I myself have stayed away from vampires since my father's death. The printer's page has always possessed a greater allure, and as you know, my grandfather successfully purged the last vampires from Venice, rendering such services all but useless here. Your name, meanwhile, often appears in newspaper accounts from Transylvania, and I read avidly of your exploits to my dear mother, Caterina.

I write now, however, not with concerns that a vampire walks beside me, but with a pressing mythological question—an academic curiosity, you might say. This entire affair has been most unusual, and so I shall start with its beginning, as is usually best for any matter where one pursues the truth.

This tale opens as follows:

Two months ago I received a most unusual missive from an individual previously unknown to me. He introduced himself as Franz Hoffman, a boy yet in the early stages of adulthood who hailed from eastern Habsburg. His uncle was a printer. He spoke of a longtime desire to become acquainted with the Venetian lifestyle and spoke very highly of my grandfather's reputation, calling him much renowned in the circles of his acquaintance; all this flattery culminated in a request that he come to Venice as my apprentice, to learn something of the trade and the city before striking out on his own.

The boy seemed lively enough and brimming with energy, and I was endeared to him through the easiness of his tone—not to mention the commendable quality of his penmanship. Upon a day's consideration, I sent a return note making it known that he was greatly welcome at the Aldine Press, and that I would begin educating him straightaway upon his arrival. I am, as you may guess, dearly invested in the future of my grandfather's press, and I was quite glad to encounter the enthusiasm of a youth who, I was already thinking, might one day take on the business himself, as no Manutius boy seemed particularly interested in its longevity.

There was only a single line in this entire correspondence that led me to believe that Franz's desire to relocate to Venice was anything besides a stroke of unexpected luck for myself and the press's future. In his initial letter, almost like an afterthought, he penned the following:

I hear that Venice is free of those of the vampiric persuasion.

Now as you may expect, I have been too firmly raised upon tales of vampires to take much notice of a passing reference such as this, beyond perhaps experiencing a brief warmth of pride to know the success and dedication of my grandfather and namesake remains known throughout Europe even decades later. I filed this letter away among my other correspondence with little thought given to that brief comment, and spent several weeks thoroughly excited by the swiftly approaching arrival of my apprentice to be.

Franz Hoffman arrived at my door a little more than a week ago. He is, you must understand, a most understated boy. He is soft-spoken and frail; he moves with a certain timidity, as though every gesture carries the distinct possibility of receiving unnatural attention. He is very blonde, and very pale. In retrospect, my grandfather or yourself might have called his complexion almost vampiric in its severity. I admit to being distinctly underwhelmed upon his initial appearance; I had expected a vivacious lad with the intensity imparted by his previous communication, filled with keen wit and self-awareness. However, as he grew more comfortable with me, I quickly observed his apprehension fall away, and he became quite lively, a truly delightful companion.

Last night, after he had shown astonishing aptitude for etching prints, I asked after his initial hesitancy. (I am, as I'm sure Paulus would tell you, an expert at inquiring after the most uncomfortable questions.) He appeared all but bursting to tell me, and relayed the tale with gusto.

He had, it seems, not selected my press by chance. Word of my grandfather's accomplishments—in both printing and vampire hunting—have traveled far, and so he believed that my company would earn him a safety he had not previously been afforded, explaining his earlier reluctance.

"Safety?" I inquired.

He nodded. "From the vampires."

Now, Signore, we begin to approach the crux of why I am writing to you.

He was not, he prefaced, a vampire himself. This is an unusual way to begin a conversation, and so I admit to leaning forward with curiosity, wondering where, precisely, his words were bound next. However, he explained, his father had been, rendering him the most unique of creatures: a human whose blood possessed the ability to permanently satiate even the most ravenous of vampires, an evidently immensely desirable trait in a country so rife with hunters such as yourself. As you well know, vampires are most easily identified when struck by the urge to feed; draining a boy such as Franz would have allowed a vampire to exist for centuries, dangerously unidentifiable.

Now I myself, though my home is a veritable archive of vampire tales, had never encountered scraps of lore either corroborating or opposing so eccentric a proposition. However, Franz was adamant in his profession of this tale. His own father, he explained, had sired him for this sole purpose, and had attempted to drain him as soon as he determined he was grown enough to possess an adequate quantity of blood, which occurred around nine years of age. Franz's mother fended him off and brought her son to the house of his printer uncle for safety. However, his father survived, and within weeks every vampire in Habsburg knew that a boy lived within their borders who could render them anonymous and immortal forever.

His childhood, Franz told me, had thus been marred by a series of vampiric attacks. Every stranger he encountered was a potential threat; most weeks, at least one attempt would be made upon his life, leading to the lingering distrust of new people he had exhibited upon arriving at my home. Both he and his uncle became well-versed in the art of vampire warding, a knowledge supplemented by the fact that Franz remained almost entirely indoors, rarely daring to venture beyond the walls of the print house, well guarded by hawthorn and mustard seeds. His uncle lacked the economic security necessary to relocate his business, but swore that Franz would depart to a safer locale once he came of age. The letter I had received some months earlier had been the culmination of that promise.

I assured him that I had not known of a vampire in Venice since my grandfather's time, and this appeared to reassure him. He is already much changed, in both mood and countenance, since his arrival; this safety has worked wonders for his health.

Upon adjourning for the evening, however, I found myself curious as to the accuracy of the mythos he implied and spent some hours scanning accounts of vrykolakas, ubırs, and dhampirs for some reference to a being like the one he described himself as. I found no corroboration for such a tale, and I am accordingly deeply curious as to your own professional opinion. I certainly wonder if this tale was merely a stab at revenge on the part of the furious vampiric father to haunt his son with eternal fear, and hope to, if this is the case, give my new apprentice what peace of mind can be imparted by that knowledge after such a childhood as the one he has endured.

Most courteously,

Aldus Manutius

Giovanni Manassi
Sent from Zhytomyr, Polish-Lithuanian
Commonwealth
9 April 1597

My dear Aldus—

Words cannot sufficiently express the pleasure I have in hearing from you. I think often of your family throughout my travels, and recently saved a child's life thanks to your grandfather's study on the use of hawthorn stakes to kill a vampire when no ash trees are readily available.

Your query concerning your new apprentice truly fascinates me. My response has been somewhat delayed by my own investigation into the topic, as well as a recent spate of vampires in Odessa that required my attention. My efforts, however, have proven successful, and I hope the news I share now will adequately satiate your curiosity.

It appears that your Franz Hoffman's fears are not only merited, but perhaps even more concerning than they initially appear. I spoke recently with a colleague of mine from Smyrna who shared a very similar tale, though in this case the vampire succeeded in consuming the child's blood. The effects were primarily as Franz feared in assuaging the creature's bloodlust.

However, this acquaintance spoke of an additional ability. He claimed such an encounter would enable the shape-shifting ability highlighted in Turkish ubır myths, a truly terrifying proposition for vampire hunters such as myself.

I advise you to guard Franz closely, though without him realizing if you are able so as to preserve his good health. Even in Venice, basic precautions would be advisable, if only for your peace of mind. Next time my steps carry me near Venice I will be sure to stop by; it has been many years since your city has needed to fend off vampires, and I fear even the most educated such as yourself could use additional assistance in constructing the most effective safeguards.

Best wishes—

Giovanni Manassi

Franz Hoffman of the Aldine Press
2343 Calle della Chiesa, San Polo
Campo Sant'Agostin, Venice

21 September 1597

My dear uncle:

I write once more with the most joyous tidings imaginable, ones I could not have dared hope for mere months before my departure.

Venice is truly glorious—I wish you were here to see it with me! I admit it has taken me time to accustom myself to the language, yet already it feels so familiar I might have lived here for years. I never truly understood how much I missed while laden by fear, and now I take every chance I can obtain to explore the world. Just last week Signore Aldus and I spent hours out on the water, and he pointed out every building by name. I confess I have already fallen more than half in love with this city.

The print-master here, Signore Aldus—he insists I speak of him by his first name, though it feels improper—is a peculiar fellow, yet I trust him as I have not trusted any save yourself. He lived alone prior to my arrival.

Although he speaks of it little, I gather that following the death of his mother, Caterina, some years before my arrival, he all but sent away his children; his father had passed several years earlier. It seems that he, too, was supposed to have moved to Rome to follow his family in their studies, perhaps wishing to free them from the grief he himself felt. However, he has chosen to maintain the print shop. Initially I thought it was from a sense of duty to his father and grandfather, but I believe now he truly loves the work. He is subdued in his affections but very passionate once he gets to speaking. I fear I have worried him with my concerns about vampires. However, he has never once disappointed me: no vampires have plagued me since I set foot upon the streets of Venice.

Signore Aldus speaks little of his mother, even going so far as to hide pictures of her from my sight. I gather that he misses her very dearly, and though he is thirty years my senior, I believe we have found some commonality in that shared status as orphans.

I must seal this letter now if it is to reach you before the first snows, but I hope next summer you find your way to visit me here. I dearly wish to show you my new home and introduce you to Signore Aldus; my life here lacks only the reassurance of your presence.

Your nephew,

Franz

Aldus Manutius of the Aldine Press
2343 Calle della Chiesa, San Polo
Campo Sant'Agostin, Venice
28 October 1597

Signore Johannes Hoffman:

I write these words as a confession. I beg that you do not do me the disservice of misconstruing them as anything less, or discounting the horror I have thus inflicted upon your nephew. I am leaving this letter beneath the floorboards of the Aldine Press addressed to you, hidden where it can be found but I doubt anyone will think to look.

I do not know if you will ever read these words—in fact, I hope you do not—but you entrusted me with the safety and well-being of your dearest nephew, and I believe just by not leaving some account, even the most damning one, I would be doing you, and Franz's memory, a profound disservice.

I said this was a confession, but I must begin with the section I do not regret. If you despise me for it, so be it; but I hope it brings you some twisted form of comfort, either by reaffirming your hatred of me or by providing some modicum of understanding.

Aldus Manutius the Younger, grandson of the famed vampire hunter and printmaker, died seven years ago.

At the time, his mother, a woman called Caterina Odoni, also gave the appearance of illness. That individual was myself.

I do not believe the actions I took here were objectionable. My entire family—Aldus included, when it became clear he was going to die—had known for years that despite being born into a woman's body, I had always been a man. I had been forced to live in a way that went against my true nature because my husband Paulus's indignation had stood in my way, but he had died (naturally, I assure you) years before. Aldus himself made the initial request that I take his place upon his death, so at least through his passing he could free me. We had always been very close, and he once told me it was I, and not Paulus, who taught him what it meant to be a man.

The deception itself was very easy. Aldus shared my features and my bearing; I had not aged a day past twenty-two. If anything, many said that Aldus had recovered into even greater health than that in which he had taken ill. Aldus's children and wife chose to depart to Rome, as they could not properly mourn the deceased while the surrounding world insisted he still lived, though we parted on amicable terms. For my part, I loved the printing press; I too loved my family, but could not bear to immediately leave a role I adored so much, and which I had only recently been able to inhabit.

Thus I came to live as you know me, as Aldus Manutius—an act that I do not consider in the least to be a deception.

The deception that took place is that I led them to believe I was not a vampire.

Yes, the irony! I am well aware. I married Paulus and bore him three children on my father's insistence, before I'd gained enough clarity of self to understand just how terrible a wife's existence would be for me, and before Venice's last surviving vampire turned me on a late-night walk. I never dared tell my husband what I'd become, particularly after his ill reaction to my declaration that I was a man. I kept my appetite at bay.

Thus it was far easier for me to take my son's place, as I had not aged; far easier for me to become indistinguishable from him, as I had many sleepless nights to determine how to do it.

I lived peacefully and unobjectionably. I suppressed my bloodlust to a painful degree, once every summer vacationing to Wallachia or Bavaria and eating my fill without drawing the attention of vampire hunters to Venice.

And then your nephew appeared.

I beg you to believe me when I say I never intended for him to be my victim. From our first interaction, Franz was like a son to me. Even when I learned the magnitude of what his blood could do, I repressed every inhuman urge and desire. I wanted only to protect him.

He felt, it became clear, no such loyalty toward me.

That night, I had given myself away. I had not left Venice that summer to satiate myself, equally afraid of leaving Franz and of taking him with me. I was starving, and when I glimpsed a rat dashing across my floor one night, I could not stop myself. I tore it open and drank its blood—a poor substitute for the human variety, but far better than nothing. I drank and I drank until its blood was spilled down my shirt, and its corpse was rough and dry, and rather than whetting my appetite the rat's blood had only made me feel its burn more deeply.

That was how your nephew found me.

He understood at once.

I had kept a sharpened ash stake by the door ever since his arrival, a precaution against any outside vampires who came for him. I tell you, once more, that I had every intention of protecting him. He seized the stake then and plunged it toward my mouth, and...

I could not help myself.

I told him to stop.

You know, I am sure, of the compulsion of vampires.

There is nothing quite as torturous to bear as the look of horror in the eyes of a boy you have come to regard as like your son. That horror was painted across Franz's face, and I knew then that he would ruin me.

And oh, I was hungry.

Every summer, I told you, I go north to eat my fill. Every summer, only that prevents me from preying on the Venetian streets. And there he stood, already snared by my tongue: helpless, delicious.

And his blood came not only with the lure of satiation, but that of power.

I could not push those thoughts any longer.

I knocked the stake from his grasp so easily I barely felt the wood bruise my fingers and drew him toward me with a single beckoning finger. He moved closer to me, closer as I pulled him near, until his chest was pressed against mine and his head tilted back, looking up at me, pure terror in his eyes.

His last word was *please*.

I did not heed it. I couldn't. I beg you to understand that. The hunger had seized me, and in that moment, there was nothing so utterly natural as sinking my fangs into Franz's bared throat.

This letter, I said, is an apology.

I cannot pretend I regret it. I have never felt as alive as I have these past three hours, made fully myself by your nephew's blood. The rumors of transformation are true; at last, my body matches who I am. I am finally, entirely myself.

I have also never felt guilt the way I do now.

Blood stains true—his blood, my thirst. Perhaps you can find consolation in the knowledge that I will carry him within me always, and his sacrifice will make me whole long after your body, and his, have withered into dust.

Do not look for me.

Most cordially yours,

Aldus Manutius

w jego grobie

This excerpt is included in the
accounts because it occurred in an area
near Silesia, that many people do not
know was plagued with vampires, and its
time frame seems to correspond with
Empress Maria Theresa's banning of
cremation in the Empire.

6. FROM THE DIARY OF ISTVAN RÁKÓCZI, KNOWN AS LUBOMIR COUNT OF OSTRAVA
- Lee D Meeder

July 21, 1755. Vienna. - I do believe my time here is over. It feels like my time everywhere has passed. It seems like all of my skills in the Arts have passed. I can no longer produce new gold. My anti-aging formulas seem to not be effective anymore. Memories are short, and the members of Empress Maria Theresa's court have forgotten when I could do these things. Today they mocked my first-hand account of the oupires in Moravia and Silesia. The favored doctor of the empress, the haughty van Swieten, dismisses it all. He ridiculed me and those who have been terrorized by oupires in front of the court, saying, "All the fuss doesn't come from anything other than a vain fear, a superstitious credulity, a dark and eventful imagination, simplicity, and ignorance among the people."

When I arrived back at my quarters, I saw the message from Ostrava. Cousin Jan has been kicked in the head by a horse and remains unconscious. This gives me an excellent excuse to leave Vienna and never come back. They can keep their supposed enlightenment.

July 22 -Emil, my faithful servant all these years, is at the front of the carriage, directing the horses, exposed to the sun, while I continue to enjoy the shade over my head. Emil has witnessed what the Intelligentsia have not. He has seen what can go wrong when the dead rise from the grave. I appreciate his company and belief.

July 23 - The weather is holding up. There has been no rain to make mud and slow our progress. Emil thinks that we might make it there in a total of 6 days. I hope Jan will hold on. As we are both descended from the Rákóczi rebel family, I tried to establish and maintain a presence in the court so that, when the time came, I could help confound the Habsburgs with bad advice and lead to their ruin and downfall, liberating Hungary and Transylvania from their dominance.

July 24 - We had a light sprinkling of rain at the end of yesterday. It was enough to collect some rain water on our way without ruining the road. My brother, Claude-Louis, le Comte de Saint Germain, wanted me to persist in Vienna until he could find a way to unite the British and the French against the Habsburgs. I laughed at his idea that the British and the French would ever stop killing each other. And they haven't. I wish it had worked. I am out of time.

July 26 - We have arrived at Ostrava. Jan's wife, Anna, greeted us, showed us where we would sleep, and showed Emil where the horses and carriage go. It is good to have some Silesian food in me. This is where I was raised, hiding from the Habsburgs. Jan does not look good. His bed is in the corner of the room, up against the wall in the shadows. There is a rattle as his chest slowly goes up and down. I don't think anybody has really done anything for him besides trying to give him water. He is not conscious enough to eat.

July 27 - I went out in the early morning to gather herbs to make a poultice for Jan's head injury. But when I returned, Jan had already passed away. I went into his room to make sure. There have been too many stories of people being buried alive. To my dismay, I found a black cat on Jan's bed, up against the wall. This means that the cat had to cross over Jan to get to the wall. This puts him at increased risk of becoming an oupire. I advised Anna that we should put a long stake through Jan's skull before we bury him, to prevent a transformation. I also advised her to lay the thorny stem of a wild rose on top of Jan, and put something heavy on him. She will not hear of it. She states that he was a good man, and he would not come back that way. I have seen enough to know better, but she will not believe me. At least she agrees to put an iron fence around the grave site to keep more dogs and cats from randomly walking across his grave and further increasing the risk. We will bury him tomorrow.

July 28 - Jan was buried in the morning. This afternoon, we received word from Hulvaky of a possible oupire strike that had occurred overnight. The oupire was strangling one of the residents, who happened to be a childhood friend of Jan's, before his friends saw what was happening and drove off the spectre. They claimed it looked like Jan. We had not heard anything from the body during the night, but we had all been exhausted and sleeping soundly.

July 29 - Anna accused me of moving her flour urn to the wrong spot. I assured her that neither Emil nor I had touched it. I am glad that she has her two sons and daughter, all married with their own children, to help look after her. While I will stay as long as I can, I will need to leave if I hear that the empress has figured out who my father really is. He was the rebel. I didn't think she would tolerate the son of that rebel taking up residence as the Count of Ostrava, so close to Silesia, which she had been forced to cede to the Prussians after the first few years of her reign. That was still a sore spot, even if Frederick the Great referred to her out of respect as "the only man among my opponents."

July 30 - Anna's oldest son reports that they ran off a spectre in the middle of the night that was leaning over their baby. The baby had been sleeping with the son's wife. His wife knew that the spectre was there, but was too weak to move and do anything about it. The baby looked listless. The son reported that when he picked the baby up, he heard a crack, like a bone breaking, and the baby gave out a weak cry. The shins did not even hold their shape. By the end of the day, the baby had died.

I am convinced that Jan has been changed to an oupire. There is only one answer for this. We must dig up his corpse and utterly destroy it by cremation, so that it cannot come back and do any more damage. Nothing restrains these creatures. Nothing keeps them in the ground. Once the alteration has occurred, only obliteration by fire will work to permanently stamp out the menace.

I told Anna this. She refused to believe that this was Jan's doing. I think that tomorrow I will have a talk with the other townspeople and we will prevail over Anna's poor judgment.

July 31 - My heart is broken. Jan made an appearance last night. He started squeezing the life out of Anna, and then bit her on the neck. She screamed, and Emil came to the rescue. Jan let go of Anna, but with superhuman strength threw Emil across the room into a wall and broke his neck. Emil died instantly. We immediately built a box for Emil with a steeply-sloped lid, like a roof of a cathedral, and smeared the top with animal fat, to keep the cat from walking over him, trying to prevent the same fate from befalling his corpse as had occurred to Jan's.

Anna only lost a little blood, so she is not too weak yet. There is hope for Anna, in spite of the bite. A surprising number of people bitten by oupires live without any residual defects. Some survive with chronic weakness or pain.

She still wants confirmation that it is Jan, even though she admits it looked like him. One of my horses is extremely steady, and has never stumbled. I will take down Jan's iron fence around his grave, and have a boy from the town ride my horse through the cemetery. If the horse refuses to walk over a grave, that grave is the one housing the oupire. While we are getting that ready, we are also going to slaughter a pig. It is St. Ignatius Day, which means that, at least, if we rub the pig's lard all over Emil's body, we can at least prevent him from turning into an oupire.

Has it crossed my mind? Why pig's lard, and not some other animal? Why only St. Ignatius Day, and not some other saint's day as well? Where did this procedure originate? These questions sound logical, don't they? Yes, it sounds like the stinking logic of Enlightenment, the bonfire that is minimizing the effect of the true sparks of mystical reality.

They informed us as we ate dinner that in spite of being beaten, the horse refused to walk over Jan's grave. I immediately rounded up several more men and shovels and went to Jan's grave to destroy his body. It was not even dark yet, but he was gone. His burial linens were left next to his grave. He had chewed through them.

We had seen this pattern before. I say "we"- I am still having a hard time accepting Emil's loss. The oupire, if its movement is restrained in any way by material in the grave, will go to any length necessary to be free of them, including their destruction. But once the oupire is free of the grave, it seems to regard the very same garments or linens as part of its new home, and seeks to leave them ready to welcome it back upon the oupire's return.

I had an idea. I took the linens and climbed up into the tower of Saint Wenceslas Church, after leaning a ladder against it. When Jan's body came back to his grave, it was angry that its linens were missing!

I had seen oupires respond to speech before. I suppose it makes sense that if their mouth, hands, and legs are still able to work, they might still be able to understand some words. I yelled out, "Hey Jan! I have your linens here! Come and get them!" Jan heard and immediately headed my way.

Did he respond to the taunt in the tone of my voice? Did he respond to the actual words? Was he simply trying to take revenge for his linen loss on the nearest sign of life to his location? I do not need to understand, because the strategy worked.

Jan wasted no time getting on the ladder and making his way up, but I reached out the tower window and pushed the ladder away from the tower. Jan sprawled on the ground after his impact. His legs and one arm were not moving. I quickly descended, took a spade, and severed Jan's head from his body. The other arm stopped moving.

I had been involved in this sort of thing before, but it was always helping out some other family in some other village. This was my family, my cousin and childhood friend whose head I had just severed. I tried to not dwell on that, because I believed we still needed to act quickly.

I found the men who had been willing to dig up the grave, and we got a big fire going under Jan's body. It didn't burn. I had never seen this before. Most oupires' bodies burned, but this one wasn't burning. We grabbed it by the feet and pulled it out of the fire. Then we proceeded to use axes and shovels to chop up the body into small pieces. With the first chop, we noticed a lot of blood in his body, so we gathered the blood into pots as much as we could. Finally, the pieces were successfully burned.

We found that, while Jan was on his excursion before returning to his grave that evening, he had drained quite a bit of blood out of two cows, and then tied their tails together. The cows were very weak. We will try to nurse them back to health, because they might be the difference between life and death for the village towards the end of winter.

August 1 - We had two more ceremonies today. One was spreading the ashes of Jan over the Ostravice River. The other was entombing Emil under Saint Wenceslas Church. First, we put three coins in his mouth, and then we laid a heavy ceramic slab on top of his body. This way, if the pig lard does not work, the ceramic slab will hold him down.

We took the blood from Jan's body, mixed it with flour, and baked bread. We were able to make enough loaves so that everyone in Ostrava could have a bite. Perhaps Ostrava would now be safe from any more oupire conversions for the next generation. I have never received an explanation of how this works, and it is over one hundred years old. However, at court in Vienna, I had heard about the furor, and the success, in the English colonies when some pioneers inoculated children against smallpox. I can only wonder if this is related somehow. Did they steal their idea from this ancient oupire prevention technique? Or did we steal this idea from African rituals of inoculation against demon possession in the villages of Ghana?

August 31. Anna did recover her strength, thank goodness. She apologized for being so stubborn about Jan. I understood how she could be mistaken about what would happen. Jan was a good man, and a leader of Ostrava. We will all try to remember him that way. One of the cows died. Just for good measure, we burned it. The other cow recovered, and is making milk again.

The arrogant Doctor Gerard van Swieten has arrived on a mission from the Empress. He is investigating our claims of the terror of the oupires. He is in complete denial. He has pointed out that four more people have died in Ostrava in August, and none of them have become oupires. We point out that they ate the bread and installed iron fences around their graves. He doesn't believe the bread does anything, and stated that it is disgusting. He has also said that we are fortunate that we don't think we have oupires anymore, because the empress is embarrassed that anyone in her kingdom would believe such a thing, and she has outlawed the exhuming, destruction and cremation of any corpses.

I plan to live out the remainder of my days here in Ostrava with my family. It feels like my connection to a special mystic underworld continues to fray, but that is what life is like anyway, isn't it?

I allowed van Swieten to go on his way. He didn't eat the bread. If he dies anywhere near me, I'll sever his head before his body gets cold. No exhuming will be necessary.

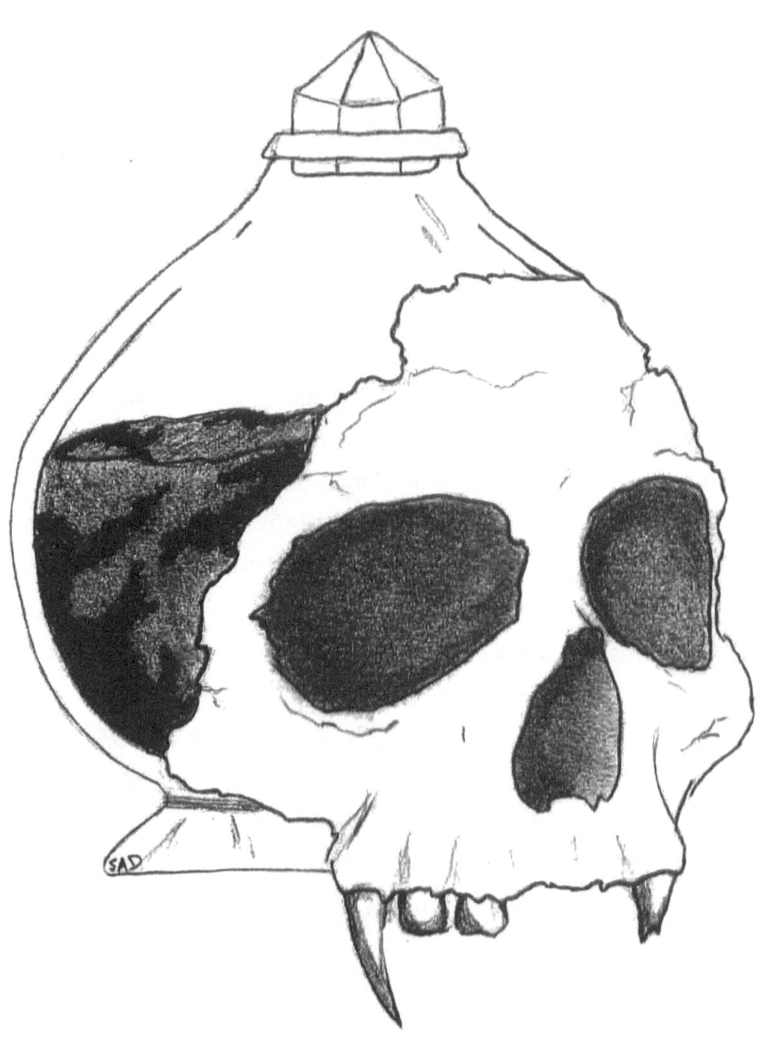

Translated from French, this is the final entry in the journal of Roseline Sauvage, notable for her extensive studies in the field of chemistry. In the following decades her experiments would be built upon by Michael Faraday in his work defining the laws of electrochemistry.

7.   A DRINK OF DEATH - Toni Owen-Blue

Second of February, 1789

I didn't think I would know my last entry when I wrote it. I'm not the first Sauvage to record my life in these pages, and I thought, like those that came before, that one day my entries would simply stop. It's the nature of this line of work: you make a mistake, your pistol misfires, a vampire has a trick up their sleeve, your plan goes awry—and it spells your death. You often don't know it's coming, and it's usually quick. I never thought I would consider such things a blessing, but now I have to look death in the eye and walk with intent to meet him. I envy my predecessors.

I wish I had more time to prepare for tonight. Not to snatch a few more months of life for myself, but for the sake of certainty: my plan has been laid with a slap-dash hand, and the concoction that is the lynch pin of it all is untested. But Lucrèce must be stopped, not because of his unholy powers, but because I see the fires of unrest smouldering in the heart of France, and if he has his way, I know that they will soon burn with a vengeance. We're not set irrevocably on that course yet, but Lucrèce wants nothing more than bloody revolution. He wants to grow fat off it, and build his terrible powers beyond the depths of mortal imagination.

The trap I've laid isn't complex but should, if everything goes as I intend, be effective. I wrote a letter to an old friend of mine, Tristan Deschamps, who attempted to woo me when I was still a young courtier. I expressed sympathy for the loss of his wife, and my regret that we had never known each other more intimately. At the end of the missive, I gave him a time and place that I would wait for him, in the hope that we might rekindle what we lost twenty five years ago.

This letter, of course, never made it to Tristan. It was always my intention that it would go astray, and fall in the hands of Lucrèce. He might suspect a trap, but even if he does, I doubt whether he will be able to resist the temptation to try and catch me unaware.

My full account illustrates in more depth why I think this. Lucrèce appears in some of my earliest entries in '66. I had killed vampires before that, but never hunted one over an extended period. I think he enjoyed being my first; he played an elaborate game of cat and mouse with me, before disappearing. Looking back to that time, I can see he was a master with over three centuries of feeding to fuel his evil rogueries, while I was a mere novice with no special talent for the work.

I met him again in Belgorod in '79, a veteran hunter by then. Yet he laughed at my new tricks, and mocked my marksmanship. He led me on a bloody chase through the city, leaving rooms of murdered women with riddles about his whereabouts written in their blood. I was on the hunt for nearly five months, before he vanished again.

The last time I saw him was in Damascus in '83, it was there we both nearly met our ends. We locked pistols, then swords, duelling through the darkest hours of the night along the banks of the Barada. It was there I cut him down the face, leaving a scar that he has to this day. But in doing that I over extended myself; so close to victory that I lunged too confidently forward. Lucrèce disarmed me with one hand, and gripped my neck with the other. I was sure I was about to meet God, for there's no human who can break the grip of a vampire.

But instead of killing me quickly, Lucrèce smelt my hair, and licked my jaw with his blood stained tongue. He bit my neck to taste me, and growled like a beast as my blood ran into him. In his moment of distraction, I pulled a cross from my coat and pressed it to the back of his head. We began to scuffle once more, and I managed to throw myself into the river.

It was during my convalescence that I came to understand my survival wasn't thanks to my own strength, but to Lucrèce's weakness. Throughout all our meetings, over our years of hunting and being hunted, he had developed a desire that I couldn't fully understand. He could have killed me that night, he could have even turned me, but he had not. It seemed to me, he would not. I knew that, if we were to meet again, that would be the key to his undoing.

So now we meet again in Paris, my true home, and I know it must be now. My concoction might be untested but, in theory, its chemical composition is sound. In the pages that precede this entry you will find the formula I have used, should this terrible tincture ever be needed in the future.

The liquid I have produced is thin, with a slight yellow cast, and a semi-transparent film on top. It smells strongly of rotted garlic and ammonia. This I have attempted to get rid of, to make the imbibing easier, but I have been unable to do so without compromising the composite's effectiveness.

I have hidden the potion within a hollow pendant that I shall wear around my neck. Usually, I would keep such things in a pocket of my coat, but tonight I will be doing away with the male garb I have favoured for all my years in this dark business. Instead, I shall favour a lady's corset and polonaise. I haven't worn the polonaise before, nor did I ever intend to. The last time I wore a gown the pannier dress was the fashion, but for the sake of the ruse, I must.

It's a new moon tonight and so, lantern in hand, I shall make my way through the back of the Deschamps' rose garden. There I will hide in wait, for as long as need be. When I'm sure he has come, I will drink from my necklace. If I'm the chemist I hope I am, I should see no immediate effects in myself, though inside the mixture will fast be suffusing itself into my blood.

When Lucrèce reveals himself I will try to flee, I think that will serve to titillate him, and allow him to catch me after a little while. When he does, he will play with me, I'm sure, and live out whatever sick desires saved me from him in Damascus. But in the end, he will drink from me, and every mouthful of my blood he takes will mean a mouthful of holy poison inside him. When the dawn comes, the chemicals will begin to quicken and will—should—mean a painful death for us both.

I have lived a long time for a hunter, and I die now with no regrets. My nephew Cyrille is ready to take my place, and pick up this journal where I shall leave it off. I only have one last wish for this life: that Lucrèce will not turn me. I don't believe I would do much harm to this world, fledgling vampires are so weak, and I know Cyrille would not allow my work to be undone. I am, in these last moments, more worried about myself. I have suffered in this life, bringing holy light to all the darkest corners of this world. To be banished to hell now, when I am about to go into God's arms, would be the cruellest of the Devil's tricks.

And yet I will take the risk with no regrets. If the price of peace in France is my soul, then that is what I shall pay.

The time has come. I must go. God save me.

```
Ichabod Crane, a small-town
schoolmaster, was secretly a vampire
hunter by night.
```

8.   BE CAREFUL WHAT YOU WISH FOR -
Henry Herz

Ichabod Crane's Diary, June 1, 1790

Oh, how I love our little valley of Sleepy Hollow, one of the quietest places in the whole world. A small brook glides through it, with just murmur enough to lull one to repose; and the occasional whistle of a quail or tapping of a woodpecker is almost the only sound that ever intrudes upon the uniform tranquility. But no longer.

Lately, the neighborhood abounds with dread tales and twilight superstitions; stars shoot and meteors glare oftener across the valley than in any other part of the country, not without cause. For as I discovered, a vampire haunts our woods.

Remorsefully, I set aside my plans to court the lovely Katrina Van Tassel, a blooming lass of eighteen; plump as a partridge; ripe and rosy-cheeked as one of her father's peaches. Instead, I vow to protect her and my beloved valley from the predations of the undead. Truth be told, I cannot claim this to be an act of pure altruism. For it is my secret hope that in ridding the town of the vampire, I shall win favor in Katrina's eyes.

Katrina Van Tassel's Diary, June 2, 1790

I rode to the apothecary this afternoon to purchase medicine for father and happened to spy the town schoolmaster, Ichabod, heading home. A kind man if, dare I say, odd in appearance. Tall but exceedingly lank, with narrow shoulders, long arms and legs, his hands dangled a mile out of his sleeves. His feet might have served for shovels, and his whole frame hung together most loosely. His head was small, and flat at top, with huge ears, large green glassy eyes, and a long snipe nose, so that it looked like a weather-cock perched upon his spindle neck to tell which way the wind blew.

Ichabod rode with short stirrups, which brought his knees nearly up to the pommel of the saddle; his sharp elbows stuck out like a grasshopper's. He carried his whip perpendicularly in his hand, like a scepter. As his horse jogged on, the motion of his arms was not unlike the flapping of a pair of wings. The skirts of his black coat fluttered out almost to the horse's tail.

My task complete, I mounted my horse. Before I could depart, that rogue, Brom Van Brunt swaggered over and seized the bridle in a thick fist, smiling and making banal conversation. While some girls swoon at Brom's broad shoulders, curly black hair and not unpleasant countenance, I find his arrogance and roughness overbearing. To escape his attentions, I told a white lie—that father urgently needed his medicine.

Ichabod Crane's Diary, June 4, 1790

Last night, as I have for a fortnight now, I armed myself and ventured forth into the shadows like a questing knight-errant; cloves of garlic in the right pocket of my long, black cloak and a pewter crucifix hung round my neck. On my left hip dangled a light cavalry saber. I holstered a flintlock pistol on my right side and slung over my shoulder a gunpowder flask. My left pocket bulged with a pouch of silver-plated lead pistol balls. Each of my high, black boots sheathed a sharpened wooden stake. I saddled and mounted my elderly Appaloosa, advancing into the darkness.

We trotted along the lofty hills rising above Tarrytown. Far below, the Tappan Zee spread its dusky and indistinct waters, with here and there the tall mast of a sloop, riding quietly at anchor. Piercing the silence was the occasional melancholy chirp of a cricket, or perhaps the guttural twang of a bullfrog from a neighboring marsh, as if sleeping uncomfortably and turning suddenly in his bed.

The night grew darker and darker. The stars seemed to sink deeper in the sky, and wind-driven clouds occasionally hid them from my sight. I approached the very place where many of the scenes of local ghost stories had been laid, the fearful tree of Major André's hanging.

As I am not a courageous man. At the sound of an eerie moan my teeth chattered, and my knees smote against the saddle. I hoped it was but the rubbing of one huge bough upon another as they were swayed by the breeze.

About two hundred yards beyond the tree, a small brook crossed the road. A few rough logs, laid side by side, served for a bridge over this stream. On that side of the road where the brook entered the wood, a group of oaks and chestnuts, matted thick with wild grape-vines, threw a cavernous gloom over it. It was at this identical spot that the unfortunate André was captured, and under the cover of those chestnuts and vines were concealed the sturdy yeomen who surprised him. This has ever since been considered a haunted stream, and fearful are the feelings of those who pass it alone after dark, myself no exception.

As I approached the stream, my heart thumped at the sight of a hunched figure scuttling silently on the far side. Remembering my quest, I summoned up all my resolution. I drew my saber and gave my horse half a dozen kicks in the ribs, so as to charge across the bridge. But instead of starting forward, the perverse old animal made a lateral movement and ran broadside against the fence. I jerked the reins on the other side and kicked lustily with the contrary foot. It was all in vain; my steed started, it is true, but only to plunge to the opposite side of the road into a thicket of brambles and alder bushes.

I then bestowed both whip and heel upon the ribs of my mount, who dashed forward, snuffling and snorting, but came to a stand just before the bridge, with a suddenness that had nearly sent me sprawling over his head. Just at this moment, a splashing tramp by the side of the bridge caught my sensitive ears. In the dark shadow of the grove, on the margin of the brook, I beheld again something black, misshapen, and sinister. It stirred not, but seemed gathered up in the gloom, like some dark monster ready to spring upon a traveller.

Though I will never admit it publicly, I shall set down here the truth of the matter. I had vowed to confront the vampire, but now facing the terror first-hand, I could not muster the fortitude to confront him. Rather, the hair rose upon my head, my hands trembled, and my bowels threatened mutiny.

The shadowy object of alarm put itself in motion and, with a scramble and a bound, stood at once in the middle of the road. Though the night was dark and dismal, the form of the cloaked vampire might now in some degree be ascertained. Sharp fangs glittered in the starlight. There was something in the dogged silence of this monster that was mysterious and appalling.

As my terror rose to desperation; I rained a shower of kicks and blows upon my horse. Away we dashed through thick and thin; stones flying and sparks flashing at every bound. My flimsy garments fluttered in the air, as I stretched my body forward over my horse's neck in the eagerness of my flight. Gripped by the horror of the moment, I resolved to find new quarters in a distant part of the country. Northward we galloped through the woods, not halting our panicked flight until reaching Peekskill.

Katrina Van Tassel's Diary, June 6, 1790

It has been two days, and no one can account for our missing schoolteacher. The degree to which I miss the odd fellow surprises me.

Still, during my evening walks in the woods on our farm, I have encountered a handsome gentleman wearing a dark suit and cape who spoke with what might have been a Romanian accent. Unlike Brom, he was both charming and sophisticated, and I found myself quite taken by him. Though I gazed into his eyes, I am still unable to recall their color. Time seemed to lose all meaning in his company. His demure refusal to discuss where he resides or why I never see him on my daytime trips to Tarry Town intrigued me. I hope to spend more time with him and to remove his veil of mystery.

It was said that any woman who loved
Edgar Allan Poe, was doomed to die.
Upon his own death bed, Poe raved
deliriously about a mysterious figure
called 'Reynolds'. Those two facts are
not as unrelated as they may seem.

9. THE DEATH OF A RAVEN -
Camellia Landman

September 27, 1845

He's clever, that's for sure. Cleverer than any
undead beast I've tracked before. He's constantly
surrounded by a veritable buffet, and he lives so
publicly that I cannot touch him. He flaunts his dark,
twisted nature so brazenly and is applauded for it at
every turn. It is infuriating, the blasted Edgar Allan
Poe.

I had almost managed to catch the creature last
night before he once again slipped from my grasp.
Never have I had to try so hard to enter into the orbit of
an undead. I had managed to secure an invitation to the
literary salon of the ever-discerning Miss. Anne
Charlotte Lynch. The salon is only for whom Miss.
Lynch deems the best and brightest of the New York
literary world, putting me in competition with the likes
of Emerson and Melville. I needed to be published

before I even had a chance for a respectable conversation with her.

I have never claimed to be a philosopher or an artist or anything of the sort. As luck would have it, a vivid description of the real darkness I encounter in my true profession was taken as, "an exquisite depiction of the human condition," and other such nonsense. There is nothing human about Poe's condition.

Upon publication, I was free to talk my way into an invitation. Everything was on track! I should have been free to pack my bags and move on. I had heard tell of quite a few of the disgusting undead out in Rhode Island. That is where I should be instead of chasing after Poe! Woe, I am instead left to stew in my failure.

I almost had him! Miss. Lynch welcomed me with open arms. I stuck to the fringes, neither standing out nor disappearing. People moved about each other with practiced ease, lively conversations springing up left and right.

Then he entered.

The energy shifted immediately. It was palpable, like he was a magnet drawing their focus as he drifted to the parlor. He perched himself on the edge of one of the couches, Miss. Lynch to his left and Mrs. Fanny Osgood at his feet. He began to recite one of his gothic poems from memory as the other guests watched on with rapt attention. As if his writing is anything more than a projection of his own guilt at the creature he is. The Tell-Tale Heart indeed.

I watched as the room fell under his spell, the women in particular. He was a spider drawing them into his web of silky words and arrogant charm until they were all ensnared.

Thankfully, I had taken precautions to defend my mind against the onslaught of demonic influence. With a silver cross hanging securely around my neck and pentacles sewn into my socks, I was immune to his allure.

I had felt such pity for all those in attendance who had fallen for the wiles of that creature. My own arrogance got the better of me, as it would turn out that it was I who should have been pitied!

I had planned on following Poe as he left the salon. He must have caught on to my intentions. As I've said, he is a most clever creature. To think what he could have been had he not been afflicted by this curse!

Everyone was mingling once again. I could tell he would soon be taking his leave. I began to make my move, positioning myself in such a way that I could easily slip out unnoticed behind him. I glanced back to check his position when his gaze met mine. And he winked! The hubristic peacock winked!

He leaned over to whisper something to Mrs. Osgood, and a screech rang out from across the room. Miss. Elizabeth Ellet stormed over in a flurry of rage, arms waving about uncaring of whom they may hit. The two women were in an argument for the ages. It drew quite the crowd, and in the midst of the commotion I lost sight of Poe.

I could have screamed, myself! He was there one moment and gone the next—he must have back slang it while I wasn't looking.

I rushed out onto the street, hoping to catch a glimpse of him as he fled, but there was no trace of the creature under the light of the moon.

And now, I find myself lamenting my abject failure. The beast saw me, plain as day. He knows that I am after him, surely, he will come up with more creative ways to evade me.

I cannot let the matter rest. If it takes months or years or the rest of my miserable life, I will slay the beast that is Edgar Allan Poe. This I swear.

With grim determination,

- N.T. Reynolds

February 2, 1847

I've just heard news that I cannot help but feel responsible for. Three days past, Virginia Poe née Clemm moved on from this world. Survived by none other than Edgar Allan Poe. I should have stopped him by now. I should have saved her. Her constitution had been waning for years under his "care." I can only think of whose life he may take next.

He had become infinitely more difficult to access upon his move to the countryside. I could not step foot into Fordham without alerting him to my presence. Perhaps now that he is no longer tied to the town, my opportunity will arise. I cannot allow him to take another victim.

I believe his next target will be none other than Mrs. Fanny Osgood. The pair have quite the history, and if Mr. Rufus Wilmot Griswold is to be believed, she has been in danger from Poe for some time now. I shall be heading back to New York tomorrow to see that she is alright.

    With fervent resolve,

    - N.T. Reynolds

September 30, 1849

    It must be fate! I had nearly given up. After so many years spent in pursuit of the same creature, I thought him untouchable. When he went south, he was securely out of my reach. Lady Luck must be on my side at last, for whom did I just pass on the street but none other than Edgar Allan Poe.

    He appeared not to notice me, walking on with his usual air of mystery. This will be my chance. I refuse to allow this beast to slip through my fingers once again. After frolicking through the country, fooling ladies with his charms at every stop, he has returned to me in an act of providence. Make no mistake, Edgar Allan Poe will not be leaving Baltimore.

    With steady blade,

    - N.T. Reynolds

October 7, 1849

    Quoth the Raven, "Nevermore."

    - N.T. Reynolds

Excerpts taken from the wartime diary
of Miss Cora Joiner, regarding her time
as a volunteer nurse at the Delannoy
Plantation Hospital north of Natchez,
Mississippi.

10. NO MIRRORS - Mina Humiston

April 30th 1863

On Caspar's suggestion I have taken up diary writing again. It is something I have not done since I was a little girl—how long ago that was, and frivolous too! At times I wish I was a little child again, happily ignorant of the evil which resides in this country. But one cannot force the sands of time back up the hourglass, so to speak, and therefore I will not dwell on it. I hope this practice will strengthen my nerves.

I suppose I ought to describe my surroundings. Wishing to remain near to Caspar and Hiram, I obtained permission to work at this new hospital. It has been set up inside a recently abandoned plantation home. The surgeons here tell me they discovered the place only a few weeks back. With it being so spacious, clean and empty they thought it the perfect setting for the sick and injured to recuperate. I can't help but to agree. The sprawling grounds are covered with beautiful oaks, wild roses, and persimmons and great Magnolia trees. The place has become somewhat unkempt, but I feel that this only enhances the natural beauty of the area.

Inside there is a wonderfully old library and two grand pianos. Already some of us here have begun "borrowing" books. I must get over there when I have the chance, before everything disappears! During a lull in activity one of the other nurses played a few pieces from memory. It was quite a lovely time. It took our minds off of the war, even if only for part of an hour. I do hope she will play again!

I shouldn't get ahead of myself. For all of its beauty this place has a horrid past and purpose. The nurse's quarters have been set up in some of the slave cabins, and in ours there was a large, rusted stain soaked into the hard dirt floor. The dirt has since been sifted to bury the spot but I still shudder to think on it. It seems all the slaves have fled, for the surgeons say that there was nobody here when they stumbled upon this spot—not a living soul. I pray they've made it to freedom, either through northern lines or farther south and down to Mexico.

It is getting very late. I must retire soon if I am to be of any use tomorrow. I am glad for the new start; I am ashamed to say that at the last hospital, I fainted at the sight of a stack of human limbs being simply chucked onto a growing pile. The sight—the stench! It took much effort to revive me and the surgeon was quite impatient. I believe he still might be. I vow not to repeat the incident; I wish to prove myself.

...there is one queer thing: the grand house has no mirrors, anywhere!

May 1st 1863

I have grown accustomed to the absence of mirrors in this place, but it still puzzles me somewhat. I wondered, at first, if perhaps the Master took them with him when he and his household fled. If so, why leave behind the countless pieces of fine art which decorate the walls? One of the matrons recognized the pieces and introduced me to the fine copies of Titian, Lambert, and Constable, and when I can, I stop to admire them.

I am glad to have brought my own mirror with me. It is only a sentimental object. I don't think myself vain, but I do wish to remember what I look like and to know if there is blood on my face. I find its presence comforting; it is like having a piece of my mother by my side, may God rest her soul.

In any case I don't mind the lack. The men are kept from gazing upon their own mangled states, and the artwork gives them something pleasant to look at as they convalesce. At the very least, I hope it takes their minds off of their suffering. There is now a rumor floating amongst the sickbeds that the "Angel of Death" stalks these halls. I find the idea awful. Even being away from the battle does not free these men from war.

May 3rd 1863

Oh, nursing is difficult work!

Physically and emotionally difficult. I shall regain my composure, only allow me to weep onto the pages first.

The men here are troubled. They don't trust the doctors and many of them fear dying here rather than on the field of battle. I cannot blame them. In most wards one can hear moans and groans, and in the surgery room it is like the back of a butcher's stall—blood drips and sprays and creates pools upon the floor. The floors have not been cleaned, and so there are brown prints leading out of the room.

The thing which sticks most in my mind is the continued talk amongst the soldiers. It is the specter again. Some say it is the reaper, some the ghost of their fallen comrades, and some the vengeful specters of the men their bullets found.

It grows worse still. A young man—a boy, really—was brought in yesterday. An amputation proved necessary. He was in a black mood because of this, and when I tried coaxing him into letting me write a letter to his family, he said he had none. A terrible thing, if it is the truth! I still weep sometimes over the loss of mother and father; I cannot imagine being so young and having no family. I digress. Despite this foul mood his condition seemed good, and we all hoped he would rally.

This morning he was dead. It is as though some feral beast attacked him, for there was a large wound on the side of his throat and over his heart as if something were trying to get into the muscle and blood inside. Indeed he was gray as a stone. Another nurse wondered if he'd bled to death. It certainly seems that way, but his sheets were clean and unblemished as undriven snow. He's lost blood...what took it?

Caspar was on hand for the burial. He and everyone else who saw the boy's body were quite disturbed. I am still troubled, for the case makes no sense no matter what angle it is viewed from. I weep for the boy and his family and for Caspar and especially Hiram. There is the fear always lingering in the back of my mind: that they should be brought here woefully injured or dead.

May 8th 1863

One should not be ignorant of troubles, but it does no good to dwell on them. I ought to focus on the good things. This task is easier to-day, for Hiram has been promoted to Lieutenant! Caspar and I are very proud, and we celebrated with a few cups of coffee in what little time we could eke out.

Caspar tells me that my role is as important as anything else here, but I sometimes wish I could do more. Hiram helps to lead the men, Caspar provides for their spiritual welfare. I only assist those more knowledgeable than I am. Perhaps it is only my insecurities which cloud my judgement...which leads me to another good part of these past few days. A new nurse, Mrs. Molly Swales, has begun working here. I believe that we are already becoming fast friends. She is long-time widowed, and only a few years my senior, but you wouldn't know it for she is so worldly and well-traveled. With her knowledge of herbs and healing, she might be considered a "wise woman." Nothing can bother her for she takes everything in stride. I only wish that were the case for myself.

I do find her somewhat queer, for upon my noting the condition of the place her expression grew grave. When I mentioned my own mirror, she advised me to keep it close. I can't see why it should help anything, but I also cannot think of how it might hinder, and so I shall keep it on my person. Most people have their own strange quirks, and so I will indulge hers, for I enjoy her company, and the wonderful yarns she spins.

May 10th 1863

Caspar visited the hospital to-day with the task of distributing letters and reading to the soldiers. He informs me that Hiram is doing well, only suffering from a minor case of nerves. I pray that those nerves won't overwhelm him as they once did when he was a boy.

We have all been very busy. Molly tells her stories to the soldiers to take their minds from the suffering. If only I could, I would pull up a chair and listen, but I have other duties. To-day I assisted the surgeons, wrote a few letters, and passed out coffee and tea to the men as well as the surgeons. I long for this war to end soon.

I ought to end these entries on good notes, but another strange thing happened this evening. As I traveled across the grounds I thought I saw a figure high up in the trunks of one of the oaks. When I looked up into its canopy I saw a gray, sickly face peering down at me. It appeared to be the boy we'd buried. I can note this calmly now, but the sight then gave me such a shock; I'm afraid that I tripped over my own skirts in my hurry to get away. Once I collected myself and looked up again I saw that there was nothing there. I don't know what I saw.

It was twilight, I am overworked and tired, and my mind was elsewhere. Still, the image of that specter leering down at me like some bird of prey would a mouse frightens me. Molly has returned to the hospital, and I am alone here in the nurse's cabin.

I hope that I see no more dead men in my dreams. Most of all I hope the others will retire soon. Some of these nights in the "sunny" south can be quite damp and chill. Therefore Molly and I have taken to sleeping close together to preserve body heat. Human touch and the comforts it provides help to keep the nightmares away.

May 13th 1863

Most all the same to-day. Hiram paid us a visit to see his men. He does have a terrible case of the nerves. He conceals them well. It was only when we were alone that his facade cracked, and he slumped against the wall with an expression of great despair. To my horror he wept. I could do nothing but hold him. He told me that he isn't sure how much longer he can continue on. He fears for the men under him, for his comrades, that every day might be his last. He must have seen how my eyes watered, for he gathered himself up and apologized, and made me promise not to tell anyone what had happened.

I promised him. I have already broken that promise, and I feel terrible for it. I told Molly my troubles, both because she asked and because I could not bear to carry them by myself. If I cannot trust Molly, who can I trust? She is a stalwart and true woman, stout in both body and heart. She comforted me, saying that if Hiram has survived this long he will surely make it, and that if he does perish he shall have lived and died a true man, and we would be reunited one day. When I continued to weep she only held me. She is a good confidant and I am grateful for her company. I suppose she understands loss because she has already lived through the death of her husband. She tells me they had been married for all of two years before consumption took him.

May 18th 1863

Terrible news! Hiram has been injured. An amputation proved necessary and they've transferred him here. He is alive, but he is not well. At the moment he is somewhat delirious. He has lost his left arm from the shoulder down, and every time I lay eyes on him I must look again, for my mind tells me that my eyes deceive me. It is a sight I will never grow accustomed to. When he is of sound mind he grows despondent, for he fears dying in a sickbed. I overheard him say that he wished he'd died on the field. I wish he wouldn't express such an awful sentiment, but indeed I think that disease is perhaps a greater enemy than the Rebs, for it floats among every one of us unseen, like some malevolent spirit.

There is no use in distracting myself, but I attempted it. I was ordered to go and rest and so I left the ward. On my way out I passed a few of the paintings and examined the portrait of a man among them. He is Mr. Delannoy, one of the original owners of this place, who perhaps died shortly after Washington crossed the Delaware. The piece quite strikes me because there is something of a hunter within his pale gaze. How talented the artist must have been to capture such a thing! I did not like to look at it for too long.

After our long shift Molly and I were allowed to retire. We washed the blood from our sleeves as best we could. I asked her to tell me one of her stories. I wish now that I hadn't. I don't know what to make of what she told me. She checked that we were alone, lit a pipe, and began an account of something that occurred in her hometown in New England. I cannot tell it as well as she did, and I do not wish to linger on the grisly details, so I will summarize as best I can:

Consumption burned through the area one winter. Entire families were stamped out by the terrible sickness. Those who fell ill reported, with much terror, that those who'd previously perished came to them in the night and sat on their chests and squeezed the air from their lungs. It was only after some of the corpses had been exhumed, and their hearts cut out and burned to ash on a stone, that the strange illnesses stopped. An awful story! When she saw I was upset she apologized, and yet still said I ought to remember her tale. Why? I hope to put it from my mind as soon as I can.

May 19th 1863

He is dead.

May 21st 1863

It troubles me deeply. Hiram, like the boy, succumbed to wounds he'd gained overnight. Wounds to his chest and throat. Could they have been self-inflicted? None of the men around him know anything, but a few have reported that "the reaper" made an appearance once more. Staff and soldiers are beginning to worry, and the head surgeon is pondering whether the hospital ought to be moved. Is there a beast lost in these halls? Or perhaps some new and hideous disease arriving from the battlefield? Sometimes I wonder if Molly knows more than she tells, for more than once she has slipped off into the night, and I have awoken alone.

I believe I have never prayed more in my life. For Hiram's soul, for Caspar and Molly and everyone here. The only solace I can take is that his temporary resting place is beautiful, shaded by oaks and decorated with wildflowers. Molly collected a bouquet of wild roses to lay on the grave—a gesture which touched me deeply.

May 25th 1863

I do hope that I am not a burden. Here are my insecurities again. I do not wish to leave here; I feel that Caspar needs me more than ever, and in spite of

Molly's secrecy I do not wish to leave her side. I was sent away early, for I am fatigued with grief. I am alone again. Good-night.

May 26th 1863

It is so early that the sun has barely risen. I hastily write this account down in order to clear my head. I dreamt of Hiram last night. I wish that I could not dream! Even the oblivion of sleep gains me no relief. I awoke—or I thought I awoke—to find my neck bent in such a way to fix my gaze upon the paneless window. Despite the darkness I could make out little motes of dust dancing around the room. They drifted aimlessly at first. Then they seemed to pick up speed and purpose, congealing into the shape of a man. I began to feel quite afraid then, for a man about in the darkness can have no good purpose.

The face was outside the window, looking in, and I recognized it. It was Hiram's visage in that colorless dust, and I wanted to reach out, but I could not move. Then the sun's first feeble rays reached in through the window, and I awoke. Nothing there, only the other nurses. Though asleep, their faces were as tense and grim as my own feelings. We are all worn down in body and spirit by this cruel war.

May 30th 1863

I am certain now that I have taken leave of my sanity and will awaken at any time wrapped in a straight waistcoat. Nobody may see this diary now, lest they think me mad!

I've been sleeping badly these past few nights. It is all or nothing; either I am too exhausted to even dream or else I am plagued by nightmares. Two nights ago it was a moving, crawling pile of limbs, and last night it was Hiram again. It began in the same way, with the dust and moonlight, and then he was there, standing over me. I found that I could move, but I was too afraid to do so. For he that stood over me possessed Hiram's face but none of his goodness. He—it—began to stoop. He came lower and lower until I came to my senses. Either we'd made some terrible mistake and buried him alive, or else he'd come back from the grave in an affront to God and nature. As such I began screaming. So useless! All I could do was scream!

Molly, sleeping beside me, awoke and sprang to action. She grabbed my mirror from under my pillow and chased the ghastly thing away.

The others, aroused and alarmed, pleaded to know what was happening. Molly, again, took charge. She told them that an ill-intentioned vagabond had come in, but that I'd spotted him and raised the alarm. She then gripped my shoulder and led me out of the cabin. She stopped at the entrance and replaced a small bouquet of roses and what must have been garlic flowers, for they smelled so strong, atop the door ledge. She then pulled me away from the cabin.

I was still in a state of hysteria, and so she grabbed me by the arms and held me steady until I'd calmed down. Her dark eyes were steely; all of her merriment was gone and in its stead was grim determination. She reminded me of her tale of the Un-Dead and then, swearing on her sanity, told me that something of a similar nature was surely happening here.

When I suggested that she was still spinning yarns she reminded me of the grisly wounds inflicted, of the specter which haunted the sick soldiers, of the curious fact of the mirrors. She returned to me my mirror and wiped the tears from my face. She told me that Hiram— how I hate to repeat it! That Hiram is in danger of becoming such a beast himself if we don't work with haste to dispatch the body and save the soul.

I guess I am mad for believing her so easily. But I know that there is something going on. I asked who this original beast might have been, who killed the boy and now Hiram and is repelled by the presence of silver mirrors. What Molly told me chilled all the blood in my heart: that the master of the household had never left! There is no worse place we could have set up a hospital, save for perhaps the lowest level of Hell!

June 1st 1863

I must continue with my work. I must pull myself together, lest they send me home. If I must leave, let it be after Hiram is cared for. Molly and I went to the grave to restore the roses. I worried that the monster, Mr. Delannoy, had disturbed the grave. Molly believes it was only an animal; Delannoy has surely been sated enough for the next few weeks. How I hate the thought of Hiram's blood running through his veins!

Molly says there is some beneficial property to the wild rose. I am beginning to wonder if it was the circumstances surrounding her husband's fate that started her down this path. She confided that she'd come here after hearing rumors from the freedmen. How many times has she carried out this sort of task? It seems like a lonely existence.

June 2nd 1863

We were occupied all night and could not get away until shortly before dawn; and when we arrived at the grave, Caspar was there. My blood ran cold to see him; I feared that he'd been made another victim. He seemed asleep, for his back was slumped against the trunk of a magnolia, and his cap was pulled low over his head. When I began to fret that he'd succumbed to his own grief, he stirred. I felt suddenly guilty and disturbed, for there was no good way to explain the task we'd come to undertake. I stood there uselessly, the lantern hanging in my hand.

Molly greeted him and then asked if he'd had any nightmares about Hiram, and he confirmed as much. Then Molly abandoned the formalities. She told Caspar that we needed to disinter Hiram's body before sunrise.

Caspar became irate when he realized she was earnest. He was about to speak when she shushed him and ordered us to hide and quickly blew out the lantern. We took refuge behind a great oak. When I peeked through a gap in the lower branches I saw the thing that had taken Hiram's form approaching. He moved so unnaturally, like a man mesmerized, and I could not look away. Caspar gasped sharply; Molly had used my mirror to show Caspar his lack of reflection. The thing then appeared to dissolve into the grave. We rushed to the spot to see that the dirt had been somewhat disturbed once more, and Molly demanded to know if Caspar believed his own eyes. He'd gone very pale, and I feared that he would faint. I scarcely knew if he could stand, and so I offered him my hand to hold. Weakly, he asked how he could be of assistance.

Molly was very grateful to him then; three pairs of hands were much better than two, especially when it comes to gravedigging. We had to work quickly, lest somebody see and report us.

I will summarize again, though it pains me to do so. I opened the lid and saw Hiram's remains. He looked as fresh as the day he died, mouth shut, jaw firm. A small bit of blood trickled from his ears, and his skin was gray.

Molly said that was a good sign, for he had not yet begun to feed on unsuspecting souls yet. Molly requested that Caspar read from his Bible while she carried out the deed. I could only stand and watch. I've never felt more useless. She staked his heart and...

I cannot bear to recall the rest. My only consolation is that Hiram looked at peace after the business was finished. I hope that he truly is.

Now Molly says that our final undertaking is to find and destroy Delannoy's corpse. Caspar has volunteered his assistance. We will need to work fast. I never wish to feel useless again. When we find this demon, I intend to be the one to stake it.

June 6th 1863

I have not written as of late. So much has happened. Molly believes Delannoy's grave is in some hidden chamber. This beast must possess some form of intelligence and surely will grow wise to our purpose. We must strike hard and fast. I believe I've developed some bloodlust, for I would like nothing better than to slide a blade into this monster's flesh. It is a violent thing to say, but it is my true feeling. I believe Caspar feels the same. He hopes to carry out this execution soon, for he will be departing within the next week. In the meantime we must see to our mundane duties. I must be here and present. I must stay vigilant; it is doubly awful that this monster should prey on helpless, sick men who cannot fight back.

June 6th, 1863

Wonderful news! I believe I have found the entrance. I entered the library for the first time in a while, to find a book that one of the soldiers had requested when it occurred to me that there was a space between shelves. It is barely large enough for a man to pass through, but a specter could. I told Molly, and she said she had not searched it yet. I had to take the book and read to the soldier, while Caspar was sent to inspect the place. I do hope that I have found it.

June 7th 1863

For the third time I shall summarize. It happened this way: It was the portal to Delannoy's subterranean tomb. It was so cramped and dark that I feared the walls would close in. We discovered the tomb, and then returned to work.

We came away from our duties as soon as we were able to. Caspar and I met first, and we mused over this odd and nightmarish situation. It seems there is no going back, as even by electing ignorance we cannot forget what we've seen. We waited, fearing that somebody may come in and demand to know what we were doing, or that perhaps the beast would spring out. I kept an eye on the door and Caspar kept watch on the hidden entrance.

Molly arrived ten minutes later, begging our pardon; she had to gather her supplies. She then hurried us down. Night was near falling and Molly did not think we could face Delannoy at his full strength. We descended with lanterns held high and entered the bloody cavern. Despite the frigid air, I was sweating. The place reeks of iron, and the walls are splashed with rust.

Opening the tomb's lid proved difficult. Dread overwhelmed me. If we could not overcome this demon with haste, a worse fate than death awaited us all. As the stone made an appalling crash of sound, Molly thrust the stake into my hands. She produced her own tool, a wicked silver knife. She must have given Caspar orders as well, for he began reading from his Bible.

I do not know what was said; all the blood in my body rushed to my ears as I pinned the stake over Delannoy's chest. I am ashamed to admit my hands shook.

In the light I saw that his eyes, pale as moonlight, had opened. He stared with such malice, baring his too-white teeth. I recalled Hiram's gray, slackened face and stiffened my resolve. As I hammered the stake in he began to writhe and moan. My hands became wet and warm with more blood than seemed possible. Bile coated my tongue.

I faltered; he sat up; Caspar dropped the book and grabbed the beast by the shoulders, holding him down, and Molly made quick work in separating the head from the body.

It was over, then. The flesh withered. The bone turned to dust. There is nothing left of the old devil save for the bloodstains which coat his tomb. Caspar's watch revealed the ordeal had taken all of ten minutes. God only knows how long Delannoy's reign of terror must have lasted.

We are all quite exhausted. We washed the blood from our hands, our arms, our sleeves. Now that the deed is done I fear all the fire within me has been extinguished. What now is our goal? To watch men become disfigured and die?

June 10th, 1863

I thought that after avenging Hiram I would feel much better. I don't. I am still disheartened. I am relieved, of course, that there will be no more unnatural deaths here, but the monster's death did not unto the damage wrought. It certainly did not restore Hiram to life.

Molly understands how I feel. There is no way to prevent that which has started long before we were born, but what is in our power is the ability to prevent that which happens in the present. She has heard other rumors from places farther south, out west, and up north.

Caspar is done with this work and wishes only to return to his ordinary role of Chaplain. I do not blame him. However, I do not feel the same way. When this war is over—for everything must have an ending—I will join Molly in hunting down these Un-Dead creatures. I am glad to have met her, and I am glad to be her partner. At the moment, however, I have coffee for men in the sickward that won't pour itself.

Part 2

CYNTHIA HAWTHORNE BLEDSOE
44 PROSPECT PARK WEST
BROOKLYN, NY 11215

August 16, 1942

Ens. Wendy Anastasios
RAF Pembrey,
Burry Port
SA16 0HZ, United Kingdom

My dear Wendy,

I would not bother you at such a time if it were not truly important. Especially considering our estrangement. It is unfortunate we didn't get the chance to speak before the war. I accept responsibility for that. I have never been good with the things family is supposed to do. I admit in the last decade I have been so focused on my work I have allowed most other things in my life to fall away. I swear it was for a good cause.

Alas, there is little time for such regrets.

You will find a parcel with this letter. Please take care with it!

This has been my life's work. I know it will seem odd to you at first. I apologize. I received this stack of records in a dusty box, from my Uncle Charles. Your great uncle. He, like myself, was a reclusive scholarly man, and he marked me as his heir early on, as I did with you. On his deathbed he handed me a fine mess.

I have spent years organizing his files and corresponding with his sources. The more I worked, the more I found. Uncle Charles had friends, connections all over the world, and the records just arrive. It was my task to collect the information. To make some sense of it all.

Now this is your task.

I know this must be quite a lot to put on your plate, but I believe you are uniquely qualified to do it. I have watched your progress through school, your focus and you ambition. Your bravery in joining the military in our time of need. I should confess now, it was I who paid for your tuition at Sarah Lawrence. My uncle did the same for me, far before it was conventional or even acceptable for women to go to university.

I leave you all I own. The houses in Society Hill, Tarrytown, the French Quarter, and

Paris. My stocks and, of course, the boat. But most of all, this legacy. You are now the record keeper, and you must continue this work for the course of your life. You must look among your family for an heir to pass it onto when you are done.

I am sorry, Wendy, to put this responsibility on you, especially now. It is a lonely one, but one I am sure you are up to.

All of my love, and blessing from the afterlife.

Your devoted auntie,

Cynthia Hawthorne Bledsoe

23ʳᵈ September, 1893

bread

cheese

beef

paper so I can keep my shopping lists elsewhere

fig. 1: Abraham's Star of David

Note to self: Stick to the day job, Joseph. You'll never make it as an artist.

24ᵗʰ September, 1893

Francis Varney moves around in sunlight easily — sun effect must be a myth. I wonder about garlic?

But Abraham's David's Star worked. I must keep mine on me. I must make sure that Eliza and the girls wear one at all times as well.

garlic

remember to get paper this time

25ᵗʰ September, 1893:

These are not good days in Ireland. The death of

The personal diary of Joseph Fishbyne, lately of Portobello, Dublin; his diary indicates that vampires have infiltrated the furthest reaches of Europe.

Case # 0011 - BLOODTHIRSTY - Caolán Mac An Aircinn

22nd September, 1893:

My grandfather, Avraham, was the bravest man I've ever known. I hope that I can live up to him, and also that I never have to.

I caught Dunleavy looking at me again today. I think he suspects.

23rd September, 1893:

bread
cheese
beef
paper so I can keep my shopping lists elsewhere

24th September, 1893:

Francis Varney moves around in sunlight easily—sun effect must be a myth. I wonder about garlic?

But Avraham's David's Star worked. I must keep mine on me. I must make sure that Eliza and the girls wear one at all times as well.

24th September, 1893 (later):

garlic
remember to get paper this time

25th September, 1893:

These are not good days in Ireland. The death of Charles Stewart Parnell, who came the closest to peacefully delivering freedom for this country, has weighed on the national consciousness. Though the Land Wars are mostly over, there is restlessness, and I worry that parasites once thought banished will worm their way back into this society. Years of steel and blood are coming, and I fear the Jews of Ireland will not be easily quit of it.

I had occasion today to reflect on my being here, in this place, rather than in Odessa, in the Russian Empire, which is where I was born many moons ago. I was asked to address a local meeting of the Gaelic League and speak about the evils of empire. My own story is in large part that of a frightened child whisked away by his mother, a congeries of bright images and transitory terrors, so instead I told the story of Avraham. It concerns a fishmonger—not a rich man nor a cunning one, despite what was implied in the years after the Tsar's assassination—standing in his own little village home against the Cossacks, whose bloodthirstiness knows no bounds. One in particular, their commander, seemed to make an impression on my grandfather. He was a great big brute of a man, a nobleman, it appears, of some ancient Greek family, whom my grandfather knew only by the nickname of Taku. This Taku led his horde from village to village, murdering Jews as he went. Why, I asked my audience, did all this happen? Why, it was because some people had decided to kill a Tsar and one of them was a Jew. Never mind that the rest were Christians. That was enough to damn us in the eyes of the Cossacks. They set about purging us from greater Russia, which had never been the kindest of homelands, with fire, sword and musket. It serves the goal of empire, I explained, to discharge one's malignant energies on the helpless, such as the Jews, or indeed the Irish. For if we were not there to absorb the shock, why then, it might be turned upon those who originated the problems—I mean of course the empire-builders.

This much I said to general acclaim. But as I spoke, my eyes had been roving around the crowd. As they did, whom should I spot but Dunleavy, squirrelled away in the back. He was nodding away with the rest of them, but I noticed that his eyes were fixed on me, and they were bloodshot with rage. Dunleavy is an unhealthy-looking man, a great swollen purple thing, like a bag of blood shoved into a tweed suit. His jowls drip and tremble, his hairy hands are always twitching and jerking about or preening his moustache. He is greatly proud of his moustache, is Mr. Dunleavy; it is long like a Magyar's or a Turk's, and depends to either side of his mouth, as if framing it, or concealing it. I believe he owns some company or other, or perhaps a shop, though now I think of it I am sure I have never seen him working anywhere. Perhaps he has old money.

At any rate, he is sufficiently prosperous that he can while away his hours at these meetings while managing to do precisely nothing for any cause but his own. Avraham told me stories about such men.

So I continued; I spoke over the applause. I told them Avraham's story, not in philosophical overview, but in all its dreadful specificity. I told them of how he told my parents and brothers and sisters to hide; how he stood out in the main street when the Cossacks thundered down, just a man in a shirt and vest and trousers, an unarmed man, and how he screamed:

"You come looking for the Jews? Well, here I am. Take me!"

They came for him in a Wagnerian tide, like valkyries on their horses if valkyries knew only hate. They ringed him round, the cowards, with their guns and swords, and he was there with his open hands. Taku was right in front of him. I saw all this from where I hid. And, though I did not say it then, I remember very well that Taku was just such a man as Dunleavy was. For all that he was one of the finest horsemen on the steppe, he was swollen and purple, over-bloated, to where I wondered how he could sit his horse. He even had mustachios. This man, this bloodthirsty brute, levelled his rifle at my grandfather. He had not even the courage to use his sword, but insisted that he kill this little man from a distance. The Irish liked this. It reminded them of their tragedy at Vinegar Hill in 1798, where their pikemen were riddled with musket shot.

How did Avraham know? He pulled out from around his neck a Star of David, and at the sight of it the monster Taku shied, and his horse bucked. All of a sudden the Cossacks who had seemed so disciplined were in a jumble; their horses tossing and snorting, the men hauling on the reins, wide-eyed.

It was then I realised something important: they were *afraid*. Not of Avraham, but of Taku. If he should stumble, then some great power indeed was at work. And indeed they broke, so that Cossacks streamed down the village street away from my grandfather, kicking up flurries of snow with the speed of their passage. The last to go was Taku. He did not, would not, could not approach my grandfather and the holiness of the symbol in his hand, but before he left he spat at my grandfather and told him in Russian:

"I will hunt your family to the ends of the earth."

This all was well-received, evidence where none was needed of the brutality of empire and of its brutish scions. Well-received by all, I should say, except Dunleavy. The smile slid off his face like grease off water as I spoke, and his gimlet eyes transfixed me with loathing.

He *knows*.

But so do I, Dunleavy. So do I.

1ˢᵗ October 1893:

Eliza and the children complain about their Stars of David, saying that they draw the gaze of passersby in the street; but better strange looks than the attention of a vampire.

Vampire. There. I've said it. Or written it, as the case may be.

I am given to understand that Bram Stoker is undertaking a novel on the subject of the vampire. How little he knows! For the vampire is not a pale, shrunken thing; rather, it is a glutton which sates itself endlessly upon blood. This is why the vampire is purple and bloated.

The girls tell me that a strange man was waiting for them outside of their school, and that they avoided him only with difficulty. Eliza told me that a well-dressed, corpulent man approached her in the street and attempted to engage her in conversation. Their descriptions match that of Dunleavy. I fear that I do not have long left before the final confrontation.

2nd October, 1893:

Moishe came to visit today with news. He has been helping me with my research, and I had asked him to look into Dunleavy. I expected that he would find that Mr. Dunleavy was not in fact Mr. Dunleavy, but had come here under an assumed name, perhaps shortly after Avraham and the rest of my family came to this country; that it would transpire, indeed, that Mr. Dunleavy was the vampire Taku, come from Odessa to Ireland to exact revenge on the family who humiliated him. Instead, he discovered that Dunleavy is a native son of a long line of moderately prosperous Kingstown merchants.

It is odd, is it not? Some evils seem to follow my people from place to place in the world, and some others, no matter where we set our foot, spring up malevolently at our arrival, new yet familiar. Yet this country has been, on the whole, kind to us. Did not Daniel O'Connell observe that Ireland is "the only country that I know of unsullied by any one act of persecution of the Jews"? I will repay that kindness by driving out the vampire scourge.

Now where did I put that garlic?

2nd October 1893, evening:

I wonder how deep the rot in the Cantacuzino family went. Was the old emperor of Byzantium a vampire too? Were his parents? His siblings? I will have to find that newspaper in the archive again tomorrow.

3rd October, 1893, early morning:

He came at the stroke of midnight, with an admittedly admirable sense of theatrics. But I was ready for him. I am wearing my Star of David to ward him off, I have cloves of garlic in my mouth to forestall his ravening bite, and a stake at the ready to put through his heart. (This had better be worth it—with the garlic, I doubt Eliza will kiss me for a week.) I awoke to see that the light of the moon and stars and gaslamps through the window was blotted by an enormous, squatting shape. As I watched, he undid the latch of the window and let himself in. (I know that lack of invitation, now, is no barrier to the vampire.) Mercifully, Eliza did not wake next to me, though the cold wind raised goosebumps on her skin and caused her to stir fretfully. If the vampire touches her, or the girls...

"I know who you are," Dunleavy said, crouching on my windowsill. "Grandson of Avraham, who humiliated my brother. There is a price on your head."

"It will be doubled after what I do tonight," I said, and I jumped for him with my stake and my Star of David wrapped around my fist. But the wretch, he took flight; simply leaped from the windowsill and took on the aspect of a bat in midair.

(Note: must tell Moishe about this. I don't think we knew they could do that.)

So now he knows who I am, and also that I know who he is. If I am to have any advantage, I must press it now. Eliza, I assume you are the one who is reading this. I am going to pursue the vampire and nail him to the ground like the crawling parasite he is. Please God, I will be able to write as much in this diary myself. If this is the last entry, know that I love you very, very much and that I have done what I have done to keep you, the girls and all of Ireland safe.

I love you, Eliza. Goodbye.

*£10 reward offered for information as to the whereabouts of Joseph Fishbyne, lately of Portobello, or Joseph Dunleavy, lately of Kingstown.

An Incomplete Record of Personal Accounts

From the journal of Engineer Vasily Petrovich Malenkov Trans-Siberian Railway, February 1893

Case # 0012 - THE WHITE HUNGER - Bill Mulligan

February 3rd, 1893

The storm has worsened. The men curse the wind, the cold, but they may as well curse God himself, for he had deigned to create this forsaken land. To what end, I cannot say. It is said that once our toil has ceased, that many lives will be saved, that the trains will move great numbers without fear of nature's wrath. If it is so, it will be built upon our blood. We have lost two more workers—bodies discovered this morning, blackened with frost, their limbs twisted as though they had died in agony. The madness that grips men as their blood chills to ice lay marked on their faces, contorted with fear. Neither showed signs of exposure before nightfall. They were hard men, stronger than me. We found no tracks in the snow to suggest they had wandered. They simply vanished from their tents, only to be found at dawn, as if the wind had lifted and discarded them.

The learned men of the church are wrong. Hell is not a place of fire.

February 5th, 1893

The Tungusic guides refuse to work after dark. They whisper of a presence in the storm. "Nangen" they call it, as best as I can pronounce the word. They will not explain. When pressed, the eldest among them spat on the ground and warned me: "Disturb not the sleepers in the ice." The overseers laughed at this superstition, but even they no longer stray far from the fire at night. I found the guides later, desecrating the bodies of the unfortunate victims of the cold, to prevent their return. Savages, proud of their ignorance.

Fresh workers have arrived, a welcome sight. The sooner we cut through this desolate land, the sooner I may relegate it to my nightmares.

February 7th, 1893

Something is wrong.

Two more men went missing. Their bunks were empty at dawn, yet no one heard them leave. No footprints lead away from camp, only the howling wind, and the endless white. A search party found a single body three miles south—half-buried in the snow, his coat half-torn away, skin waxy and mostly unblemished, like some porcelain doll. His eyes were open, and his expression...I will not forget that face. Their throats were torn, possibly by some carrion feeder, though what life this land can sustain is a mystery to me.

I have watched men die in agony, tortured for their crimes, yet none of them matched the horror in that man's face. What death would induce such terror?

Work is at a standstill. The days here are short, and nothing—not threats, not entreaties, not promises of gold—will make the men leave the safety of their tents. Though how safe are they? The workers huddle in numbers far greater than the shelters can provide. This cannot go on.

February 9th, 1893

Tonight, I saw it. I cannot believe what I now know to be true. I pray that the cold has driven me mad. I should rather spend my last days in an asylum than face this truth.

I had taken first watch with Antonov. The wind had quieted, the night deathly still. Then I heard footsteps crunching through the ice, slow and deliberate. Antonov saw them first: figures emerging from the treeline.

I thought them survivors from another camp, but as they stepped closer, I realized the truth. Their movements were stiff, as if their limbs were half-frozen. They wore ragged, outdated uniforms. Some in tattered coats of Napoleonic make, others the remnants of the Tsar's army.

Antonov whispered a prayer, but the figures did not react. They stood at the edge of our shelter, watching, never speaking. In the firelight, their eyes shone like those of a beast. Then one of them opened its mouth.

No breath. No steam in the freezing air. Just black gums and long, broken teeth.

Antonov fired his rifle. They did not flinch, even as the bullet tore through the collar of a man wearing a dark blue habit-veste. But when I stepped forward with my torch, they recoiled. I do not think it was the fire—so puny a flame could

141

not suffice to hold a dozen men at bay. I believe it was the light they feared.

I was close enough to see their features. I now know why our men died with horror carved on their faces. Whatever these creatures once were, no trace of humanity remains.

We fled back to camp and warned the others. I ordered the men to keep the fires burning until dawn.

February 10th, 1893

The guides were right. This land is cursed.

I spoke again with the oldest among them, Gantumur. He told of an ancient burial ground hidden beneath the permafrost. The dead here do not rot. They *wait*. The cold keeps them in slumber, but when the balance is disturbed, when the ice is cut too deep, they wake, to walk, to feed, to drink the warmth of our blood and assuage their endless cold.

We have cut too deep.

How came these cursed men to this forgotten grave? No soldier of Napoleon walked so far in his doomed, foolhardy invasion, and yet I see the tattered uniforms of the Garde Impériale. I cannot be certain, but I believe I witnessed Bulavin's Cossacks, Pugachev's rebels, and even the wretched souls of the short-lived Baikel insurrection, men who had fought and died on our motherland's soil. But men no longer. Were they brought here? Why? Gantumur mutters something about this land being used to contain the bodies of those who walk though they are dead. I would once have thought these the ramblings of an uneducated fool...Science and logic deny such things. And yet...

Gantumur says there are ways to stop them, but it must be by the hand that freed them. I suspect I am to assume the blame, bear the guilt of those whose orders I follow. I am expected to destroy them or sacrifice myself in the attempt, hoping to appease the restless spirits.

I have no intention of dying. But in the desperate eyes of the men beneath me, I see few options.

February 11th, 1893

Today we fought back.

Gantumur entrusted me with a spear of leaded steel, an ancient thing ornately fashioned, the Lord's prayer carved into the hilt. It feels unnaturally cold and heavy in my hands. With the last of their strength, the workers tore a hole into the earth, large and deep enough for a man.

The Nangen appeared moments after the setting sun. They have changed; faster, hungrier. The blood of our fallen comrades has replenished them after so long a fasting. I allowed myself to walk within yards of them, able now to fully comprehend the horror.

Their faces are smooth, the frozen skin and flesh sanded away from so many years in the grinding ice. In the oldest, little more than skull remains. Their teeth are unnaturally long. They say that teeth grow even after death, but these are the fangs of an animal. A predator's teeth, formed for merciless slaughter.

I had judged them nothing more than restless corpses, but now I sense the hungry intelligence within. They smiled at me until they saw the spear in my hand, and then rage overcame them. A Cossack leaped for my throat, and I ran toward the safety of my men, jumping over the freshly chiseled hole. I spun around and plunged my weapon into his chest.

Any mortal man would have died instantly, but the creature hissed and fought me. I forced him to the snow, then kicked him into the makeshift grave. With the same iron hammers we used to build our railroad, we pounded the spear through its chest, pinning it to the frozen earth. The men pushed dirt over him, filling the hole. The ground shifted for a bit and then grew still.

We celebrated until we noticed that the army of the Nangen had doubled in size. Among their number now stood our fallen comrades from the first night, their faces lean and hungry. The ancient rituals had failed us. We now knew that death was not the worst of our fates. Those demons with lips smiled at us. There could be but one end to this fight. We retreated to camp, deflated, all hope gone.

February 14th, 1893

I have made my decision. Or, rather, it has been made for me.

The men are terrified. The dead return each night, coming closer, testing the edges of the firelight. They do not attack, not yet, but they are waiting for the flames to die, for the living to weaken and lose whatever advantages life gives us.

I write this final entry, so that whoever finds this journal will know the truth. If I fail, tell the Tsar—tell the world—this railway should never be completed. Take our tools and build a wall.

I have organized the men with strength remaining to dig graves, to dig until their hands are bloody and frozen. They forged railroad spikes together for enough spears to man a Roman legion. Tomorrow, when the Nangen retreat from their silent watch, I will order the weak to flee the camp, to make a desperate flight for freedom. I do not expect them to succeed, but at least they won't add to the enemy's number.

With a handful of men, I will make our stand. I am an engineer, it is my duty to study a problem, to bend the earth to my will. We shall scatter fires among the graves, to make the enemy mass his forces at places of our choosing, negating their advantage in numbers.

It is a mad plan, with little hope of success, but it is a plan. Should we destroy them all, it will most likely come at a cost. I can only pray to a God who has abandoned us, that I freeze in this lifeless white hell, for if I should join the ranks of the blood-drinking dead, if I should be reborn in a body immune to cold and hardship, our world of warmth and plenty will fall before our army.

We should not have come here.

*The final pages are stained with blood, the ink smudged. Vasily Petrovich Malenkov was never seen again. The camp was later found abandoned, the fires long dead, the snow undisturbed.

Case # 0013 -ALL THE DEVILS AT ONCE - Gwendolyn Kiste

Friday, May 27th

I'll say it, even if no one else will: Abraham Van Helsing is a scourge.

The man kills one vampire and suddenly considers himself an expert in the field.

Pardon me: the man *watches someone else* kill one vampire, and suddenly considers himself an expert. Because everyone knows he wasn't the one to wield the stake. That honor goes to the Texan with the bowie knife who didn't live long enough to tell the tale. That's why Van Helsing is telling it for him. He's considered a hero because he's fashioned himself as one.

Now we might be miles from Prague, even further from London, those glittering cities so faraway they might as well be in a dream, but that doesn't mean we haven't all heard about Van Helsing. When you help vanquish a count—a man of power—word tends to get around. Bored villagers are good for one thing, and that's talking. And when I ventured into the marketplace this morning, all they could do was gossip.

"He's coming," the ladies at the fruit stand whispered, their calloused hands aflutter.

"Who?" I asked, searching the wooden carts for an armful of apples that weren't bruised or half-rotten.

"Abraham Van Helsing," they said, looking far too pleased with themselves.

I seized up on the cobblestone. "Why in the world is Van Helsing coming to our village?"

The ladies glared at me, the same way they'd looked at me ever since I was a little girl. "For the vampires," they said with a snuff. "He'll be here by sunrise."

At this, I nearly belted out a laugh in their faces. Of course, he would be traveling at night. What an amateur.

With my head down, I abandoned the apples and ventured down the street, sneaking through the back door of the tavern. Eliska, the owner's daughter was waiting for me, her dark hair in a braid, her cheeks already flushed.

"Valeria, have you heard?" she asked me, her voice breaking apart. I only nodded. She and I hid ourselves away for the rest of the day, reading from our old occult books, the spines splitting in our hands.

She paced back and forth in her tiny bedroom. A spinster's bedroom, the local men would say. "Should we be worried?"

"We should always be worried." I reached out for her hand. "But we'll figure it out. We always do."

Eliska gave me a small smile, and for a moment, everything seemed all right. She and I have been friends since we were practically toddlers. My only friend, the only one I ever needed.

Van Helsing is everywhere now. On my way home, you couldn't turn a corner in this village without hearing that poisonous name on someone's lips.

"Van Helsing will save us all," my sister said at supper, her greedy eyes gleaming. "He'll teach us how to protect ourselves from harm."

Like we aren't already doing that. My sister pretends there isn't a garlic wreath hanging on our door, a dozen wood stakes tucked away in every drawer, hawthorn bushes lining the property like a fortress. This house is a vampire ward incarnate, and that isn't because of my sister or her dubious husband or any of her sour-faced children.

It's because of me.

Not that she ever remembers. Not that anyone here remembers.

Saturday, May 28th

The ladies from the marketplace were right. Van Helsing arrived ten minutes before dawn.

"Isn't his carriage magnificent?" they all crooned at the tavern when I stopped by to visit Eliska.

I scowled through the window, watching his black horses whinny nervously on the street. It looked like an entirely ordinary carriage to me.

Eliska beamed at me from behind the bar. "Are you going to introduce yourself to him?"

I shrugged. "What for?"

"Perhaps so you can teach him a few things."

I couldn't help but grin back at her.

Here's the thing they won't tell you: nobody becomes a vampire hunter by choice. You do it because you have to.

Because there's something in the shadows of your village, and nobody else is willing to take care of it.

And here's the other thing they won't tell you: almost all vampire hunters are women. They're the killers you never suspect. The wives and mothers and sisters and daughters. The ones who spend the day cooking stew in a kettle and folding herbs into a poultice. The ones who spend the evening tucking their children into bed and then stealing onto the midnight streets, a wooden stake waiting in their pockets.

We know the risks. In the evening gloom, we might meet monsters, and we might meet men, and either way, we know we're in danger. But our husbands and fathers are skittish as colts, cowering behind their tankards in the taverns, puffing out their chests at the mention of vampires, sinking back into the shadows the moment someone calls for volunteers to dispatch one.

Tonight, the village was still busy welcoming Van Helsing, so nobody noticed when I slipped away at sunset, loitering in the nearby graveyard. It shouldn't be so easy to find a vampire. But they're drawn to death, to the soft earth still stinking of rot and mourning. The moon had barely risen in the sky, when a gaunt creature crept out from behind the village's only mausoleum.

"Good night," I said, and buried my sharpest stake dead-center in its heart.

When I arrived back in the village with a handful of dust—proof of my exploits—the men merely curled up their lips and ordered another round. "Van Helsing would have done it better," they told me, and flicked a single gold coin my way. The meager pittance this village gives me for saving their lives.

Monday, May 30th

Yesterday morning, Van Helsing held a meeting right in the middle of Sunday mass.

"We must convene as soon as possible," he told the men.

I did my best not to sneer. I for one was never permitted to hunt vampires on the sabbath. Or even mention them for that matter.

"It's sacrilegious," the villagers would say, their eyes narrowed, their holy fists clenched.

But they made an exception for Van Helsing. Half the patriarchs in this village skipped church, treating our esteemed vampire hunter to an early round at the tavern.

Eliska got the grim honor of serving the slathering wolves their sour ale, as Van Helsing regaled them with tales of train trips through the Carpathians and madhouses where the men dine on flies and climb the walls like spiders. By the time I arrived, the locals were devouring every word the professor spoke, as though he was the wise father they never had.

"Your vampire is a very interesting specimen," Van Helsing told them. He said it like we only had the one vampire to worry about. He still thinks of it as an isolated problem like a single case of the cold rather than the bubonic plague.

"He's a fool," Eliska whispered to me, and the two of us giggled like the schoolgirls we used to be.

One small mercy: at least he isn't staying with them. Each night, the village has been rotating who gets the honor of hosting Van Helsing, shepherding him from doorstep to doorstep like a common vagabond.

But one thing I wasn't expecting was a knock on our own door. "Good afternoon," Van Helsing said when I answered, tipping his hat to me.

"You have the wrong residence," I growled, ready to slam the door in his face.

But then my sister materialized at my side. "So wonderful to have you, Professor," she said and took Van Helsing's useless hands in hers.

"He's not welcome here," I said, pulling her aside, rage boiling in my guts.

My sister stood a little taller. "Why won't you do this for us? For our family?"

She forgets everything I've already done. She and her husband claim they take care of me, despite the fact they're living in my home.

"You should help us," my sister said, that hateful look glinting in her eyes. "We wouldn't want the locals to start their talk about you again."

There it was in the space between us, the words left unspoken. The villagers never liked me. I save their lives, and they detest me for it. She and I both know there are places for people like me. The madwomen, the difficult women, the ones with forked tongues and truth brimming in their veins. And everyone knows what happens in those places. They'll chain you to walls. They'll lash you with belts. Then they'll forget you ever existed in the first place.

I backed away from my sister. "So long as it's only for one night," I said, and she smiled at me, bright and false as a sermon, just like she always does when she gets her way.

Tuesday, May 31st

It's already tomorrow, and Van Helsing hasn't budged from the wingback chair. *My* chair.

"This is such a delightful home," he said as he perused my bookshelf. I tried to hide the best tomes—the folklore and the fables and the encyclopedias with entries on beasts that go bump in the night—but he managed to pilfer a few of my favorite occult titles anyway.

"I think I'm going to like it here," he said with a smile.

Thursday, June 2nd

At supper, Van Helsing finished off the last of our cured meats from the cellar. He went through a month's supply in just a few days.

"I don't want to be an imposition," he said and then took a second helping.

Monday, June 6th

It's been a week, and Van Helsing isn't going to leave. Not anytime soon. Not unless we give him a reason to.

He won't hunt vampires either. "All in good time," he promised again last night at the tavern, and because they're fools, the men believed him.

Meanwhile, Eliska and I met a trio of vampires in the graveyard that nearly had us for dinner. Long after midnight, we retreated to her room in the back of the tavern, massaging tinctures into our wounds, bandaging up our bloodied hands.

In other villages, the women band together. They help each other. But it's just the two of us here, and sometimes, it's barely enough.

We curled up in bed, her long hair cascading over me, her scent like lilies in the morning. "We'll figure it out," I said, and I wondered who I was trying to fool.

Wednesday, June 8th

Sometimes, I wish I was a vampire. Then I could rip out the throats of the men who've wronged me.

Friday, June 10th

Tonight, I waited for my sister and her family to retire to bed. Then I crept down the stairs, practically an intruder in my own life.

"No more," I whispered. I wouldn't endure that man for one more night. But as I wavered in the doorway, everything in me held tight, I suddenly heard that terrible melody as mournful as a dirge.

Weeping. Van Helsing was sitting in the parlor, and he was weeping. Thick tears on his ruddy cheeks, snot clogging up his nostrils like a wayward child at naptime.

And all the while, he kept repeating the same words.

"Devils or no devils, or all the devils at once, it matters not; we fight him all the same."

He was afraid. Of course he was.

Something softened in me. "Is there anything I can do?"

He shook his head. "There's nothing, my child," he said, and I wanted to remind him how I'm far from a child these days, but by then, he'd returned to his weeping, so I turned back to the stairs and disappeared into the dark.

Saturday, June 11th

At sunrise, Van Helsing emerged from the parlor, his eyes limned red.

"It is time," he said, and all day, he readied himself with wooden stakes that were too thin and garlic that had long since lost its potency.

"He's going to get himself killed," Eliska whispered, as we watched him in my backyard, muttering under his breath. He invited a few of the men from the village to join him tonight, but as always, they politely declined.

"Good luck, professor," they said brightly and raised their latest round of ale to him.

Only Eliska and I followed, tracking him to the graveyard, the one place where you'll always find a vampire in this town. And tonight didn't disappoint.

There were more of them than I anticipated. At least four figures, gaunt as a grave. A thin stake quivering in his hand, Van Helsing seized up the moment he spotted them. No surprise there. When he vanquished the count, he had brave men by his side. Far braver than him. He wasn't used to doing it alone.

They descended on him, quick as lightning, and Eliska and I charged forward. We told ourselves we were ready. We told ourselves we could handle this.

We were also wrong.

I'll never forgive myself that we got separated. Me, tumbling over tombstones near the beaten path. Eliska, facing off in the shadows by the mausoleum. I managed to destroy one of the creatures, and that was enough to scare the others. They backed away from me, setting their sights on Eliska instead.

I parted my lips to call out to her, to warn her, but Van Helsing saw this as his chance for chivalry.

Still quivering, he wrapped his arms around me. "We must go. *Now.*"

I thrashed against him, but he was stronger than I expected. Taller and broader and more brutal. He wanted to save me. He didn't understand he was condemning my best friend.

"Don't," I said, but it was already too late. As he dragged me away by the waist, Eliska turned back once, just as the figures surrounded her.

"Valeria," she cried out, her voice splitting in two, and then they were upon her.

Monday, June 13th

The funeral was a quick little affair. No flashy sermons, no floral garlands, not for a tavern keeper's daughter. She was nothing to this town. Nothing to everyone except me.

"It was a simple mistake," Van Helsing said, and the other men slapped him on the back and told him he did his best. As though anyone in this village has given their best in years.

I waited alone until nightfall. Until the gentle stirrings in the earth. It never takes a new vampire long to claw their way out of the grave. They're stronger and more eager than the living will ever fathom.

"Hello, Valeria," Eliska said, coffin dirt still clinging to her like a lover. I stood back, already knowing what I was supposed to do. I should finish her off. I should let her rest, once and for all.

We went walking together instead, twining between gravestones, hiding out behind the mausoleum.

"It doesn't hurt as much as you might expect," she whispered, and my heart twisted in my chest, because I wish it hadn't hurt at all.

We roamed the cemetery until it was almost morning.

"I miss you," I whispered.

She gave me that small smile. "You don't have to," she said, her scent of lilies almost overwhelming. "We can be together now."

I knew what that meant. She wants to give me her profane gift. She wants us to share the night forever.

Part of me wants that too.

Tuesday, June 14th

In the waning afternoon, I find Van Helsing in the parlor, sitting there like a still life.

"I need your help," I say. "I need the whole town's help, actually."

Instantly, he perks up. "Whatever you want, my child."

He's the only one who can gather everyone together. All the men, and my sister too, following him through town at sunset, like rats in thrall to the piper. He doesn't tell them there are vampires. In fact, at my behest, he lies and says we're meeting another vampire hunter at the crossroads.

"Almost there," Van Helsing says.

The sun has just vanished among the trees when we reach the graveyard.

"Why are we here?" my sister asks, and then she gets her answer. Eliska emerges from behind the mausoleum. And she's not alone. She's brought every vampire she could find, all the ones who hide in the shadows. She's even recruited a few new faces. After all, it's not just the living that want to meet Van Helsing—the undead are eager to get a look at him too.

"We can fight them together," Van Helsing tells the men, but he still doesn't understand. This village wants to sit back while others do the fighting for them.

In a flash, it's chaos, the men exhaling their useless shrieks, the creatures closing in. They take my sister first, her throat torn out in an instant. And they save Van Helsing for last, shattering his spine, shattering him.

But I'm not like the others. When it's over, there isn't a scratch on me. Not a single drop of blood. Not even a bruise.

The villagers—what's left of them anyway—will talk about this night. They'll say I walked away with fire in my eyes and laughter bubbling up my throat like sweet grog.

They'll say I left half the locals to be devoured whole, with only the moon as their witness.

Maybe it's all just rumors. Or maybe it's the truth.

All that matters is that I'm the only one left to tell the tale. Van Helsing used to know something about that. Now the world will have to take my word for it.

As dawn cracks through the edges of the sky, Eliska gives me one final smile. "We can still be together," she whispers, but I only shake my head.

"Another time," I say, and disappear into the long, desolate shadows of the grave.

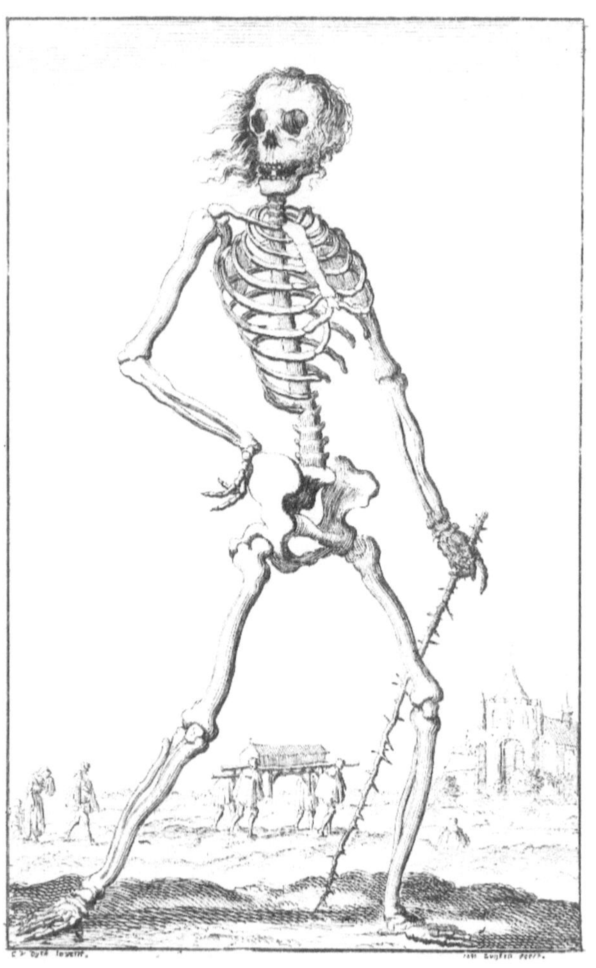

Captain William Connor Bryant served as a British Army Military Police Officer during World War 1. In 1917, he was tasked with finding a group of AWOL soldiers suspected of smuggling contraband threatening Swedish neutrality. What he uncovered was something far more sinister. This is his final diary.

Case # 0014 - ATTRITION - Johan Robertsson

Stockholm, October 19th 1917

One could argue that there is little honour in starving people, but a war of attrition hinges on hunger. My superiors believe that our trade blockade is the only thing preventing the Swedes from an alliance with Germany, which is why it is of utmost importance that the embargo holds.

I have confirmed the names of the six British soldiers suspected of bringing in the foodstuffs. According to the telegram I received yesterday evening, they are all of rather excellent character, which surprised me. Apart from Private Woodfield having been written up for violating uniform regulations, their records were all spotless. I was very disappointed to find Private Mansfield on the list. He served under me in France, and I came to hold a great deal of respect for the man. Not someone I would expect to desert their post. Well, I can admit when I am wrong, and these scoundrels are likely exploiting the embargo to overcharge the poor Swedes on rations. Most ungentlemanly.

I have made a friend at the customs agency (cigarettes go a long way here). According to him, the Finnish steamer intercepted this morning carried two of the suspected soldiers and several crates of contraband. Our men have been detained, and I have arranged to interrogate them about the whereabouts of the others. I will draw no small satisfaction from returning them to England and seeing them judged for their improprieties.

*Undated Entry

Most unexpected turn of events. Most irregular. The two detainees are dead. By their own hands by all accounts. Most ungentlemanly.

Stockholm, October 20th 1917

I am ashamed to admit that I am in a bit of a state this evening. The aforementioned interrogation never took place as our fellow soldiers, Lewin and Talbott, had deemed themselves guilty, as it were.

That in itself would be disturbing enough, but as I and Inspector Karlsson soon discovered, our Finnish steamer was carrying a most unusual cargo.

Karlsson, a large man of few words, allowed me to attend the search, which took place at 2 PM. A modest vessel, it was swiftly surveyed. Karlsson discovered a crude hand-drawn map in the cockpit. I traced it when he stepped out for a cigarette.

The lower deck cargo hold held three wooden crates in slightly varying shapes and sizes, suggesting they had been hastily assembled. When Karlsson pried open the first one, expecting tins and barrels, we both had a start. There was a dead man inside. He wasn't wearing clothes. Ghastly sight. Blueish gray. Bullet wound to left middle torso. Bottom of box casket filled with congealed blood. He wasn't dead when they put him in there. Second box, similar find. Third box. Private Mansfield. Alive.

Stockholm, October 21st 1917

Private Mansfield has expired, God rest his soul. I wasn't able to get anything out of the poor chap before he succumbed to his injuries (bayonet by the look of it). Karlsson is nowhere to be found and local authorities have no reason to divulge any further information. It is a great, grim mystery as to why someone would smuggle dying men across the Baltic Sea in the middle of a war. Or why they would turn on their own and dispatch Mansfield in this horrid manner. What disturbs me most is that there seemed to be little to no effort to deliver these three alive. At this point, I am no longer looking into dubious activities of opportunist soldiers. This is murder. I need an answer to whom and why, lest I fear poor Mansfield's fate will haunt me to my dying day.

The map I traced suggests that the cargo was to be delivered in town. After some deliberation, I have decided to assume the identity of Talbott, one of our dead soldiers, and make the delivery myself. I have secured a private's uniform and three fitting substitutes for our coffins, paying some local riffraff (rather handsomely) to load them up with stones and wool.

With a bit of luck, I can discover and expose this fiendish plot in one fell swoop.

Stockholm, October 22nd 1917

May the Crown and our Lord forgive me. This is now far beyond my orders. I am risking career, honour, and perhaps my life, and in case this journal ever were to find its way to my superiors, my main defence is that I am simply doing what is right. To leave this matter would be a sin of the highest order; a blatant disregard of the principles and duties required of me as a soldier in His Majesty's service; and above all, an obscene dishonouring of the dead men found upon that ship, Private Mansfield in particular. No man deserves such a fate, thus, not completing my investigation would be most unbecoming. Ungentlemanly.

I followed the map to deliver my substitute cargo. It led me to a man named Albrekt, a peddler of various illegal wares, and clearly of low character. As I committed to the role of Talbott, we only communicated via his very fundamental grasp of the King's English, but I know enough Swedish to understand when I'm dealing with a charlatan of the highest order.

It was clear that Albrekt was expecting the bodies as he went out of his way to avoid inspecting the crates. I had decided to soak the wool blankets in a few pints of pig's blood from the local abattoir. The smell sold the ruse. However, he was visibly upset when I admitted that none of the victims were alive. It struck me as very odd to expect wounded men to survive without warmth or comforts in wooden boxes barely fit to transport apples. At this point, he did what any dishonourable coward would and fled. The chase was short lived. Once I caught him, I made the regrettable decision to extract answers by force. To the cretins credit, he did not divulge much.

The boxes were headed for a small village in the northern territory of Dalarna.

Mora, October 24th 1917

I have travelled to Mora by train, a day's journey north of Stockholm. Since I cannot travel in uniform outside Stockholm, I wear local attire, my Webley concealed in an improvised holster. Beyond the capital, the embargo's effects are palpable. Hunger prowls behind every pair of eyes I meet, like a primeval god stirred awake by the sanctions. I am very careful not to draw its wrath.

Tomorrow, a local named Larsson has agreed to take me to Eldris, the location named by Albrekt. Despite being all but skin and bones, he only agreed to take me once I had offered all remaining chocolate, cigarettes, and a scrap of cheese I've carried since Copenhagen. That leaves me with no other bargaining chip but my pistol.

Approx. 0.5 km outside of Eldris, October 25th 1917

Larsson drove me in his little carriage but refused to take me the entire way to Eldris. His rural dialect made him very hard to comprehend, but it was obvious that he was afraid. Perhaps he is wise enough to realise that being seen aiding a British gentleman wouldn't curry him any favours. Then again, I have seen boys in trenches waiting for the whistle with more composure.

It would have been dishonourable to force the man, so I travelled the last kilometre by foot. I have made my camp on a hill overlooking the village. Counting hearths and candlelight, it's no more than twenty houses in a valley, fields to the south, forest and mountains to the north bathing in moonlight. I can see a pair of lanterns where the road reaches the first animal pens.

What ungodly reasons would a small farming village have to trade in wounded, foreign soldiers?

*Undated Entry

Awoke 03.14 AM. Noises in woods. Steps, breathing, 4-5 feet. Bear/wolf? Drew pistol. Cocked. Considered warning shot. Heard voice. Man. Old man. Sudden shout from the valley. Villagers with lanterns. Three men. Person in woods withdrew. Two villagers?

Oct 26

Barely any sleep. I am struggling to make sense of last night. I wrote down the sequence of events, but I'm already questioning half of it. In the light of day, an object has appeared on the field near the tree line to the north. I did not bring my binoculars, but I know a fallen soldier when I see one.

I fear the only course of action is confronting the villagers.

*Undated Entry

I have seen one of the missing soldiers! He is being held in one of the pens on the western part of the village. I am currently being detained in one of the farmhouses. The villagers seized me as soon as I approached. They confiscated my side bag, but did not discover my concealed weapon. They left this notebook but took my pen, hence the coal. They are as hard to understand as Larsson, and seem just as afraid. They kept referring to someone named "Gamlingen," which I roughly translate to "the old one," likely a village elder. Hopefully, I will soon be given the opportunity for diplomacy. If not, I will have to put these wretches in their place.

*Undated Entry

It has been nearly six hours. No food, no water, no elder. There is much activity outside. It seems they have realised that their shipment is not coming. Some of the men are armed with sickles and pitchforks, too many to shoot my way out.

Searching for an escape, I discovered a cellar door. It led to nothing but a hole underneath the floor, but its contents have disturbed me deeply. It was filled with clothes and shoes. Among them uniforms, two of them ours.

Oct 27

I have decided to depict the events of the last ten hours as objectively and matter-of-fact as possible, as much for the benefit of the report as for my sanity.

Around 10 PM last night I was bound and escorted by three villagers to the pen holding the other soldier. I identified him as Private George Woodfield by the regulation-violating beard. Upon entering the roofed pen, Private Woodfield showed no sign of registering my presence. At first glance, I feared that he was dead as he hung off the floor from his wrists, strung up by the rafters. His face was bloodied and battered, and he was in uniform. I considered that Private Woodfield might be dead, but then he coughed. My assailants bound me to a wooden fence, then proceeded to hoist Private Woodfield down. When I protested, I received a swift punch to the chin. At this point, Private Woodfield suddenly got his wits about him, likely energised by hearing the King's English. As they carried him past me, he spoke. Though his speech was slurred, this is what I heard him say:

"I will bring you as many as you need! Please!"

I saw their lanterns head north before they disappeared out of sight. Remembering the body on the field I saw the previous day, I decided to go for my revolver. At the time, I hoped to intervene and save Private Woodfield. However, I did not manage to free myself before I heard the men returning in a hurry. I concluded that they were no longer carrying Private Woodfield, which brought new resolve to my efforts. I broke a rusty nail in the pen fence with my boot, and sawed through the rope. This took me approximately ten minutes during which I could hear Private Woodfield's distant pleas for mercy. Fortunately, they hadn't bothered locking the gate.

There was no lantern in the pen, nor anywhere outside. But the moon was nearly full, and I managed to make my way out into the field headed for the dark tree-line. This is when I heard a sound I struggle to describe. Animal-like, but not like any animal I have ever heard. It was followed by Private Woodfield, shouting at the top of his lungs. I produced my Webley and ran in the direction of his voice. Within twenty seconds I stumbled onto Private Woodfield blubbering in the slick grass. He was tied to a stake driven into the ground. Realising there was no use in pulling him free, I fired my pistol through the rope at point-blank range.

This is when I thought I was losing my mind.

In the muzzle flash, I saw a figure standing no more than ten feet away, between us and the forest. Writing this, I cannot think of any explanation for its queer appearance, all I can do is account for the dark, the flash, and the chaos of the situation to preface my description. I saw a man, or something in the shape of a man, well above six feet tall, yet hunched over. It looked as though it was covered in an animal pelt, draped across its narrow shoulders. Either that, or some kind of deformation to its back. The most striking feature by far, however, was the elongated face. Huge black eyes.

It shuffled towards us in the moonlight with a terrifying determination. When Private Woodfield grabbed me, yelling for me to shoot, I fired. The first shot may have missed, but I heard the impact of the second one. In the flash of the third, the creature was still standing. And I swear on my dear mother's grave that it bared fangs at me. I grabbed Private Woodfield and dragged him towards the village not knowing where else to take refuge.

When we reached the houses, the villagers were waiting. Once within the light of the lanterns, I made it abundantly clear I was armed by firing a warning shot, knowing full well this left me with a single round. Luckily, they cowered, and let us pass. I returned to the house where they had held me earlier to retrieve my things. I found my side bag had been ransacked, leaving me with my single round. In return, I recovered my pen and found my journal where I had stashed it. But when I made for the door, Private Woodfield had collapsed with his back against it, refusing to let me go back outside, as the villagers gathered on the other side. At this point he was raving, bleeding heavily from his neck. For a brief moment, I thought I had shot him in the commotion, and tried to apply first aid. That's when I discovered that he had been mauled across the side of the throat. He was bleeding out. When I kneeled at his side, his voice was but a whisper. This is, to the best of my recollection, what he said:

"They lured us here. He's cursed them, stolen their minds as he did Lewin and Talbott. The old man of the woods. Kill everyone. Starve him."

Then Woodfield dozed off. He bled out within minutes. Not knowing what to think, I am ashamed to admit that I hid in the house all night, cradling my revolver. There has been noises outside, screaming, and running, and dying. It is quiet now. The old man of the woods—Gamlingen—has come to my door. He whispers in the dark, whispers that he will let me live if I bring others.

Well, old chap, a war of attrition hinges on hunger.

Elsie Jackson was most active in the 1920s, specifically from the years 1925-1928. While she disappeared shortly after the stock market crash of 1929, the notes she left behind were invaluable to decades of future vampire hunters. The wealth of knowledge, specifically in the ways one can detect vampires, helped to catch the infamous Butcher Vamp of Baltimore in 1953, and many of Jackson's techniques are still used by vampire hunters to this very day. Below is a selection of Jackson's journals with particularly revealing information regarding the detection of vampires.

Case # 0015 - DOUBLE SHADOWS AND BREATHS NOT TAKEN - Juno Crew

6th April 1928

I have been following this current vampire from speakeasy to speakeasy across the city for a week and a half now, and yet I'm still not sure who exactly it is. There are a few people who show up at most of the gin joints, and I've narrowed my suspicions down to three of them—the three that have been at every saloon where there's been a body.

First of my suspects is Leo Winters, who speaks like someone trying his best to pretend he's British when he's really American. He never talks about himself, and I don't think he was simply born with those sharp canines. Theresa McCoy flashes her smile at all the men, and they fall at her feet. Whether it's just her good looks (she is an absolute doll), or a thrall, I can't yet tell. And then there's Warren Day. He is the most confounding of my suspects, which also puts him up much higher on my list. He seems perfectly ordinary, smiles and talks just like any other man. Slurs his words after a few drinks, and I think I saw him try and sneak a peek down my dress when he thought I wasn't looking.

It is one of the three of them, of that I am sure. And I highly doubt it would be two or more. They do not look as if they know each other much at all. And besides, vampires don't work well in groups. They are incredibly territorial. I once saw a group of four vampires tear each other to pieces, no intervention from me necessary. So yes, I think it is one of my three suspects. My gut tells me it's Warren, but I absolutely cannot make a move until I know for sure. I will not hurt an innocent person. Not again. I will go back out tonight. I think this vampire of mine will be on Lenning Street tonight, given its past travel patterns.

7th April 1928

I killed the damn thing. It took me the better part of the night, watching all three of my suspects, but my gut was right, in the end. It was Warren Day. It was strange, though. While I was right, most of the usual traits of a vampire were not present in Warren. He didn't have particularly sharp canines, he didn't throw around his thrall like it was a game of catch, and his eyes and his voice were perfectly normal.

I haven't met too many other vampires, though, that weren't in the process, or about to start the process, of feeding. It is very possible that Warren was, indeed, a rather average vampire, and this is just how they present when they are not about to drink blood. In any case, I did see some things of note, while watching him watch his targets. He licked his lips quite often, as if his mouth was exceptionally dry. And although he drank several drinks over the course of the night, I never once saw his throat move as he swallowed. The most damning thing, though, was that he blinked only half as much as the average human, and when he did blink, it was in erratic fits. It wasn't something I'd noticed at first, too caught up in watching his mouth for teeth, watching for the way he spoke to others. But watching him last night, he'd stare into space for minutes at a time, before rapidly blinking, as if it was something he'd forgotten he had to do.

In the end, I got him alone by pretending that I was one of his marks. I sidled up to him, giggled and smiled and took the hooch he bought me, and followed him out to the back, where he thought he might paw at me or something similar. Once I got him alone, it was easy enough to finish him off. Everyone seems to think that the only way to kill a vampire is with a wooden stake, but in reality all one needs is a nicely sharpened silver dagger. Some people use guns, but I don't like burning powder. They make too much noise and are much harder to conceal in glad rags anyhow. Besides, I'm just fine with a knife. I didn't even get any blood on me last night, though the bastard bled quite a lot. And no wonder, too. He'd been gorging himself every night for a week and a half straight, maybe longer.

13th May 1928

Need a haircut soon. It's almost down to my shoulders, and I want it back up by my ears again. The blinking trick has worked rather well so far. But it is by no means foolproof. Some vampires seem to have caught onto this habit of theirs, and some of them are much better at hiding it than others.

But there's another tell I've noticed, too. Vampires don't breathe. At least, not like humans do, or animals for that matter. It's the same with the blinking. Some of them know that they should be doing it, but it doesn't come naturally to them. They have to remember to take breaths in and out.

That's how I caught the gal last night. Loretta Bass. She was good, too, the sort of doll who's pretty, but ordinary, in the way that means your eyes just sort of slip over her. And she blinked like normal, too, drank and laughed and spoke just like the rest of us in the gin mill last night. She even smoked with us, breathed in the smoke and blew it back out in a puff. But when she wasn't smoking, she wasn't breathing. I watched her for an hour, and she blinked like normal. But her chest never rose or fell like mine does, like any human does.

It was a few hours into the night that Loretta got up, leading a man like a dog on a leash out the back of the ritzy speakeasy we had all found ourselves in that night. I wasn't even supposed to be there hunting that night. I really just wanted a nice night out, some hooch, maybe a nice man to smile and laugh with. Maybe even bring home for a night, if he was particularly agreeable on the eyes and the ears. But Loretta had unsettled me, from the moment she walked in, and if there's one thing I've learned, it's that I always trust my gut. So when she got up, her victim trailing behind her, I followed.

She'd led him out back, had him pressed against the wall, had extended her fangs but thankfully, hadn't yet sunk them into the skin on his neck. Her thrall kept him calm, hypnotized, docile as she went to feed. I had to act quickly. Usually, it's better to stab a vampire. I get more control over where the knife goes, can twist it just right to send the poison of silver straight to the heart of the creature.

I didn't have time to do that, though. So I threw my knife at her, hoping to land a solid hit. I did. Hit her right in the shoulder. But shoulder wounds don't kill vampires, so all I really did was make her mad.

She screeched and dropped her victim, who slumped against the wall, seeming to be in a state of shock. I didn't care. I was focused on Loretta. I killed her quick enough, managed to get my knife back and stab her in the heart. Got blood on my nice dress, which was disappointing, but I think it should wash out alright. I'll tell the cleaners I got my monthly, and they shouldn't ask too many questions.

I left the victim slumped in the alley. He was something of a pig anyway, and I only saved him on principle. I'm to go out again tomorrow night, this time with Marian. I hope it will be better than last night. I do want to enjoy myself once in a while.

1st August 1928

Oh, it's been a whirlwind of a week. I've been going out almost every night with Marian. We've been dancing together, and I got her to find a real sheik.

That was three days ago, and I would've been lonely with Marian all over her new man, if I hadn't met Theresa. She's a gem of a girl, and I believe if I were a man I would already be helplessly in love with her. She's the one I kept seeing a few months ago, tracking that one vampire. Warren something or other, I think. I don't have time to look back through this journal and check for sure.

But three days ago I properly met her, and oh what a gal she is. I think I may tell her about my hunting. She's sharp witted, and I could use a partner. The better I get at finding the vampires, the more there seem to be. She's a university girl over at Barnard, and her book smarts might be useful later on. I will think more on this.

I killed two more vampires last night. They were hunting together, a rare sight. And then, of course, they turned on each other. I saw them squabbling in a fenced up yard, over on the east side of the city. The argument, which involved much more posturing and hissing than it did actual words, seemed to be over a victim, a young man passed out from blood loss in the grass. They were too busy with their hissy fit (oh I do make myself laugh) to notice me, so I got the jump on them. So yes, it's been a hell of a week.

5th August 1928

I did it. I told Theresa about the hunting. And the crazy thing is, she wants in. She wants to join me. I told her yes, of course. I'm going to start training her soon. And she's going to look through Barnard's library. See if there's anything that can help us.

My tells, the ideas I have, they aren't foolproof. Vampires are still getting past me. Sometimes I only find them because they have their fangs out, or they're covered in blood. Sometimes I only find them because I'm too late to save someone. I can't keep doing that. Hopefully, Theresa can help. The library has a phone, so I can check in on her or give her specific things to search for if I need to. I'll drop a dime to her tomorrow, and see what we can find.

27th August 1928

Theresa's been able to find so much in Barnard's library. Oh, I could just kiss the gal. One of the most damning things she's found has been that vampires, they don't have blood. Not just that they need to feed on blood to survive, but they do not have any blood of their own at all. Which means that they're pale, washed out. And they have no veins of their own. Not veins that are visible, at least.

It's hard to see in the dark, when they like to come out. But when you know what to look for, it's easier. When you know what to look for, it's so much easier. Theresa is a genius, working like she is. She wants to be a politician someday, she told me. The first female president. I think we're really getting somewhere.

29th August 1928

Theresa is dead.

I am going to kill the bastard of a vampire that did this. I didn't notice. I didn't notice until it was too late. There's something else missing, something both me and Theresa overlooked. There weren't any vampires around when she was killed. I left for the water closet, and came back and she was gone. Out in the back, already drained of blood. But we weren't hunting, there were no vampires there. Me and Theresa both watched for blinks and swallows and breathing. And everyone looked normal. Everyone looked human. So we must have missed something, something important about vampires. There's no other way.

30th August 1928

It's the shadows. Everyone says vampires don't cast shadows, but I know they do. So I ignored it. Or at least, I didn't think deeply about it at all. Especially at night, in shady gin mills or ritzy speakeasies, streets with lights that flicker as it is, it was easy to ignore, to not think about it. But vampires don't just cast shadows. They cast two. Two shadows, every time. That's how I got the son of a bitch that killed Theresa.

I don't know how I'm to go on without her. It hasn't even been a month, but I feel so off kilter without her. I think I was dizzy with that dame, even though she was a woman, and I'm certainly no man, and we really hadn't known each other that long at all.

I've heard of this sort of thing before, women who fall in with other women, who live together as if they were married. Men, too. People say it's not right, they'll go to hell, but I've killed enough unholy things that I don't know if I believe in hell or not anyway. And it felt so right, it can't be that wrong. Not that it matters much now, she's a stiff in the funeral home, and I'm just some gal again. I don't even want to go out now, even though Marian's been bugging me about coming out with her and that fellow of hers.

I think the vampires are getting stronger, which isn't good. At least, I think they're catching onto the fact that I'm hunting them. Which also isn't good. But I suppose I gotta keep going. Theresa wouldn't want me to stop hunting on account of her death, I know that much. I think I will go out with Marian tomorrow. A couple smells from the barrel might do me some good. I could use some good hooch right about now. I'll watch everyone's shadow, too. Just to make sure.

Part 3

Wendy Anastasios
44 Prospect Park West
Brooklyn NY 11215

December 15, 2002

Kay Robinson
19216 Boudray Walk
West End, QLD 41018
Australia

Kay,

Since the Second World War there has been one global conflict after another. Civil rights and women's rights. The rise of the middle class with the post war technological boom. And the social justice revolutions that, as my nibling, you are keenly aware.

After America put a man on the moon, one would think it easy to believe just about anything is possible, but as it is with most things, exploring the heavens became old hat. Something fantastical became mainstream.

And yet, what I'm about to tell you will sound not only unreal, but completely unreasonable, or even mad. But I assure you, it is real. They, are real.

Before you read any further, open the box you received with this missive. Along with legal papers you'll need to sign, you will find a neatly but securely bound tome, a large envelope full of notes and scribblings and four ledgers from my solicitor; bank accounts, properties, and the like; they are all yours now.

Now, assuming you have looked through the box, let me first say this: we've always had a simpatico, haven't we? When I visited you and your parents in Brisbane in 1976, you were six and precocious and driven and the most empathetic child I'd ever met; a delight compared to your cousins.

When you were a teen, you said I understood you as no one else had. And I did. And I'm so sorry we couldn't have spent more time together. But my life had taken me over. It had become a thing of its own. What I could do is fund your scholastic progress and your creative endeavors, as my Aunt Cynthia did for me, and I was happy to do it. Happy to watch you bloom into the grand adult you have become.

To the box. There's no way for me to sugar coat this Kay, so I'm just going to pull off the Band-Aid in one sharp tug. Vampires are real. The stories you'll read in the tome I have sent, are real. Collected and confirmed.

Yes, I am serious. No, I'm not mad. I know it's a lot to learn.

Your great great uncle Charles passed the legacy to your reclusive great aunt Cynthia, who passed it to me when I was serving in the Women's Army Corps after college. Aunt Cynthia and I made such progress. Everything is so much easier to understand now. You need only confirm a story sent to you, then slip it into its proper place. I am old, my health is faltering, and I have received so many new records that the work has begun to pile up. Again.

I will take to my newest, and most secluded, acquisition on the Isle of Skye to finish my days in peace. It is with a heavy heart full of sorrow that I hand the lot of it over to you. And yet also with a spark of pride knowing you are more than qualified to do this job.

I have informed my connections, all over the world, that they will be dealing with you from now on.

It is my hope that even with this big responsibility, you can find a joy in life that I never could, aside from those brief moments I shared with my sisters, their families and you.

With all my love,

Auntie Wendy

Wendy Anastasios

P.S: A bit of advice: no one truly knows my exact financial worth, and I've worked hard to keep it that way. It would probably behoove you to do the same.

The fragment reproduced below was recently found amongst assorted papers donated to the New York Public Library. It is attributed to a Ms. Lavinia Jones, originally of Abilene, Kansas. From what little is known of Ms. Jones, it appears that she led an adventurous and unconventional life for a woman of her generation. Originally training as an actress, she then joined an agency of Private Investigators. The below appears to record one particular experience she had during the period she was working as an investigator.

019-0-16 - SWEET SISTER - A.R.C. Mitra

October 15, 1943 – Manhattan

I've been trailing her for a month now, and I don't want to lose her again. I almost did, back in Chicago, but I was able to catch up. I've followed her here cross-country, all the way from Sunset Boulevard, where she was singing in a real nice club. Not like her, to perform anywhere particularly flashy, anywhere where she'll get a lot of attention and be seen by a lot of people. It's just not how she operates. Not good for her particular kind of business. But I'm thinking she couldn't pass up the nice dresses and the jewels a girl gets when they work at a joint like that. It was a miscalculation, because they put her face on a poster outside the club, and it was my dumb luck that I happened to walk past it while I was on a job.

She must've figured out I was onto her right away. She's always been able to sense it; that's why I haven't been able to get her so far. Or maybe I came on the scene right when she was about to split anyway. In any case, she was out of there pretty much the day after I saw that poster, and I had to move fast. Which I did.

I haven't been fast enough yet, though, to nab her.

Makes sense she'd come to New York City. It's awful easy to hide in plain sight in a city this crowded. And Manhattan's filled with lonely people. The bigger the city, the lonelier the people. Peel back the fronts of apartment buildings on any given street, and you'll see isolation and despair inside. I've been doing this job long enough to know that. I've seen some things.

It's the perfect feeding ground for her.

How long have I known the vampire? All her life.

How long will I pursue her? For the rest of my life, if I have to.

October 19, 1943

I got lucky last night. I knew she'd made it to downtown Manhattan, but I didn't know exactly where she was. I'd been asking around, old photo in hand, using the line I always did: *looking for my sister; she's run off with a married man, mom and dad are so worried.*

Finally, I struck gold. An old man behind the counter at a grungy little shop on Mott Street squinted at the picture and said she came in every now and then for cigarettes. She was such a pretty little thing, he said, and seemed so much the worse for wear, that he usually just gave them to her. She worked a few blocks away, at a lounge in the basement of one of the more decrepit buildings of Chinatown, the kind of place people went to drink and hide in the darkness for a while.

Pretty little thing. That was her exactly. Of course that was her.

I found the place, and I've been hanging out there, last night and tonight, sitting in the back of the bar, trying to blend into the shadows. I'm wearing an old black velvet dress, and a hat with a veil that covers some of my face, so no one can really get a good look at me. I'm as unobtrusive as possible, just another woman in the big city who's a little worse for wear. I've been propositioned a couple of times already, of course, but that goes with the territory. No one's going to think twice about me sitting back there in the evenings if they think I'm a lady of the night, as they call them. That's fine by me.

She hasn't shown up. I hope she hasn't gotten wind of me asking around. Maybe the old man at the store told her. I've been eyeing every singer and cocktail waitress in this joint, but none of them are her. It's been a long time since I've seen her in the flesh, but I'd recognize her anywhere.

October 20, 1943

Still no sign of her. I just fended off a couple of boys in uniform; I told them they couldn't afford me, and they thought that was so funny they left me alone. I watched their retreating backs and wondered how much longer they'd be in the city. Would they be killed in the war in Europe before the year was up? I'm sure they wondered why I seem so uninterested in making money. I'm getting a little worried that I'll attract more interest the longer I stay here. Maybe this would've been easier if I'd had a male operative who could pretend to be my date, although this particular job is probably too dangerous for a man.

Sitting around here leaves a lot of time for thinking. Thinking about this business, how long I can stay in it. It's a tough job for anybody, the private investigator gig, and the little agency I've been working for—well, we take on work others won't. Real dangerous stuff. I had reasons for getting into the business, obviously, because in the back of my mind I'd always known eventually I'd go after *her*. I got the training I needed. And I'm *good*. Being a woman isn't nearly as much of a disadvantage as you'd think. Actually, it helps. Men never see it coming, when it's a woman. All the men I've tracked down before were awfully surprised when they realized what was happening. I'm small enough, still young enough, attractive enough for them to let their guard down. Get sloppy. Funnily enough, I've got exactly the same advantage *she* does. Guess that's why her victims tend to be men.

I know the Agency must be getting impatient. I took a leave of absence; told them I had a personal thing to take care of. Family issues. God knows if I'll still have a job when I get back to LA. But just now, when I'm so close to her I can taste it, I don't really care. My bigger concern is that she's left the city already, and the longer I stay here, the colder her trail is going to get.

October 21, 1943

She was there tonight. I knew her as soon as I saw her up on stage, framed by dusty gold velvet curtains. In the dim light, through a haze of cigarette smoke, I knew her. She was almost glowing, resplendent even in that tacky lounge with its threadbare carpet, and cracked leather seats, and peeling red fabric wallpaper; with its back room where men went to bet money they didn't have or make bargains that'll make your blood run cold. She was wearing a little pale blue dress, a white fur stole draped across her bare shoulders, and her hair was blonder than I remembered, almost silver. She was singing low, sultry tunes that made you feel sleepy and warm, like when you'd had one too many whiskeys on a cold night. I retreated further into the shadows so she wouldn't spot me and adjusted the veil attached to my hat to cover more of my face.

It had been such a long time since we'd been in the same room. I've been tracking her on and off, throughout the years. Perusing newspapers for strange accidents and suspicious deaths and sudden illnesses, especially of young men, and especially if in the weeks leading up to their deaths, they'd been seen in the company of a young woman no one knew much about and no one could now locate. Reports of men who had abruptly dropped their friends and families, who had lost jobs and broken engagements and left marriages, whose health had declined dramatically in a short period of time, who had seemed suddenly plunged into a pit of despair before their unexpected deaths. The promising newspaperman who'd jumped off a bridge; eyewitnesses thought they saw a blonde woman standing behind him as he climbed up onto the ledge, but couldn't be sure. The salesman who'd driven his car into a lake, observed in the company of a woman at a local diner earlier that evening. The three Privates, seen in the company of a female USO performer on the eve of their departure for Europe. They were found dead in their quarters the next morning, shot by their own army-issued weapons.

I hadn't seen her in person since that party in Palm Beach two years ago, where one of the waiters collapsed and died in a back room. An overdose, they said. And of course, she'd slipped away in all the chaos, slipped through my fingers once again.

October 22, 1943

She's found the next one. Of course she has. There's always one, wherever she goes. It's the pianist. Young guy, nothing extraordinary, and an average player at best. I asked around and found out his name is Johnny Donaghue. He's already a little worse for wear. Every night, he's knocking back liquor like it's going out of style, drunk fingers stumbling over the piano keys, burnt-out cigarette dangling from his lips. She's a fast worker, and she's sure as hell been working on him. He's got this dumb blank look on his face whenever he looks at her, like she's the only woman he's ever seen.

I feel sorry for the kid. He's on borrowed time. If he gets lucky, maybe I'll get to her before she finishes up with him, but I don't like my chances.

I tried following her tonight when she left the club, but she disappeared backstage, and I couldn't manage to finagle my way behind the curtains to follow her.

October 23, 1943

Earlier this afternoon, I went over to the building where the lounge is and checked out the area. The lounge has a back door that opens into a little alleyway; that's how a lot of the staff must enter and leave. I thought maybe I could catch her back there. So I slipped out partway through her performance, made my way to the back door, and waited. It was pitch black there, and smelt of rotting garbage and stagnant water. I could hear rats scurrying across the pavement. Now that I was close to getting her, I realized that I'd never really decided what I was going to do with her. Turning her over to the cops—what would that achieve? They'd never be able to prove anything against her when it came to all those men.

Well, there was one thing I could do. I reached into my coat pocket, and my fingers curled around the little revolver nestled there.

I waited for an hour, at least. I listened to the dripping of water through a broken pipe. It was getting cold. There were intermittent sirens from cop cars and ambulances zooming down the street.

Then, finally, a flurry of activity. The back door opened, and I saw a couple of the waitresses come out, then some of the other performers. No one paid any attention to me, leaning against the grimy wall some distance from the door. But she didn't come out, and neither did Johnny Donaghue.

Had she known, somehow, that I was there, waiting for her? Was she on to me?

October 24, 1943

I thought she might be gone today, if she knew I had caught up to her, but she was up on stage again tonight, and I was back at my post at the back of the bar. After she was done, she didn't leave right away. Instead, she came down off the stage, and I saw her speaking to Johnny Donaghue, standing really close to him, speaking rapidly into his ear. Every now and then, she'd pause, and look vaguely over at a group of men in one corner, and Donaghue's eyes would follow her, and then she'd lean back in towards him, and speak some more. The group of men were regulars, they were always sitting in that same corner. I had an idea what was going on, and it turns out I was right.

Eventually, Donaghue got up, and he nearly tripped over the piano stool. He was pretty toasted from all the scotch he'd been drinking. He walked over to the group of men, swaying as he did, and then, without warning, launched himself at one of them, yelling incoherently, something about them going after his girl. The whole thing was pathetically predictable. Another man came bursting out from the back room. I figured he was Donaghue's boss, because his suit was more expensive than Donaghue. He was followed by two big, rough looking men, who pulled Donaghue off the man he had thrown himself at and dragged him out.

She was standing by the edge of the stage, watching the whole thing very coolly, with an empty, dead look in her eyes.

That was when inspiration struck. I bolted out of there, and ran around to the back of the building. I got to the alleyway just in time to see poor Johnny Donaghue being thrown out the back door and straight into a rain-filled pothole. Swearing loudly, he just sat there for a while. Then he managed to hoist himself up and began to stumble towards me. I don't think he even noticed me, because he went right past me. He reeked of liquor and filthy water.

I followed him. After a couple of blocks, he stopped in front of a particularly decrepit old apartment building. He stood there, swaying slightly, at the foot of the stairs that led up to the front door. I wondered if he'd make it up or if he'd just give up and go to sleep right there. But, eventually, he dragged himself up and managed to get the door open, then went inside. After a while, I saw a light come on behind one of the filthy windows on the sixth floor.

Either she'd come to him, or he'd go to her. He was my best bet for getting to her. It was an old trick my first boss taught me, back when I was learning how to do this work. To get to a predator, stick close to the prey. And boy oh boy, was he this week's prey. She'd already proverbially fattened him up. No doubt he'd lost his job tonight, and from the state of the building he lived in, I doubted he had much else. Now he had only her.

That's what she does. She doesn't do anything as lurid as drink the blood of her victims. Her feeding is far more subtle. She'll smile sweetly and look at you with those big green eyes, and push the hair away from her face with those slender fingers, and you'll want to protect her, want to help this little woman alone in the big bad city. You'll give her everything— your love, and your care, and your sympathy and your concern. And she will take it from you, and it will sustain her. For a while.

But she needs more. It isn't enough, for her, mere adoration. She wants it all. She wants your life. She'll take everything from you, and you'll throw it all away, willingly, because she has become your everything: mother, sister, lover, god. And then she'll take you to the edge of an abyss, and very gently, tenderly, she'll give you the slightest push and watch you fall.

October 30, 1943

I don't know why I'm writing all this down. To keep a record, I guess.

She did come to see him, two nights after I followed him home. I had rented a little car so I could keep an eye on the building. It was late, past 2 o'clock in the morning, but I was wide awake. There was no way I was going to nod off and risk missing her. A cab pulled up in front of his building, and she slid out of it. She was wrapped in a black fur coat, already dressed for the funeral. She stood beneath a streetlight for a moment, illuminated by the sickly yellow light of it. Then she walked up the stairs to the front door of the building, and slid inside.

I waited a few minutes, then followed. Next to the door was a list of apartments, and I saw *J. Donaghue* scrawled next to "6B." I tried the front door. It was locked. This was a standard problem in my business, and I always had a couple of lockpicks on hand. Even still, it took me a lot longer than usual to jimmy the lock. When I finally got the door open, I saw there was a staircase directly across it. I began to walk up the six flights of narrow stairs. It was dark inside; the only light came from a single naked bulb downstairs. I reached inside the pocket of my coat and felt the metal of my revolver. I still didn't know what I was going to do. I just knew that this had to end.

Finally, I was standing in front of a door with tarnished brass letters reading "6B." I pressed my ear against the peeling paint of the door. I couldn't hear a thing. There was nothing for it. I raised my hand to knock, and then, on second thought, tried the doorknob. To my surprise, the door was unlocked, and it swung open.

Johnny Donaghue was already dead. I knew it as soon as I turned on the light and saw him sitting limply in a dusty old armchair, head hanging forward, a glass lying on its side by his feet where it had fallen from his hand. In the time I had taken to pick the lock and walk up all those stairs, she'd finished him off.

She was nowhere to be seen. The back window was wide open, cool air streaming through. She must have gone down the fire escape. Of course, I tried to see if I could revive Donaghue, but he was a goner. I called an ambulance. Then I got the hell out of there.

I can't really remember driving back to the motel I was staying at, although I must have done so automatically. I do remember that it had started raining, big heavy drops splashing onto the windshield. I felt so tired then, like all the sleep in the world wouldn't be enough. I needed a drink.

I dragged myself back to the tiny room in the motel and shrugged off my coat before turning on the little flickering lamp by the door.

She was there.

"Hello, sweet sister," she said.

That old stupid nickname she used, just to incense me. Her voice was soft and smooth, musical, almost. It had always been like that, since she started talking. "So, you've found me. Or—" she looked around the shabby motel room with something like disdain "—I've found you."

She was standing in the middle of the room. I stared at her, and she looked back at me; identical green eyes looking at each other. It struck me once again how alike we looked; I was just an older, scruffier version of her. There was a neon sign across the street, and it cast its alternating red and green light through the window behind her. Turning her skin and hair green, then red. Green, then red.

She looked good. Even better than when she was in the lounge. Her face looked full, her cheeks pink, her eyes shining. Of course she looked good. She'd just fed.

"You killed my parents."

I don't know why I said that. The words came out of me involuntarily. But looking at her then, all I could see was her, twelve years old, in a cotton dress with flowers in it, standing in the center of the kitchen of our little house in Kansas.

We'd been in that house less than a year, after the Jones' adopted us. The Jones' were the only parents I could remember. And right then, I was back there, coming in through the door to see her standing there, with Papa lying at her feet, his head in a puddle of blood. The rifle was still in his hand. Mama lying on the floor by the kitchen sink. Murder-suicide, they said at the inquest. No one ever really understood why.

She was my sister all right, but at the orphanage, and in the foster homes we'd been in, I had always avoided her, because I had always known something was wrong. The animals she befriended, who'd then die of some illness. The boy at the orphanage she used to play with, who'd drowned in a pond one afternoon. And every time she'd look just like she did standing in that kitchen in Kansas all those years ago, just like she looked right then in that motel room.

Satiated.

"*Our* parents," she said. Her voice was serene, as if she was correcting my grammar.

I'd known the truth all along, of course. Even still, I was grateful that she'd admitted it. My little sister, the vampire.

I should have reached for my coat, with the gun still in the pocket. I don't know why I didn't. But the more I looked at her, and the more she looked back at me, the colder I felt, until my hands were so numb I could barely move my fingers.

"Goodbye, sweet sister," she said. She walked across the room and past me, so close our shoulders nearly brushed against each other. Then she was out the door, and by the time I snapped out of whatever spell she'd worked on me, she was long gone.

The vampire has gone back west, and I'll follow.

How long have I known her? All my life.

How long will I pursue her? For the rest of my life, if I have to.

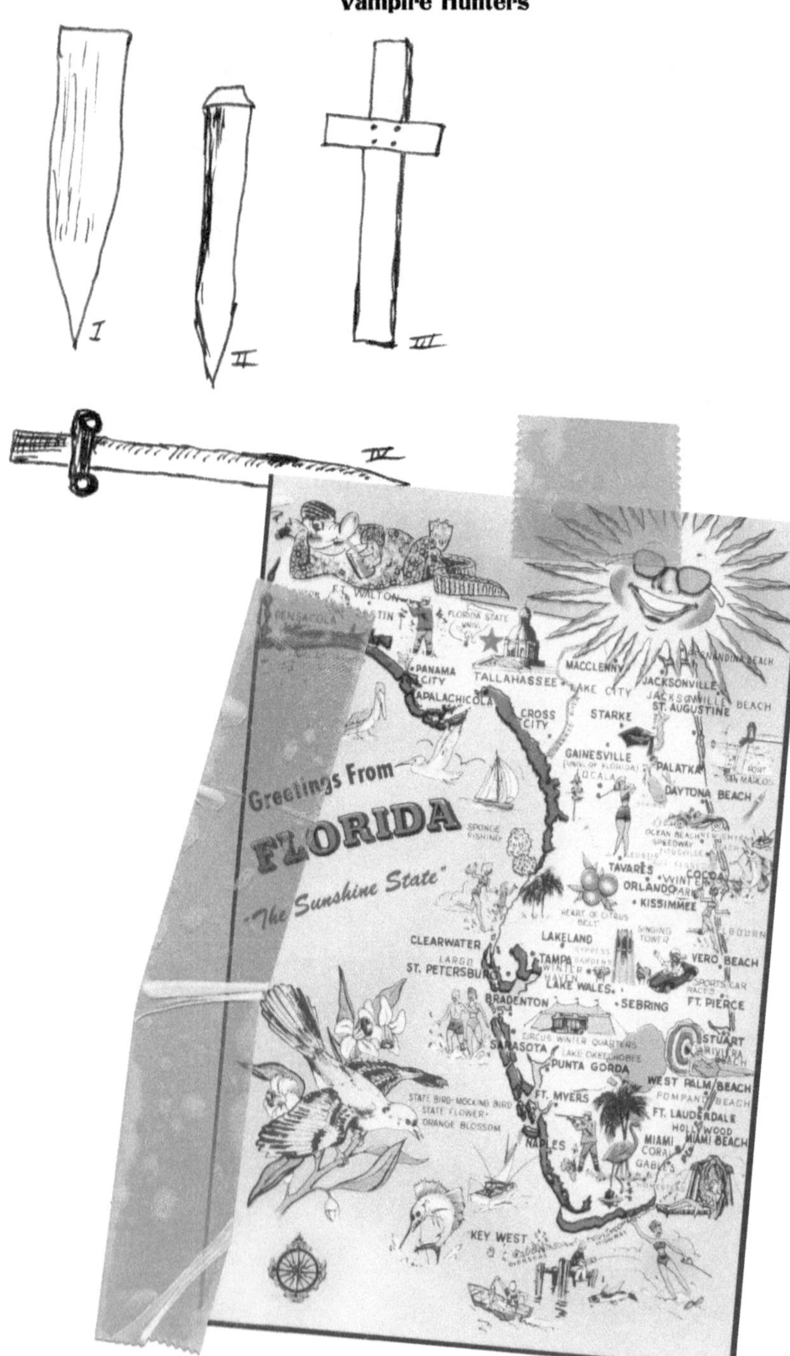

Greetings From
FLORIDA
"The Sunshine State"
PENSACOLA
FT. WALTON
PANAMA CITY
APALACHICOLA
TALLAHASSEE
FLORIDA STATE UNIV.
LAKE CITY
MACCLENNY
JACKSONVILLE
JACKSONVILLE BEACH
ST. AUGUSTINE
CROSS CITY
STARKE
GAINESVILLE
(UNIV. OF FLORIDA)
OCALA
PALATKA
DAYTONA BEACH
TAVARES
ORLANDO
WINTER PARK
COCOA
KISSIMMEE
HEART OF CITRUS BELT
CLEARWATER
LARGO
ST. PETERSBURG
LAKELAND
TAMPA
WINTER HAVEN
LAKE WALES
VERO BEACH
BRADENTON
SEBRING
FT. PIERCE
SARASOTA
PUNTA GORDA
STUART
WEST PALM BEACH
POMPANO BEACH
FT. MYERS
FT. LAUDERDALE
HOLLYWOOD
STATE BIRD - MOCKING BIRD
STATE FLOWER - ORANGE BLOSSOM
NAPLES
MIAMI
MIAMI BEACH
CORAL GABLES
KEY WEST

The author of this diary — identified only by the inscribed 'A' on the cover of the book — was the grandmother of a donor who wishes to remain anonymous. A significant number of pages are missing from the book. The following are the only entries which are still legible. The reason or location for the missing pages is currently unknown.

019-0-17 - CAPE CANAVERAL - Carter Lappin

August 2, 1969

So far, I find that I am not very impressed by Florida, though perhaps I am being ungenerous considering I haven't yet seen much of it. If the roads into Cape Canaveral are anything to judge by, I'm expecting the rest of the state to surely be crowded, hot, and smell strongly of bug spray and engine exhaust. Even now I feel a drip of sweat sliding down my forehead; I must be quick to catch it before it drops and stains my book.

I don't know how long I have to write, so, though brevity has never been my strong suit, I will try to be fairly quick about it. I am waiting for Michael to return from the stand with his cigarettes, and my requested newspaper. I suspect he is taking his time about it—he seemed very eager to escape the friendly chatter from the attendant who pumped our gas.

The attendant is finished now, though he lingers, washing down our windshield with exacting care and probing each tire individually for unseen imperfections. He wants, I know, to get another chance at an audience, but is afraid to lean in my window to talk to a woman alone in her car.

He told Michael, earlier, that much of the hubbub around here is caused by the lingering excitement over the recent moon launch over at nearby Cape Kennedy. I let him believe that Michael and I are fiancés travelling as tourists for interest in the same. It is an easier explanation than the truth—both of us unmarried and yet travelling together as employer and assistant (Or, on days which he doesn't drive me entirely insane, as friends). The attendant told us that we make a lovely couple, and if we go visit his cousin, he can get us a discount on nearly-new rings. It seems to me that he pumps gas only for the chance to talk to someone new and exciting.

On the subject of gas—nearly 33 cents a gallon! I entered that particular payment into my expense book with a heavy and somewhat resentful hand. Soon we'll have to resort to walking to each new sighting for fear of spending our entire travel budget on fuel.

But I see Michael coming now. Perhaps I will write some more later in the car, provided Michael's driving doesn't make me feel sick again. I will have to make up a story to get him away from the station attendant. I fear the man is often too polite for his own good. It bodes not well for his future in fighting vampires, but I suppose we all must start somewhere.

August 2, 1969 adnm.

Michael has promised to drive with an uncharacteristic care so that I might finish getting my thoughts down on paper, as is my custom. We shall see if he holds up his end of the bargain.

The newspaper confirms my thoughts. The obituaries, tucked behind pages and pages of celebratory space-race back-patting, show a clear and distinct pattern. There are vampires in Cape Canaveral. I only hope it is not like the coven I encountered in St. Louis. What a mess that was!

Just in case, I have started carving myself a new wooden stake as we travel the last few miles, though I've set it down temporarily in favor of the pen. Michael worries about me using a knife in a moving vehicle, though Michael does worry about everything. Still I am taking extra care, and even keeping the wood shavings piled in the dip of my skirt so as not to get them all over the floor of the car.

I have a few leads to follow up on, but I think they will have to wait until tomorrow. By the time we get into town it will be dark, and we've been driving for a long while yet. I'd prefer to sleep in the day and hunt in the night, as they do, but unfortunately I am still but human and so will need to get at least some sleep tonight.

On another note, Michael is smoking a cigarette and refuses to share. I am going to toss it out of the window.

August 3, 1969

It is just past midnight, but I rather think that I am done with sleep for the night. It seems I didn't need to go looking for vampires after all, as they found me instead. Convenient, I suppose. Someone must have tipped them off. Perhaps I was recognized from my time in California. The specifics will no doubt haunt me until uncovered. It will be a task for another day, though.

Michael and I had been sharing quarters due to my unwillingness to pay for two separate hotel rooms. We are posing now as brother and sister to explain the two beds, though the pretense at being space enthusiasts remains in place. As is our custom, we hung garlic from the eaves around the door and windows, and went to bed thinking ourselves safe for the night.

(Michael will hate me for documenting it here, but he wore those terrible pajamas of his—the one whose red stripes have faded to pink and which have been cut down at the knees to accommodate for his always being hot under the covers. They make him look like a twelve year-old who has unexpectedly sprouted up during the night.)

The vampires here were more clever than I had anticipated. To avoid passing through the abhorrent smell of garlic, they came, instead, from the room below, each squeezing through the space where this old hotel had apparently boarded over a defunct dumbwaiter system. They needed only to break through the thin wall in order to enter our room. If the process hadn't been so loud, I dare say it might have worked to surprise me.

As it was, both Michael and I woke quickly enough, and I was able to have my brand-new stake in hand moments after the vampires made entry. Michael hid behind his bed as I dispatched the intruders with speed.

The noise, I fear, will have woken our neighbors. I have sent Michael out into the hall to waylay any curious folk, and myself will begin in a moment to dispose of the remains and to properly seal the new hole in our rented wall. Michael will make fun that I've stopped to write this first, but I needed a moment to collect myself.

I am tempted to think that my work is done already in this town, though I know it to be a dangerous assumption. Likely I will spend all of today (as it is, technically, a day later, now that the clock has ticked past midnight) hunting down leads while the other good and honest folk attend church. I will not be satisfied with myself until Cape Canaveral has been emptied entirely of the vampire threat, or indeed, until I can properly wake myself up! I wonder where Michael has hidden his cigarettes...

August 3, 1969 adnm.

I have found little of interest today, and Michael has pointed out it is making me rather grouchy. What little contacts I have in this hot town (Hot! What an inexcusably hot town it is!) are inclined to believe the small grouping which pre-emptively hunted down the vampire hunter (by this, of course, I mean me) were indeed the only vampires in this sunny locale.

I can't quite believe it. There is a feeling to the air. Someone or something has taken an interest in me. I will soon find out who.

August 3, 1969 adnm.

Michael and I have stopped for food at a diner which has the best blueberry pie I have ever eaten. I have tucked the business card of the place between these pages so that I might remember to stop here again should I ever pass through the area.

The afternoon edition of the newspaper is showing no new deaths, or at least none that can't be attributed to natural causes or misadventure. Michael, who is growing tired of the humidity as well but trying to hide it out of a sense of masculine pride or misplaced optimism, has suggested that it may be a few days before we can be completely sure that I have removed the threat.

A few more days in this town! Apparently there is a museum nearby that Michael is eager to visit. I may let him drag me to see it, though I will not make it easy for him.

Drat. I have spilled gravy on the page. Some documentarian I am.

August 3, 1969 adnm.

Am going to bed. Garlic on doors and windows, and now along the walls. Stake under pillow. Tomorrow will see about acquiring large but cheap painting to cover hole in wall so as not to pay a damage fee to the hotel. Michael is wearing his awful pajamas once more. Good night.

August 4, 1969

I have allowed Michael to talk me into going to the space museum. The newspaper shows nothing of note yet again. Michael has brought me back breakfast from yesterday's diner, along with a slice of that blueberry pie. I feel bad, now, for having stolen and smoked two of his cigarettes while he was out.

One of my contacts has called me back. He may have a lead on another vampire here in town. He has promised to investigate further and get back to me later in the afternoon. Still plenty of time, Michael assures me, to get to the museum and back. He has brought his camera. I fear we will be there longer than my patience will allow for. Still, it is not as though I have anything better to do, and I have always hated being idle.

August 4, 1969 adnm.

My contact left me a note at the front desk of the hotel. Presumably he had attempted to hand it to me personally, but, as anticipated, Michael was extremely difficult to drag away from his educational pursuits. Do you know that the Apollo mission brought 842 pounds of moon rocks back to Earth with them? In another life I'm sure I would have lost Michael to astronautics, so fascinated by this was he.

As it was, I mollified him by purchasing a gray hunk of rock sworn to be an exact replica from a souvenir salesman at a stand outside of the museum. Michael looked so pleased I fear my carefully constructed facade of distance will never recover.

In any case, I have forgotten the original purpose of this entry. There is a woman vampire here in Cape Canaveral. People have seen her on the beach at night. I suspect she holes up somewhere near there in the daytime. Only two bodies have so far been found in the vicinity; a notorious conman who purported himself to be a former mission control technician at Kennedy, and a homeless man. I am lucky to discover her before too many more have been killed.

I am making a new stake. Michael dislikes it; I am getting wood shavings all over the floor.

August 5, 1969

I believe I have found the vampire. Indeed, she seems inclined to stay around a specific stretch of the beach. Luckily, the moon is full enough to see by, and the darkness shouldn't give her too much of an advantage over me.

I have left Michael at the hotel. Perhaps I will stop for another slice of that pie on the way back.

August 5, 1969 adnm.

The vampire has been dispatched. When I approached, she was looking at the sky over the Kennedy Center. The stars were very bright.

She asked me if I was the vampire hunter. I suppose I should be flattered to be so well-known amongst my foes. I agreed that I was. She didn't yet seem inclined to fight, and I thought to get a better look at her before the confrontation occurred.

She told me then that she wished she could have been an astronaut. Would she be able to see the sun from up there, she asked me? Would it burn her there, too? When she looked at me, sharp fangs glinted at the corner of her mouth. It strikes me now that she seemed sad.

Tonight, she told me, NASA's Mariner 7 will make its closest approach to Mars. They'd sent it out so long ago, thought they lost it more than once. But now it was up there, doing one final scan before dropping to forever orbit the planet it was made to observe. She couldn't see it from our spot on the beach. She had thought she might.

I've never had a vampire talk so much before they tried to kill me. I didn't like it. I still don't. I could hear the waves in the darkness. For once, Florida didn't seem so hot. It seems to me that the night can bring both good and bad sometimes.

Michael keeps trying to talk to me about it. I suppose he thinks I'm acting strangely.

August 6, 1969

We are leaving Florida. Michael is not satisfied, but I told him I am confident that there are no more dangers here in town. There is, however, talk of a vampire sighting by way of Pennsylvania. That, I think, should be our priority. Michael has eventually agreed. I am only waiting now for the attendant to finish filling up the gas tank, and for Michael to buy one more pack of cigarettes on the way out of town.

He has his moon rock on the dashboard, right next to the silver cross I have hanging from the mirror.

The work goes on. I will update again if anything of note occurs.

The following passages are excerpted from the diary of Mia Caldwell, who followed her great-uncle Ferdinand into the vampire hunting business. The excerpts were shared by Mia's niece Althea, the only member of her family from whom Mia Caldwell did not eventually become estranged. Mia's words are included here as an example of a vampire hunter who developed an unusual relationship with the quarry she hunted. What began, it seems, as a way to exorcise her own darkest impulses, developed into something akin to a religious mania, though not the type one might expect to see in a vampire hunter.

019-0-18 - SICK - A.C. Wise

Select Acts of Devotion, February 18 to September 30, 1985

-Teeth pulled; canines etched with flowers; etchings darkened with shoe polish to achieve an effect like scrimshaw (full regrowth – 21 days)

-Skin removed in a long, single piece from upper right leg between buttocks and knee; skin stretched, dried, and inscribed with mixed lines of poetry (healing – 5 days)

-Left leg flayed from hip to knee; multiple bones fractured in situ; bones repaired with gold in kintsugi style (healing – 17 days)

-Flesh slit along the torso with arcing cuts between each rib; wounds stuffed with dried herbs and flowers (healing – 3 days)

-Back flayed; peeled sections of flesh pinned to shoulders in the approximation of wings (healing – ongoing)

Ritual of Care, October 1, 1985

I descend the basement stairs and find Godfrey kneeling on the cold concrete near the drain. He's naked, as is the lightbulb overhead. Its glow highlights his veins—a map I am still learning to read. His head is shorn, extending the map across his skull, rivers and tributaries in faint blue beneath his near-translucent skin. My breath catches at the sight of him. He is beautiful.

I reach the bottom of the stairs and stand before him. He looks up at me with eyes black all the way to the edges. A silvery light shines in them, reflecting from the bulb overhead. He shivers, though not with the chill. The need in his expression breaks my heart.

"How are you feeling today, Godfrey?" I ask—the opening salvo of a familiar call-and-response.

"Sick," he answers, as he always does.

I touch his chin, keep his head tilted up toward me when he wants to look away. The tips of his fangs dent his pallid lips, and his expression is one of shame.

"You are sick, Godfrey," I respond. "But together, we will make you holy. Together, we will make you whole."

I set a metallic bowl of water on the floor beside him, and circle around to his back to regard the recent work we've done.

The skin is pink and raw, crisscrossed with healing scars. I dip a cloth into the water, cleaning as gently I can, the wounds that still weep pale fluid. Godfrey would heal faster if he fed, but food is something we are both intent on denying him. He will not take blood of any kind until it is necessary; he will go without until he can no longer survive.

On either side of the scars, the skin I peeled aside lies pinned against his shoulders. I dip the cloth into the water again, making sure each pin is clean and secure.

"I was thinking." There's a faint tremor in my voice as I speak aloud my inspiration. "I could sew the skin here permanently, build upon it with other grafts, give it structure by removing and rearranging some of your bones. We could give you true wings. What do you think, Godfrey?"

His shoulders twitch, pulling against the scars. One of them reopens, and I wipe the resulting fluid away. It is not a flinch, but a hitch in his breathing, his entire body shuddering between ecstasy and silent tears.

He needs the pain, craves it as much as I do. It's what binds us together, makes us both clean, at least for a while. When I'm hurting Godfrey, we can both push the shadows away for a time and allow ourselves to believe that they'll never come crawling back in.

"Yes," he says. "Yes, Mia, please."

There's a hissing sibilance when he says "please," perhaps a lingering effect from having his teeth removed only to regrow. I set the cloth aside, the water now the same pale pink as his scars.

"Wait," I tell him. "I'll find a needle and thread, and we'll begin."

His gaze follows me up the stairs. There's a weight to it—gratitude and wonder. I've seen it before, and I know the way it makes Godfrey's eyes liquid, black ink that could overspill and run down his cheeks in place of tears. That gaze propels me, giving me wings of my own. I ascend the stairs lighter than air. This new act of devotion will make Godfrey a living relic, an undying saint. He will not be sick anymore; he will be the most glorious creature anyone has ever seen.

I will set him free.

October 1, 1985, Addendum

I will recount here how I became what I am, as best as I can recall...

The First Beginning, April 8, 1972

"You are sick, Mia, but together, there is great work we might do. It will help make you whole."

My Great-Uncle Ferdy wore a look of great sadness, of weariness and pity, as he said those words. I was ten years old, and moments ago, he'd walked into the front room of my grandparents' house just in time to stop me from killing my little sister, Chloe.

I had my hands around her throat. Chloe wasn't crying, she wasn't fighting me. Maybe she thought it was a game. I saw trust in her in big, blue eyes.

I remember distinctly how soft Chloe's skin was against my palms. I didn't hate her; we hadn't been fighting. I was curious, excited, watching the scene as if I stood just behind my own shoulder. I wanted—needed—to know what it would feel like when she died.

"Mia," Great-Uncle Ferdy said. His voice was soft; he didn't yell. "Let's go outside."

He steered me gently toward the front door and directed Chloe into the kitchen where the rest of the adults were gathered.

"Do you know what would have happened if I hadn't stopped you just now?" he asked.

We sat side by side on the step, my grandparents' front door—painted deep forest green—behind us, the shadow of the house falling over us from above.

"Chloe would be dead."

"Would that make you sad?" he asked, and I shrugged.

"If you had the chance, would you do something like that again?"

I hadn't really thought about it, but I gave the question the consideration it deserved. Great-Uncle Ferdy treated the conversation seriously, speaking to me like an adult, so I treated it seriously as well.

"Yes," I told him. "I would."

He regarded me for a moment, touched the air beside my head. The gesture was like a magician pretending to pull a quarter out of someone's ear, but there was nothing there. He looked at his fingertips, frowning, rubbing them together then wiping them on his pantleg like he expected them to be stained.

"You are sick, Mia," he said. "But together, there is great work we might do. It will help make you whole."

I knew Great-Uncle Ferdy had fought in the same war as my grandfather, while my grandmother worked in a factory making parts for planes. I knew that in war, people killed each other, and there was a good chance Great-Uncle Ferdy knew what it looked like to watch someone die.

"Will you let me help you, Mia? Will you work with me?"

I didn't know what work Great-Uncle Ferdy did. He was my grandmother's older brother. I assumed, like my grandfather, he was retired.

"Will you tell me about the war and killing other soldiers?" I asked.

"I will tell you everything you want to know," he said, his tone serious. "There will be no secrets."

Great-Uncle Ferdy held out his hand. It took me a moment to realize he expected me to shake it, a promise sealed.

"Okay," I said.

His hand engulfed mine, his skin dry and warm. His face reminded me of a basset hound—deep, lined pouches under his eyes, other lines weighing down the corners of his mouth. He was very tall, and very thin. It seemed impossible that he and my grandmother were related. Great-Uncle Ferdy's shoulders were perpetually stooped, like he was trying to avoid something hanging over him, or he was afraid of being seen.

"The first thing you need to know," he told me as he let go of my hand, "is that vampires are real."

He waited to see if I would question or contradict him. I did neither. I trusted him. He smiled, keeping his lips closed, just the edges of his mouth creeping upward. His shoulders relaxed, just a little, and it was the only time I can recall them doing so.

"I'm going to give the darkness in you somewhere useful to go," he told me. "I'm going to teach you how to hunt."

And now...
The Second Beginning, January 4, 1985

I spent nearly a year training with Great-Uncle Ferdy, and another thirteen years working alongside him. The secret family business, which he learned from his own father—he jokingly referred to it as "pest control".

It began in his basement, which smelled overwhelmingly of laundry detergent and potting soil. Along one whole wall, grow lights hung above shelves filled with copper-colored flowerpots. Every winter, Ferdy forced bulbs and then planted them in the spring.

Within that wall, opposite the washer and dryer tucked beside the basement stairs, Ferdy showed me a hidden door. The room behind it was narrow, mostly taken up by a big wooden workbench. Behind it a pegboard hung with stakes and blades and rosary beads and jars of holy water. There were surgical tools as well—scalpels and retractors and bone saws—instruments for cutting off heads to bury upside down and removing hearts to watch them burn.

There were target dummies stacked beside the workbench, and hooks and chains—the kind used in butcher's shops to hang up meat and let it drain. Ferdy pulled out one of the target dummies.

"Let's begin."

He taught me to fight. He taught me to protect myself, to strike first and quickly, never to hesitate or show mercy. He procured whole pig carcasses, hung them up on those big metal hooks, and taught me how to cut out their hearts.

After a year, he brought me on my first job. We worked together well. Even though I was only eleven years old, Ferdy trusted me, and him being in his mid-sixties hadn't slowed him at all. But thirteen years later, during one of our hunts, he slipped on a short flight of concrete steps outside a warehouse and broke his hip. He took it as a sign to retire. I inherited his "pest control" business, and continued to work alone.

As Ferdy intended, vampire hunting kept me sated. Mostly. I could kill, and it was for the greater good. I could cause pain, knowing the hurt I spared others. But through it all, there remained a faint sense of want. Like an itch somewhere I could never reach.

I distracted myself with research, building on what Ferdy had taught me. I learned all the ways to kill a vampire. And inferred between the lines, I learned the ways one could be kept alive indefinitely as well. I could, in theory, keep a vampire on the brink of death, nearly killing it, but bringing it back, again and again.

I kept the knowledge close, held it against my heart, and never acted on it. Until I met Godfrey.

Within my second year working solo, I followed a series of whispers and rumors to a half-constructed resort on the outskirts of Tulum. The developers had run out of money before completing the project, leaving behind poured foundations and the skeletons of walls. The complex stood open to the sky, guarded only with fluttering construction tarps, the jungle encroaching through holes where doors and windows were meant to go.

I found Godfrey squatting there, both figuratively and literally. Moving through the maze of half-constructed walls, I found him crouched over his latest kill—a stray dog that looked as starved as he was, ribs showing prominently through caramel-colored fur. Godfrey was barefoot, shirtless, wearing dirty khaki shorts. His face was smeared with blood, near-black in the moonlight. Pools of water gleamed on the floor all around him where the tarps had sagged and let in the rain.

His eyes gleamed too, like an animal caught in headlights. He didn't run. I didn't lunge at him the way I normally would.

"Please," he said.

I'd never seen a vampire weep before; I didn't know they could.

"I'm sick," he told me. "I don't want to be this way."

I felt the sky turn. I felt a moment of promise and possibility, the way I'd felt with my hands around my little sister's neck, the way I'd felt when Ferdy first taught me to kill.

The universe was a vast set of gears and the teeth had finally slotted perfectly into place. I was sick, and Godfrey was too. But together, there was great work we could do.

Godfrey crawled forward. Even in his weakened state, he could have killed me, but he grasped hold of my pantleg, leaving bloody handprints behind.

"Please," he said. "Help me."

"I will," I said. "You are sick, but together, we will make you whole."

His Glorious Wings Span the World, October 21, 1986

"Mia." Godfrey says my name, his voice soft as a cat's paw, waking me from slumber.

He's in my room, where he's never entered before, though I've long since given him permission. Crouched at the end of my bed, his silhouette is a gargoyle's—naked, his bones prominent, his head shorn. Light seeps through the curtains and his skin glows—moonlight and streetlight showing his veins and scars as a delicate map we have built together.

"It's time," he says.

Godfrey's wings rise behind him, made from his flesh, draped over his bones, shaped and built and stitched over the course of almost a year. They rattle when he moves, a hollow and awful sound. They look painful, heavy, dragging him down.

They are beautiful.

There have been other acts of devotion over the past year, other rituals of care, but his wings are our greatest work of all. How carefully I slit his skin, removed his bones, tended him while he healed. How I brought him to the edge, over and over again, but always withdrew, leaving him in beautiful agony, but keeping him alive.

He has been my perfect prey, and I his perfect predator. Together, we saved each other from our hungers. Together, we healed.

I slip from my covers. Godfrey goes ahead of me, his shoulders bowed under the weight of his wings, reminding me of Great-Uncle Ferdy and his stooped posture. The wings barely fit, scraping the walls as we climb the narrow stairs to the attic. In the middle of the floor is a ladder, leading up to a skylight that unlatches and lets us onto the roof.

Shingles scratch under my bare soles. A breeze tugs at me, and I wrap my arms around my body.

We survey the neighborhood. The house is three stories tall, but it feels much higher. Fully in the streetlight and the moonlight, no longer filtered through my window, Godfrey is more beautiful than ever. My gaze traces the evidence of every cut I've made in our time together, each an act of worship. I was a sculptor; every near-death I granted him made him more himself, chiseling away everything unnecessary and transforming him into this perfect creature.

And now, it is time to let him go.

Without him, what will I become?

Without me, what will he become?

Godfrey runs. My heart lurches and goes with him.

At the edge of the roof, his wounded calves bunch, then straighten. His soles arch, his toes pushing off and launching him into the sky.

His wings snap wide. They tear. Godfrey screams, and his gold-bound bones shatter inside them, leaving his flesh in ribbons as he falls.

His wings snap wide. They hold. They catch the cold October air. His bones strengthened by gold keep him aloft, and he soars.

Both things happen, both are true.

Godfrey hangs against the velvet sky, held in place by the pinpoint stars as I have held him down in time. He is perfect, an insect caught in amber.

He opens his mouth wide. A scream, a triumphant yell. The moonlight catches on his fangs, and the moment stretches to eternity. Godfrey falling, Godfrey flying. Godfrey set free from his endless torment.

He is no longer sick. Am I?

The shadow of his wings falls across the town. He is perfect. He is what we have made together. I creep to the edge of the roof and watch him fall, watch him fly.

224

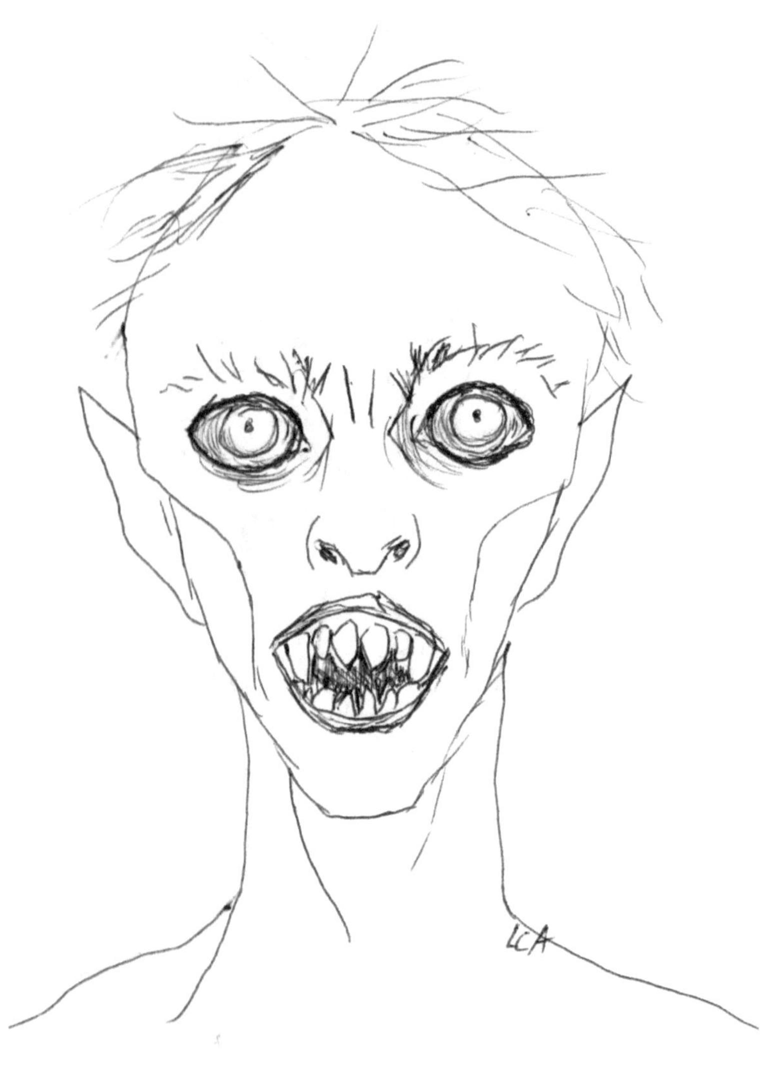

Jeremy Jackson Lawlor, known as "J.J." to his friends and family, enlisted in the U.S. Army in March 1989, seventeen months before President George H.W. Bush led the United States into the first Persian Gulf War. After four years of service, including "boots on the ground" in Kuwait and Iraq, Lawlor received an honorable discharge and returned home to a small town on the outskirts of Pittsburgh. Elizabeth Lawlor Tunney, Lawlor's younger sister and a resident of Grafton, Ohio, received a letter with no return address in December 1997—the last correspondence she would ever have with her brother.

019-0-19 - PARTY TIME AT 413 DALLYN ROAD - William J. Donahue

November 29, 1997

Dear Liz,

I wanted you to know what happened—wanted *someone* to know, at least. Everyone's story needs telling, no matter how insane it sounds. Perhaps the batshit stories deserve to be told more than any others, especially when they're true.

You and I never really shared the details of our adult lives, but you've always been smart and perceptive, so you must know how I've been making ends meet as a civilian. When you find something you love, or at least something you're good at, you stick with it. So that's what I've been doing since returning stateside, even though I took off my dog tags and combat boots four years ago. I prefer the term assassin to contract killer, because the word sounds more honorable, almost noble, like it has the strength of tradition behind it.

The movies about my business got it all wrong. The work is dirty and gritty, the money's tough to come by, and humans make unpredictable targets, which means things rarely go according to plan. You'd think the first one would be the hardest, the first kill, but that's not quite true. No one ever tells you how messy it's going to be, how personal, how intimate. The second one—*that's* the hardest pin to push over, because by then you know what to expect, and you have to go through with it anyway.

I used to enjoy the work when it came, but that changed with my most recent job, which turned out to be my final job. Central Pennsylvania this time, about three and a half hours east of where we grew up.

Usually a client gives me a name and an address and that's about it, maybe some special instructions about how they want it done—bullet, blade, or garotte. But as long as I put the period at the end of the sentence, so to speak, my checks cash, and I move on to the next one. This time my client asked to come along for the ride. Insisted, in fact, and it's not like I could say no. A paycheck's a paycheck, and a man's gotta eat.

It was snowing that day, into the late afternoon. Heavy stuff, the kind that sticks and piles up quick. I picked up the client, an hour late because of the ice and snow. Her name was Audra. Didn't give a last name, but they almost never do. She had twenty years on me, easy: long black hair, gray at the roots, skin a few shades darker than yours or mine. Her age aside, she looked like she took good care of herself: slim, muscular, chiseled face. She intimidated me a little, to tell the truth, like she could give me a run for my money.

Audra didn't say much for the first hour of the drive, other than repeatedly asking me to turn up the heat. A heavy wooden box sat on the floor between her feet.

Dusk comes early in February, especially on the gray days, and the founders of the speck of a town we rolled through—a place called Kestrel—must not have believed in streetlamps. If not for the hints of daylight peeking through breaks in the cloud cover, it might as well have been nighttime.

Out of nowhere, Audra blurted that she would handle the killing. I was to step in only if she faltered, "to make sure the circle is closed," she said. I'm not used to sitting on the sidelines, so if I wasn't there to do the deed, why the hell was I there? Audra explained that the job required two people, and that most of the folks she had worked with over the years had either died, been maimed or injured beyond repair, or took themselves out of circulation, so she needed help from the outside. So, basically, I was a glorified chauffeur. Then she said this job would be unlike all the others I had done.

Nothing surprises me in this line of work. Whether the son of a bitch owes someone money, knocks up someone's daughter, or gets in the way of a business deal, I honestly don't give a shit about the why. To me, a target is a target.

Her response, word for word: "This target is a vampire."

I've seen some gnarly stuff in my life, Liz, but the supernatural doesn't fly with me. UFOs, Bigfoot, the Bermuda Triangle—bullshit, bullshit, bullshit. I just thought this woman was crazy, plain and simple, but crazy doesn't mean much if the money's right. I was about to make some stupid joke, really let her have it, when she unlatched the box between her feet and retrieved a foot-long wooden stake etched with Christian symbols. It reminded me of a bedpost: a big block on one end, I guess for pounding with a mallet, and a sharpened point on the other.

I asked for the backstory of the job—this vampire— doing my best Bela Lugosi impression just to be a dick. She told me she belonged to a group called the Red Chalice. I'd never heard of it, but I haven't heard of a lot of things. Almost twenty years ago, someone started causing all kinds of trouble in her hometown, north of Harrisburg. First a young girl disappeared. Then two boys from the high school, both dead and gone. Then someone desecrated the church. Even worse carnage followed, but I'll spare you the gory details. After ruling out the usual suspects—the town drunk, the sheriff's unruly daughter, a long-haired motorhead—the townsfolk settled on the newcomer.

What they found when they confronted him at his home changed Audra's life forever. That night had been her introduction to the Red Chalice. She had been a "vampire hunter" ever since.

Crazy, right? Just you wait.

She said she had a decent number of kills to her credit. Said she'd taken part in more than a dozen "slayings"—her word—five of which she'd been the one to do the wet work. The first had been in some small river town north of Philadelphia. With her second, she had to intervene when her partner lost his nerve, in an Ohio town called Ashtabula. She'd killed numbers three, four, and five—a family, I guess—on the same night at a bungalow in a place called Sistersville, West Virginia.

I shared with Audra the details of my kill count, as a soldier and as a civilian, which was north of fifty. Naturally, I offered her some pro tips. She just smiled at me the way you might smile at a drooling toddler, as if I were too simple to get the punchline of a third grader's knock-knock joke.

Her work was "God's will," as she saw it, and she said knowing that was all she needed. Calling the son of a bitch we intended to kill a vampire or a demon wasn't going to make the job any less of a homicide, not that I cared. Beggars can't be choosers. She told me if things went well that night, maybe I could "find redemption" by becoming a formal member of the Red Chalice. Zero chance of that, I told her, because I was a free agent, a rogue, a ronin. I was Han freakin' Solo before he went soft.

If you ask me, the battle between God and the devil, with angels and demons at each other's throats until the end of time, it's just more horse shit, more fairy tales. I don't believe a word of it, and that's exactly what I told Audra. She turned to me and said, "You will believe. If you live to see another day, I promise you will."

I turned onto Dallyn Road, our final destination. Wide tracts of farmland passed by, each paired with a seen-better-days house pushed back from the road. A mailbox bearing the number 413 came into view. The house it belonged to was dark with the exception of a weak yellow pendant light on a porch dotted with hex signs. The next closest property—a lightless farmhouse with a big red barn well on its way to falling down—sat maybe three-hundred feet away.

Based on Audra's hype, I figured the house would mirror a haunted castle or maybe the broken-down mansion from *The Munsters* or *The Addams Family*. Instead, it looked like any other house. An innocent person was about to cash in, not that it was any business of mine.

I slowed the car, looped around, and came back toward the way we had come. I killed the headlights and parked in the gravel at the side of the road.

Audra dipped an index finger into a small glass container and withdrew a dab of liquid—chrism, she called it. An unfamiliar prayer slipped from her lips as she smeared the oil on her forehead then dragged the tip of her finger toward her throat.

She passed me a wooden stake. I waved it away and patted the Glock in my shoulder holster, but she insisted, nearly stabbing me with the stake's tip. She commanded me not to fire my weapon, even though I always use a suppressor to be discreet. The plan: She would go in first, with me just a step or two behind her, and with any luck we would find the "creature" still asleep in its crib. Then she would drive the first stake through the target's heart, the second through its mouth, four more for each hand and foot. Once she finished the job, she'd go about burning the house down, right down to the pilings. Then I could take my money and return to my "meaningless and tortured life," her words, which made her come off like a first-class bitch.

She strapped the stake to her chest and retrieved something else from the box: an oversized wooden hammer. The massive head reminded me of Thor's enchanted whopper from the comic books I read as a kid. I pulled the Glock from its holster, checked the clip, then felt for the extra clips in my jacket pocket and the handle of the eight-inch Bowie strapped to my thigh.

The party at 413 Dallyn Road was about to start.

Cold flooded the cab as Audra opened the passenger door. It couldn't have been more than twenty degrees out there. She skulked across the frozen lawn, toward the porch, and lifted something from her belt: a hatchet.

Things were about to get messy.

A few steps later she was kneeling by the front door and taking way too long to pick the lock of the worn brass knob. She was going to get us both killed, so I nudged her out of the way and kicked in the door. Splinters flew. A shirtless man with mussed hair stood on the other side. My first reaction: If that's what a demon looks like, Hell needs to reinforce the ranks.

Sleepy and harmless, the guy resembled an insurance adjuster who'd just woken up from a nap. Audra wasted no time. The hatchet's heavy blade cleaved his left arm and the meat of his shoulder. Blood spattered everywhere: the walls, the floorboards, the front of my black leather jacket. She swung at the side of his head. The blade clanged off his skull, and he dropped like a sack. I took a step forward to plug him in the head, just to make sure, and she stopped me with a stare. Swear to Christ, the son of a bitch sprang to his feet, as if nothing had happened. He snuck in a shot straight to Audra's chin, quick and hard, the kind that should have knocked her out cold. The blow stunned her, but she stayed on her feet.

Three shots from my Glock brought him down. Smoke fumed from the suppressor's muzzle end.

The poor SOB writhed on the floor, sucking his last breaths through a hole in his throat. Audra knelt beside him and traced her left thumb across his forehead in the shape of a crucifix. She then drove a knife into his temple, the blade almost as big as my Bowie's. His legs trembled for a few seconds before his body went limp.

Audra worked the stiffness out of her jaw. I figured she was about to thank me for saving her ass. Instead she called me a "goddamn idiot." We were a hundred miles from anywhere worth getting to. Even if someone had heard the shots, doubtful because of the suppressor, we had a solid ten-minute head start on the law. The only problem, Audra seethed, was that we still had more than ten minutes of work to do. I was confused, because our target was toes up on the floor, his body riddled with my bullets and his brain turned to mincemeat by the blade of her knife. She said we'd only killed the vampire's familiar, a bodyguard of sorts, endowed with some of its master's powers.

The whole damn shitshow got curiouser and curiouser.

She looked past me to the open front door. The sky had gone almost completely dark. She hurried through the kitchen, toward a door that led down to the cellar.

Audra held the stake ahead of her, the hammer affixed to her belt, as she turned the knob to an unremarkable fiberboard door just off the kitchen. She felt along the wall for a switch, found it, clicked it on and off, no light. A small black flashlight emerged from her jacket pocket. She descended the staircase, and I followed her down, one creaking stair at a time.

The room smelled stale, musty, not unlike any other cellar. Still, something about the air felt strange. At the bottom of the stairs, she took a deep breath and whispered words I couldn't hear. A prayer, I figured. The flashlight beam wandered the perimeter and settled on an oblong shape in the center of the room. It was a coffin, partially sunken into the concrete floor. Shiny and black, featureless, like a slab of onyx.

She tiptoed toward the room's center. I trained the barrel of my gun on the casket, index finger grazing the trigger. Flashlight fixed between her teeth, she motioned for me to come beside her and pry up the coffin's cap. I flipped it open and found nothing but a worn satin lining and a thin film of dirt. And that awful smell, like the rot of death. Under her breath, Audra cursed me for kicking in the door and firing off my "pop gun," mumbling something about a window having closed.

Her flashlight beam ping-ponged around the room—every corner, the rafters of the unfinished ceiling, the mouth of a crawlspace set into the cinderblock wall. She backed toward the staircase and began her ascent. I followed close behind, looking over my shoulder.

A flash of movement, the wind against my face. I didn't quite see it happen, but Audra's headless body fell backward, taking me with her. My left foot got caught in the space between the staircase and the post. Something inside gave way, and the bone snapped.

I've never experienced that depth of pain, Liz, either before or since. Certainly not since.

The flashlight tumbled to the floor, its beam facing the wall beside the stairs. Pinned beneath Audra's body, I had an unobstructed view of the thing descending from the ceiling and perching on the edge of a plank halfway up the staircase. A bat-like creature, maybe seven feet tall, all claws and teeth and yellowed flesh. Patches of long gray hair dotted its liver-spotted scalp. All muscle and sinew, the thing had the sculpted build of a predator that needed to work for every meal—a cheetah, a wolf, a shark in the water. Its upturned nose resembled a bat's. Fang-like canines jutted from the corners of its mouth, making it appear to smile. My stomach turned as its claws scored the dry wood.

I fired three times, four, five, again and again until the magazine emptied. At least one or two shots landed before the thing exploded into a profusion of bats. Hundreds of them flew down the staircase, past me, through me, like a rain of razors, their teeth and talons shredding my skin. A hot blade sliced the side of my face, and my hearing went funny.

My hand found my ear, or where my ear had been, and came away sticky and dark. Blood. My severed ear sat on the dingy tile floor, just out of reach.

I'm losing my mind—that's what I thought, Liz.

Turns out the insanity had only just begun.

The bats came together in a funnel, a twister, right in the center of the room, and formed a silhouette just beside the onyx coffin. I fumbled for the magazine release and was about to reload when a stick-like claw, the skin as yellow as chicken fat, closed gently around my hand. I looked up into the creature's eyes, as bright and green as sunlit emeralds.

I forgot the pain in my leg, my ear.

The creature had no speech, yet it growled in perfect English. It flung Audra's body off me as if it were nothing, nothing but air between us.

Looking back I don't quite remember what happened next, only the pinch of its fangs finding the artery in my throat—the slightest of stings—the sound it made as it drank, the burning sensation I'm embarrassed to say bordered on pleasure. It then held its hand above my face, and traced a sharpened claw along the underside of its wrist. My tongue tasted salt and metal and rotting meat, as the creature's blood—

viscous, almost solid, as cold as lake water—filled my mouth, coated my throat, found my stomach.

The creature reached across me and lifted something from the floor. It held my ear between its fingers, as if studying it, then kissed the ear and pressed it to the side of my head. When the creature removed its hand, the ear fused with my flesh—remade. As if a switch had been flicked, my hearing returned to normal.

The creature—a vampire, all of it was true—climbed the stairs. Bony claws scraped the wood. It looked back at me and winked, cocking its thumb and index finger in an imaginary trigger pull.

I lay at the bottom of the stairs, as if paralyzed. The disease had started its work. My broken and bloodied body was already transforming, mending itself. I had the presence of mind to wonder if I wanted to be mended, if I wanted to be transformed. I studied the pistol in my lap as a siren began to caterwaul in the distance.

Nine months have passed since that night.

I now wander from town to town, under the cover of night, staying for as long as I can, until the air changes, until I've been made, and then it's on to the next. Someday I imagine there will be a knock at my door, and on the other side will be another Audra, another disciple of the Red Chalice, in her hand a sharpened stake intended for the center of my chest.

Until then my body count will continue to rise, though my kills are no longer in service to my country or my bank account. Seven so far, if I'm counting correctly, each of them doomed and drained. Like I said, a man's gotta eat.

I can feel the disease still evolving inside me. If I walk the earth for long enough, will I one day wake up to resemble the bat-like thing in the cellar of 413 Dallyn Road? When and if that day comes, the man you once knew will cease to exist entirely. Based on who I was and the way I lived my life, I guess that's no great loss.

We'll never see each other again, Liz, because I don't trust myself. I'm a stone's throw from Grafton for now, and I'll stay close for as long as I can, keeping an eye on you and your family. Don't worry; I promise to come no closer than I already have.

Your loving brother,
J.J.

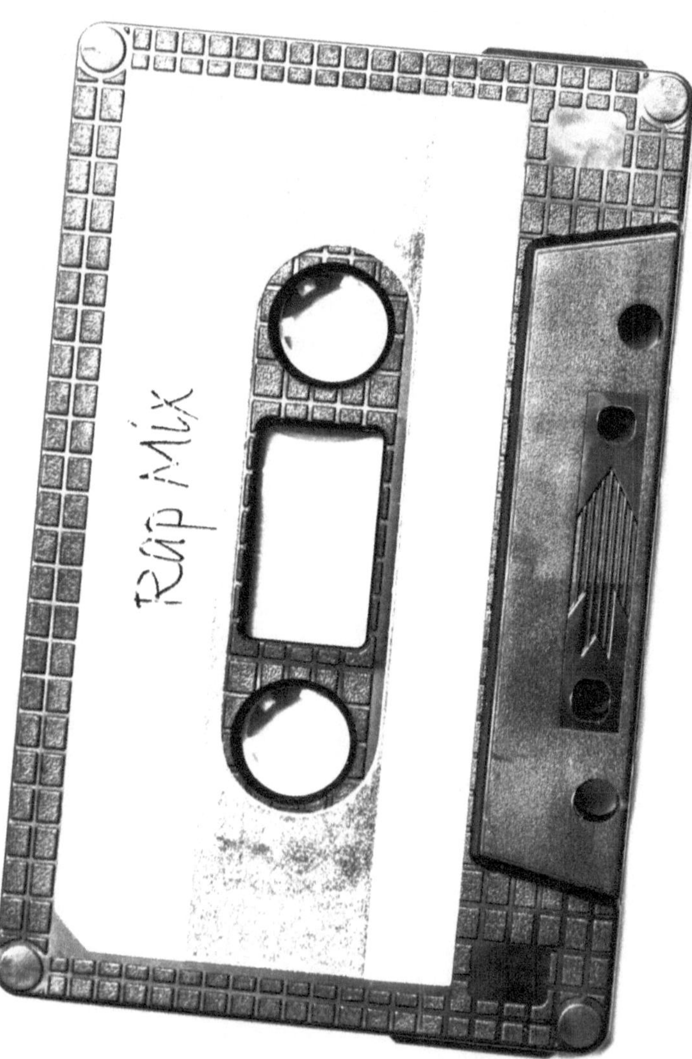

Rap Mix

February 13, 1998. The following items are included as part of Beacon Police Department's Case No. 187172. Exhibit 084, recovered after the fire at 108 Sheridan Lane in the bedroom of Etta May Washington (14, current status: missing): a battered Adidas shoebox with the words KEEP OUT written across the top in large, black marker. It is covered with various punk-themed stickers; the anarchist A, the Nirvana smiley-face, a Banned Books Week sticker from the Beacon Public Library, etc. A description of each individual item within the box has been transcribed below, by intern Ramona Wilde.

019-0-20 – BAD BLOOD – TT Madden

Item description: a cassette tape labeled "Rap Mix". Date of recording unknown. Transcript:

[Inhuman screeching. The sounds of a struggle; thudding, crashing, glass breaking. More inhuman screeching. Multiple men shouting. A feral grunt. The repeated sounds of something hard striking flesh, which, the more it is repeated, devolves into a sick, thwacking, squelching sound. The sounds of violence are intercut with snippets of Public Enemy's "Harder Than You Think," the fight clearly having been recorded over it.]

Voice 1: *young woman, confirmed through voice analytics as* Etta May Washington: [panting] Goddamn. Holy shit.

Voice 2: *older man, suspected identity* Aaron Washington: You good, kid?

Etta May: Yeah, I'm good, Unc. Lemme just...lemme sit down.

Aaron: You did good. Your pops would be proud.

[A long pause.]

Etta May: Thanks, Unc. [Deep breath] You think I should go to the doctor?

Aaron: Lemme see? [pause] Ain't need no damn doctor, girl. You fine. Ain't trust them to take care of us. And before you worry, no, you ain't gonna turn into one-a them. You just always gotta remember—

[There is a sharp whistling sound, something whipping through the air, and then a thick squelching followed immediately by a hard thunk.]

Aaron: Chop off the head. Then we burn 'em. Only way they stay dead. Get that gas, then I'll fix up that arm.

[The rest of the cassette is a mix tape containing popular rap songs.]

Item description: An unknown object that appears to be organic, floating inside a mason jar. The object is surrounded by fluid that appears to be formaldehyde. Will send to the lab for further tests. The object itself inside the jar is oblong, measuring six inches long and two and a half inches wide, dark coloration, with a thicker base near the bottom of the jar, tapering slightly at the top. Conjecture: object is not an object but an animal. A giant leech.

Item description: Newspaper clipping of an obituary from the Beacon Banner newspaper, December 27th, 1997. No picture is provided in the obituary itself, but paper-clipped to it is a wallet-sized photo. Its edges are rounded with wear, and it depicts a smiling African-American man from the waist up. He has a mustache and is wearing a polo shirt and an apron, standing before a charcoal grill.

Transcript:

The Washington family is devastated to announce the unexpected passing of their patriarch, Dr. Samson "Sammy" Washington. A well-known figure in the community, the professor of history at Beacon High School and Holstenwall College spent much of his spare time volunteering for the free clinic. In lieu of flowers, the family asks that any donations be made to the survivors of the Tuskegee Experiment.

Item description: a Blockbuster receipt for the film BLADE. The following is written in pen on the back:

Interview with the Vampire

Near Dark

Ganja & Hess

Lost Boys

From Dusk Till Dawn

Bram Stoker's Dracula

Item description: a cassette tape labeled "diary." Date of recording unknown. Transcript:

Voice 1: Etta May Washington: Uncle Aaron told me he'd tell me everything today. After your funeral, Daddy. He's talking to Momma right now. I can't hear what they sayin', but it looks like it's a lot. Momma's crossed her arms. Unc's wavin' his hands around. I can only hear a few things they shout, when their voices get loud. Momma's sayin' somethin' about the doctor. Unc's sayin' she should know better than to trust a doctor, that a doctor woulda made it worse. I dunno why, but something inside me agrees with Unc. The paper even changed the name of where Momma wanted your donations sent.

[This next section of the tape appears to have been recorded some indeterminate amount of time later. The sound of an engine can be heard in the background, tires crunching over gravel.]

242

Etta May: Where are we, Unc?

Aaron: We almost there. [Long pause] You still got that tape goin' girl?

Etta May: Yeah. I dunno why. Makes me feel like I can still talk to Daddy, I guess. You want me to turn it off? Momma doesn't like me doin' it.

Aaron: Nah, girl, keep it on. Ain't no secrets here. [slightly louder, as if closer to the recorder] Ain't that right, Sammy?

Etta May: Then can I ask why you and Momma were yellin' earlier?

Aaron: Cause there some things she don't want me to tell you, but she knows you gotta know.

Etta May: Like why you didn't want Daddy to go to the doctor?

Aaron: Yes, ma'am. Cause doctors don't help people like us, Etta May.

Etta May: Why?

Aaron: I'll show you. We're here.

[The squeal of brakes. The engine turns off. A car door opens, shuts. In the quiet, crickets chirp, frogs croak. Night-birds caw and sing. Two sets of feet crunch through gravel, and then softer grass. The sound of a key in a lock, and the rattling of chains, and the long, slow squeal of hinges opening. A thick ka-chunk of a heavy switch being thrown. There is a long pause.]

Etta May: Unc?...What am I lookin' at?

Aaron: This, Etta May, one of them things that killed your Daddy.

Item description: An anatomical diagram resembling Da Vinci's Vitruvian Man, drawn on 8 ½ x 11 paper, torn from a spiralbound notebook, folded into fourths. The subject is nude, sex indeterminate. The body largely resembles a muscular human, with the exception of the genitals, extremities, and head.

Where the genitals should be, there's a smooth surface. Like a Barbie doll. The figure has hands, but those hands bear sharpened claws protruding from the fingertips. It's difficult to tell in the drawing, despite its realism, but it looks like the claws are sprouting out of the fingertips, like they're bursting from beneath the skin, not part of the finger itself.

Where the head is supposed to be is instead a large tentacular appendage. It is longer than the figure's other limbs, curling above the body and tapering to a point. The appendage's thickness isn't equal throughout its entire length. There are bulbs in the skin throughout the length of the appendage that create the sensation of undulation.

Written on the back of the anatomical drawing is the following:

Garlic?

Crosses?

Holy water?

Mirrors?

Silver?

Wooden stakes? Anything stabby works just fine

Fire?

Sunlight? Slows them down, but doesn't stop them

Chop their heads off? Uncle Aaron said chop 'em up and burn 'em, like Evil Dead. We have to be completely sure.

Item description: The cover page of school report, top-left of the page torn off, as if pulled from a stapled whole

Report on The Tuskegee Syphilis Study

By Etta May Washington

[Written in red pen across the top] *I'll give you a passing grade, but try to stick to a nicer event for your next report.*

- Mrs. Hopkins

[Drawn across the white space of the school paper is a crude map of Beacon, with three locations circled in a different shade of red; the western part of the lake connecting to the woods, the swamp behind the hospital, and the police station. At the bottom is one word, also in red; nests]

Item description: Unlabeled VHS tape found in an unmarked cardboard sleeve at the bottom of the box. A transcription of the tape follows:

[The video opens up on a night scene of the woods, lit only by the light on top of the camera and torches from somewhere offscreen. There are lights in the distance, the big H of Beacon County Hospital visible beyond the trees. The woods are swampy, and you can hear the buzz of bugs and the squelch of boots in the mud. Two men walk into frame, and while the identity of one is currently unknown, the other can be confirmed to be Aaron Washington. He looks at the camera.]

Aaron: You alright there, Etta May?

[The camera bobs up and down, but there's no verbal reply. Aaron's eyes look to someone to the right of the camera, offscreen.]

Aaron: You watch her, you hear? That's your only job, is you watch her.

Unknown voice: Got it, boss.

[Aaron turns back towards the woods, and the rest of the group follows him. He is wielding a machete in his left hand.]

Aaron: It's just up ahead.

Aaron lifts up a fist in the universal signal for stop, and everyone obeys, following his lead as he crouches down. Aaron scooches to the side, and then points ahead into the dark.

Aaron: You see that there, Etta May? Errybody, lights off for a moment. Etta May, use the night-vision.

[The camera zooms in on what appears to be a large mound, a pile of trees that seems to have fallen on top of one another, maybe during a storm. The screen flips to a sickly green that reveals it was no accident the way these trees have fallen. They were laid there with a purpose. It looks somewhat akin to a beaver dam.]

Unknown voice: Yo, Aaron.

[The camera jerks, zooms back and then forward again, this time focusing on a pair of moving figures carrying a large package between them.]

Aaron: Didn't expect this tonight. Well, at least it oughta make the rest easier. You pay attention, Etta May.

[The camera carefully tracks the two men, nurses, their scrubs reveal, and together they toss the thing they're both carrying into the swamp water as if it were no more than a bag of trash. But as the package falls and the sheet covering it flies open, a man is revealed inside. A living man. He flails as he falls, splashing down, and then the nurses high-tail it out of there.]

Aaron: Watch the nest, now.

[The camera looks back to the strange tree-structure, the beaver dam thing, and then something crawls up and out of it. It is the creature from the anatomical drawing, except unholy and alive. Like the drawing, it's naked, its smooth crotch and bizarre tentacular head clearly visible in the night-vision. The tentacle-head whips around aimlessly like a worm pulled from the earth. The head suddenly stops its whipping, focusing on the cast-aside man, and then the creature lunges for him, its body less like it's actually walking and more like it's being pulled by the tentacle-thing where a human head should be. Even from this distance it is obvious to see the front of the tentacle open up and reveal itself not as a tentacle, but as the circular, tooth-rimmed mouth of a parasite.

The first creature is followed by more, half a dozen more, and they surround the flailing patient, some of them dropping their bodies down to him, others standing straight up, extending those terrible heads more than double the lengths of their own bodies, to feast.]

Aaron: A'ight, they're distracted. Let's do this. You stay here, Etta May.

[Half a dozen men creep into the frame of the shot, and then more, and then even more, and one of those monsters turns at the sound of squelching mud and then the men are running, screaming, slashing with blades and hacking with axes and bashing with bats and hammers. They charge together like armies of old, the creatures attacking with claws and those strange heads, mowed down by sheer numbers.

One of them breaks free, and charges Etta May—the camera— but is struck in the back by something unseen and falls to the ground. Aaron stands triumphantly above it, bringing the machete down into the creature's head, back, neck, chopping it to ribbons until it stops moving altogether.]

Etta May: Goddamn. Holy shit.

Aaron, covered in blood, looks at Etta May, at the camera.

Aaron: You good, kid?

[The video cuts to black.]

Part 4

Texts from Kay Robinson to Haruto Wilco Bledsoe - 6/8/2024

Hey Haruto

I'm just going to get right into it. Remember Auntie Wendy who died in 2002?

I was twenty-six, and no one knew this except mum, but she left me everything she had - a fortune in money, homes, investments, all of it. And it was healthy, to say it politely.

But it all came with it a responsibility that mum didn't know about - that my life must be spent behind a desk, doing research, chronicling and verifying. I thought I was fine with that. Only, I can't sit on the sidelines any longer.

I know you've done well for yourself, but I've learned of your accident, forcing you into a wheelchair for the foreseeable future. I'm sorry. But to be honest, H, your accident has given me clarity. I need to do this now, why I still can.

So, I sent you what Auntie Wendy sent to me. Her letter explains it better than I ever could. But I'm not just sending her words, I'm sending you it all. All the money, homes, investments, and H, this is the rub, you're getting all the responsibility, and it's a hefty burden to bear.

I'm sorry, but not sorry. Once you realize what you're looking at, you'll understand why it needs to be done, and then I think you'll understand why I'm doing this.

I've set up safe houses for myself all over the US and Europe. I've taken the money I'll need to survive; I've been training, and I'm joining the fray, the fight for good over evil. This is my calling; I can feel it!

I'll be in touch as soon as I am settled. If you need help, you can reach out to Ed Crimi, Megan Flannery and the people at Vampa in Doylestown. They know their stuff there. May all the gods help and be with us both.

Love you, cuz. Take care and don't worry about me.

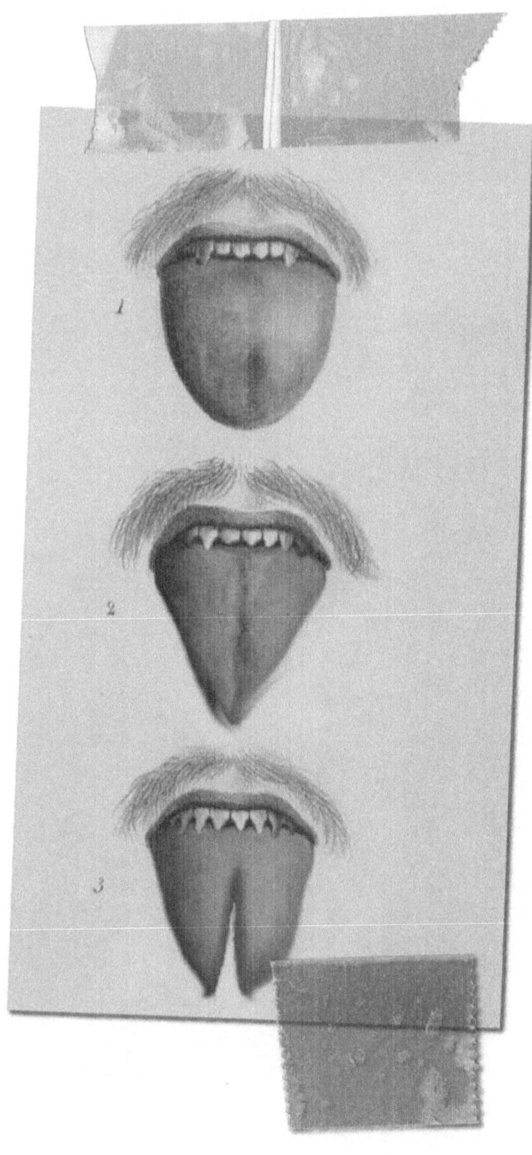

The following excerpt comes from journals found at the scene of a crime in the small Midwestern town of Odenton, Ohio. There is no record of a Professor Kestrel at Sopron College.

21. BIRDS & BEASTS - Hope Madden

August 31

That's not how it's done.

There are reasons for the way we handle our prey, chief among them self-respect. Respect for tradition. Respect for our legacy, our history, our legend. And if that's not reason enough, we feed the way we do because it does not draw attention to us, either individually or as a group.

Protect your own.

I loathe that I am in the position to have to address, to correct the kind of outrageous, reckless idiocy that would run afoul of that one, simple principle.

And yet, here I am.

Slipping from young Chloe's room, lingering in the shadows, drunk with blood and longing for the beautiful melancholy and delicious horror of the discovery, I waited for her parents to check that she was tucked safely into bed. Would it be the mother, doting, once beautiful? Or the father, protective like a dog on guard?

As I paused in the darkness of their hallway, I overheard (I will record it as faithfully as possible):

-Mother: You don't want to hear me say it, but it serves him right.

-Father: Jesus, Jessica! A young man is dead. He hardly deserved it.

-Mother: I disagree.

-Father: My god.

-Mother: But how did it happen? How was he drained of blood like that? Some kind of new disease?

-Father: Did you read that somewhere? Great. Now there'll be another vaccine.

None of the tedious conversation would have pierced the anticipation of their discovery had the woman not asked: *How was he drained of blood like that?*

Yes, quite a question, Mum. It so provoked my imagination that I nearly missed the screams and sobs as they found their own precious child, likewise drained, but not to the point of spectacle. Just enough to satisfy my needs and to leave a poetically tragic corpse.

That is how it's done.

Who would be so careless as to drain a body entirely? The beast may as well have left a handwritten warning: I exist and have come to murder your kind.

September 1

Awake and alive, barely. Was unable to sleep soundly, even after last night's feast—or perhaps partially because of it. I fear young Chloe was less chaste than she claimed. Unpenetrated, certainly, but is that all there is to chastity, really? The truly untasted leave such satisfaction that I don't begin craving the next meal for days. And yet today, I awake unsatisfied and peckish.

It was also, of course, news of this rogue stalker that plagued my sleep. There is nothing so comforting, nurturing as the hours in close quarters with no one and nothing save your own council. Unless you're troubled. Then time passes without rest.

Whose passions have never gotten the better of him? Could I extend this vampire that grace?

No. He will find none in me. His behavior, and the bitter taste of Chloe's vague impurities have left me restless. I will make the short trip to Odenton, Ohio—site of the "grisly murder" of one Brian Engle—take stock of the damage and sleuth out my foe's whereabouts. I'll pass the time productively, at least.

September 2

The least accurate reporting seems to be the victim's hometown coverage, the Odenton Voice. As prone to speculation as to grammatical error, the outlet did provide certain details:

- Brian Engle, 19-years-old
- Date of death: August 29
- Employed: Lawson's (convenience store)
- Identified by mother: Deb Daugherty, 119 Tomb Road
- Last seen outside Tri Delta sorority house, 12:25 am.

August 29

Speculation:

1.   Revenge
2.   Satan worship

Both inaccurate, luckily. I am grateful for the Odenton Voice's help in disguising my foe's sloppy predation.

Revenge: because apparently the boy was connected to another notorious young man in town, another dead boy named Evan Connor.

Satan worship: because it was clearly a murder, but an unusual one, as there was so little blood at the crime scene. Somehow that led authorities (or the local news outlet?) to ideas of the occult. How quaint that the truth would not be considered a feasible cause, and yet Satan worship doesn't defy reason. That's perhaps what I love most about small Midwestern towns. In so many ways, the thinking is practically medieval. I so miss medieval times.

The boy was last seen across the street from a sorority house. Clues concerning the true culprit may lay there, but because the stench of overripe meat sickens me, I strategize so that I may avoid a visit to Tri Delta.

Wouldn't it be fun to comb the Sopron College library for an incoming freshman? Someone willing to be a research assistant to, say, a Criminal Justice professor trying to piece together the mystery of this boy's death? An assistant who can carry her own fresh scent into a sorority house and ask questions?

September 3

Whoever it is I'm hunting deserves credit for thinking of stalking Odenton. When a town is small enough and Midwestern enough, trust in authority is so delightfully blind.

Robin. That's the name of my research assistant. Petite—tiny, really—with dark bangs hanging into her big, dark eyes, so like a fawn. Her odor is sweet enough to put me on edge. Normally I avoid places like Odenton because ennui gets the better of me. Depression offers me more struggle than a meal ever has. And the girls in towns like this, perhaps due to their own boredom, tend so often toward wanton behavior.

And yet, miraculously, I discovered Robin, whose scent is unmistakable. Purer than Chloe. The anticipation of feasting on my little bird will end in satisfaction perhaps greater even than that of unraveling this Brian Engle mystery and terminating my errant foe.

When I posed the question, "What compels you to investigate with me?" she responded, "I'd love to gain some experience, but more than anything, I want to be of use. I came to college to find ways to serve a purpose."

As she spoke, she blushed. She's almost too perfect to bear.

When she left, I moved to the crime scene: an unremarkable flat above a vacant shoe store in the small downtown stretch of Odenton, a few blocks from the college. The inexpensive furnishings—a combination of the well-worn and the newly mass produced, all of it a dismal beige—suggest that the room was leased furnished.

The space had been cleaned; the pungent chemicals scorched my sinuses. But beneath that odor, true virgin blood. Not sweet, not like my Robin, but rich with the complexities isolation nourishes. I prefer something less complicated.

Reckless self-indulgence marks the stalker drawn to this blood. And a male. My opponent sought struggle, violence.

A conundrum at the scene perplexes me. The scent of blood is strongest a few feet away from where the remnants of chalk dust suggest a corpse outline. The floor below a small table is unmistakably discolored, no doubt from a bloodletting.

Why would my opponent waste so much blood? And how did it come to pool here, so far from where the body was drained? I haven't the answers, but I commit to writing my thoughts now in the hope that they will bring clarity as more intelligence is collected.

September 4

Robin began her investigation with the mother. She flew to the nest, concerned for the grieving old woman. You could see the bubbling goal to find some justice for the crone.

Per my little bird's notes:

A backpack was found with the body. The police haven't returned it to Deb. Evidence. But its contents included a notebook, and a handgun wrapped in a Cleveland Browns beach towel.

Deb wasn't surprised he had a gun. Confirms she'd seen the notebook around the house, picked it up once from the living room floor. Says it's filled with hateful things. Made her sick— she "lost her soup"—and won't read it even if they do give it back to her. Says she'll burn it. "Hateful things," she says again.

Deb says Brian "fell about" when his friend Evan died. [NOTE to Professor Kestrel: Evan Connor ran his Escalade into the Tri Delta fundraiser, running down and seriously injuring two people, then exited the vehicle with a semiautomatic weapon, spraying bullets into the crowd of volunteers, killing 6 before police shot him in the head and killed him.]

Deb says that Brian idolized Evan, that it made Brian feel more confident that Evan had trouble with girls. "You'd think it would make him feel worse. This kid—good looking, parents have money, dresses nice, drives a nice car—if he can't get a girlfriend, what chance did Brian have? I thought they musta been gay. He made Brian feel important, I think."

What does Deb think happened to her son? "They murdered him. That's all I need to know."

She shares one more piece of information. Deb received a text from her son at 2:48 am. She didn't see it until the next day. It read: I love you.

"He didn't, though," she says without emotion.

Maybe he realized, in his final moments, that there was one person on earth he really did love? So sad.

I thanked Robin, bade her leave her notes for me to study, and asked her for solitude.

I'd planned to follow Robin, witness her nightly ritual, stoke my desire. But I had none. Even Robin's scent couldn't settle my stomach. Why choose a weakling like this Brian Engle, a would-be predator—competition, if anything, except that he would target the bruised and the overripe rather than the pure. What stalker would degrade himself in this way? This beast I track is beneath my kind.

I called Robin back, suddenly worried. My foe's behavior couldn't be predicted. Surely, he'd left Odenton. You don't stay behind with the flesh you ruined. You move on. But who could know with this madman?

Worried for my own beautiful meal, I hand Robin the one weapon that could save her. Yes, it means I cannot draw the silver blade for my own defense, but any stalker feasting on garbage the likes of Brian Engle will make for an inferior opponent. To me. But not to my lovely Robin Red Breast.

Her gratitude at the blade, though she protested the gift, moved me. Again, she blushed.

September 5

I could smell the whores on her before she entered my rooms. Of course, today's assignment was Tri Delta. I thought to ask her to go home, bathe and return. But I reminded myself that this time, I manipulate my meal for reasons larger than my own enjoyment, so I suffered the stench.

Her information was rushed. She sounded drunk. I chose not to hide my disappointment, but inwardly I cursed my own shortsightedness. Exposing Robin to all of this would no doubt taint her purity, each day ruining her slightly. I wanted to take her then, days ahead of schedule but before the taste would be seriously affected and wondered whether this abomination of a vampire and his chaos had begun to taint me as well. My thoughts raced, but stopped with the news:

One sister remembered seeing the boy, Brian, the night he was murdered. It was she who'd identified him to police as having been outside the sorority house. She had been driving three friends back after an evening of self-ruin and would never have noticed the boy except that a woman called to her.

A woman.

From the street, a woman complimented her parking.

"Everyone loves a good parallel parker."

This is what the mystery woman had called out.

This sorority sister had waved at the friendly woman, then noticed the young man with a bicycle and a backpack, scribbling in a notebook and looking terribly unhappy.

This mystery woman, then, had been the last to see the young man alive.

"Maybe I should find this woman?" Robin suggested, but my skin turned colder at the idea of it. It was instinct.

I asked Robin what the woman had looked like.

"They couldn't remember."

Disgust darkened my mood. So, my foe is a female. Never would I have predicted such careless brutality from a female, but why not? Ours is not a gift meant to be bestowed upon the female. They haven't the necessary respect for tradition nor the endurance for endless nights. How many of my kind have been undone by the romantic notion of making for themselves a mate for eternity?

...

I sent Robin away—the scent of rot on her sickened me and my mood was sour.

Robin asked me coquettishly if I wanted to drive her home, that perhaps she wasn't in good shape to be behind the wheel. I regretted again having mixed predation with this quest for justice and mourned the possible loss of such a sumptuous feast. The fact that Robin would not be at peak freshness, that excruciatingly delicate moment of untainted yet aroused perfection, will be blamed on my foul foe.

My enemy. This mysterious woman.

In no mood to follow my Robin, to stoke my flame, I remained in my rooms, contemplating until daylight threatened.

September 6

I've given up on finding my opponent before her next meal—she could be in Majorca or Istanbul or anywhere by now. But I believe now my foe is female, and I have an eternity to play this game with her. But tonight, I take Robin before she ripens further.

These last hours before a meal can be such a heady mix of hunger and anticipation, a drowsy, drunken feeling that leaves me disinterested in this chase. I will demand that Robin halt the investigation, for her own safety. I'll insist she remain with me, under my watch. I ache already with the promise of her flavor.

She comes. The smell precedes her—not of sluts but of...pastries. Of yeast and sugar.

September 6, later.

"He was decapitated—"

The announcement arrives before she does; she shouts it up the steps leading to my rooms.

I shall transcribe while it's fresh.

She'd been to Polly Wantsa.

It's a breakfast and lunch place downtown. Homemade donuts, great soup. You can walk there from campus and from the police station. It's only about three blocks from the apartment where Brian Engle was found. Eva Parkins works there since she graduated. I actually just went in to say hi but when I noticed how many cops were there, I thought I'd see if she'd heard anything about anything.

She says that's when the cops come in every day, just descend on the place. The cafe is about to close, so whatever donuts are left, she just gives the cops because she'd throw them out otherwise. They walk around like it's an office meeting, grab the coffee pot and fill each other's mugs, and talk about whatever they're working on. It's wild.

She said Brian Engle was decapitated. That's all they talked about that day. That's why there was so much blood so far away from the body. They didn't share it with the newspaper because people would freak, and assume it's devil worship. Everybody always says devil worship. It never is, of course, but if it's tricky at all, cops here say it's Satan.

Between hunger, the queasying smell of sweets and my almost unmanageable contempt for the recklessness of my foe, I admit I stopped listening. What need was there now in investigating? I'd wait for a scrap of news or rumor about another similarly disfigured body and be off on my next adventure. This game had become tedious. But then...

Brian texted his mom 'I love you' at like 2 am or something, but he'd been dead for hours. The killer had propped his head on a wine bottle on the end table—where all the blood spilled. I think he did it to use the face to unlock Brian's phone and text Deb.

My own head spun. What post-apocalyptic savagery! And from a woman! No predator with a shred of self-respect would tear through or toy with...it's unspeakable, repugnant.

The buttery sweetness that clung to Robin sickened me further.

But why that text? Maybe the killers felt guilty? About Brian's mom, you know? I could see that. I mean, it seems like Brian Engle was a terrible person. But even if you know you're killing a terrible person, he was a baby once, right? Someone loved him once. Maybe they just wanted to make it hurt his mom less.

Her romantic nature nearly pulled me from my malaise, made me remember wistfully my so-recent plan to feed tonight. But no. The image of the boy's head impaled on a wine bottle sickened me all over again, and I sent Robin home.

September 7

A boy in town has gone missing. The whispers, chattering, the harsh mechanical chirping of it from mobile devices as they passed under my window wormed into my sleeping thoughts. *Owen...devil worshippers. Owen, the friend. He's an OK dude, though...He didn't do anything, just wouldn't narc out his friend...Hope somebody takes his head off too.*

These awful words carried by bats and birds, spilling like wind from the gaping mouths of decapitated heads, bleeding into soup bowls. I awoke dreary and anxious. I'd fasted long enough.

...

Hours pass without Robin. Where is she?! I could roam the streets in search, but the idea of the spoiled and the stale that populate this town fills me with paralyzing disgust.

She arrives, my Robin! And what song does she sing?

...

My little Robin was less acquiescent, less in awe than is her custom, and I missed it. I betrayed my anxiety over her delay, causing her some alarm. But certainly, she recognized it as concern for her safety. I apologized—gallantly, I think—and allowed that the irritation in my voice was simply the consequence of my protectiveness. Perhaps she softened at that, but perhaps not.

She was kept, of course, by a later than usual interview. Had I not been so hungry, so concerned, and so vexed by this gorgon, I'd have seen that my little bird was simply following my instructions. She met with another convenience store clerk; one whose shift begins at 11 pm. He has rounded out what we can gather concerning the hag I seek.

From Robin's recording:

Woman? One did come in one night, a couple days before Brian died. I only remember because she asked for him and nobody ever asked for Brian. No women, definitely. I thought maybe she was a teacher or a social worker or something. She smiled when she said his name.

Robin spoke. Her calm, measured tone in the recording bewildered me. She asked why he sounded surprised that the woman would smile.

Brian wasn't the kind of guy you think about and smile. Suppose that's sad. He was a human being, had it kind of rough. But you're only a victim until you victimize somebody else. Then you're just a dick.

Did she laugh at that? Just a hint of a laugh. My little bird is hardening.

Brian didn't like people. And people, you know, kind of felt the same way about him. Especially after that other kid, that Evan asshole, gunned down those girls at the college and got shot. Him and Owen, they were the only people ever came here to see Brian.

Owen?! The missing boy. Could Robin see my anguish? The clamor outside my window as I slept, another missing boy. The demon was still in town, then. The thought should exhilarate me. The chase is on! I can end this monstress before her chaos continues. Why, then, the ice running along my spine?

I believed the interview was over, but I heard Robin's voice, muffled. Coquettish. Was she flirting with this Gunther to entice him to share more information? My eyes reevaluated my little nestling. What had I done? She seemed almost stale to me now, too much of her purity leached by this experience. But soon, the store clerk's voice retook my attention.

The late shift gets boring. Sometimes I scroll through the day's security footage. People would come in once in a while and razz Brian. Give him a hard time. Once a bunch of high school kids came in. Each one grabbed a dozen eggs, and they all lined up politely like they wanted him to ring them out. Then they opened their dozen and threw them at him, egg by egg. He ducked. A couple girls climbed up on the counter and pelted him on the floor. Then they all left. They didn't laugh or yell or anything. Just bombed him with eggs and left.

What did he do?

He sat on the ground crying. Then he got up, locked the door, and cleaned everything up.

He didn't call the police?

Nope. But he started carrying a backpack to work after that.

His manifesto?

That and a gun.

My hunger, my disappointment in the ripeness that had already begun to harden and spoil my prized feast—all of it flooded my voice as I demanded: Why did you not ask him what she looked like?!

She had, she practically snapped at me. But it was after she'd stopped recording.

What else had happened between my little birdie and Late Shift Gunther after the recording had ended, I wondered. I knew the stare I leveled in her direction was too much, too stern, too forceful, but in my anxious state I could not help myself.

She barely flinched.

"He said she was hard to describe. He couldn't picture her. He tried, like right there while we were standing, squeezing his eyes shut and pinching up his face. It was almost comical. But he just couldn't remember."

I understood. Twas the beast. Could be no other.

She will kill tonight. I can feel it, as if she were in this room with me. I could use that instinct, track her tonight. I could save this Owen. His fear, the stench of it, and her hunger—I can almost smell it, it rages through me. I could take Robin with me, be this boy's savior, end this demon and see, once again, the unpolluted worship in my little bird's eyes as she looks at me. Surely, she'll see something of the miraculous in me as I slay the hag.

I jot these, my last notes, as I plan it. We'll escape to some secluded place. A cabin she remembers from her childhood. She'll protect me from the light. I'll let her believe she is nursing me, saving me. She will regain what purity is possible. And at the moment of her willing submission to my bite, as she looks adoringly at me, I will terrify her. I will violate her, and her blood will spray over every surface that once reflected her childhood innocence.

Postscript

I talked to her, the woman who'd come to Lawson's looking for Brian Engle. The one who appreciates a good parallel parker. She was waiting for me, leaning against the bike rack and holding a little silver dagger just like the one Professor Kestrel had. It probably should have scared me but the way she looked at me was so comforting.

She knew I was looking for her. I asked if she'd seen Brian Engle the night he died, and she laughed, not in a mean way but a kind of surprised, happy way, and said of course. She said she'd killed him. She told me she was going to kill Owen Panzera in a few hours. But first she needed to see to something.

I probably should have run. Maybe I didn't because she had a knife, but I didn't feel afraid at all. She said we needed to go to Professor Kestrel's apartment. I asked if she was going to kill him, and she said no. She said I was going to do it.

Then I laughed. The whole thing seemed so funny, so dumb, like I'd been playing Scooby-Doo for days and suddenly realized it. She laughed too. She told me I was going to take the knife I had, the one that looked like hers (how did she know?), and I was going to run it from his belly to his throat. We both laughed at that. She asked me what look I thought would cross Kestrel's face when I gutted him, and I stopped laughing because I couldn't picture him. I couldn't remember what he looked like at all.

I closed my eyes and tried to remember what she looked like leaning up against the bike rack, but I had no idea. Brunette, blonde, young, old? I couldn't have described either one of them.

She said Kestrel saw me as a pet lamb to admire until he got hungry. She told me he was going to eat me tonight, just like she was going to eat Owen Panzera tonight. Kestrel would come up with some reason that I should stay with him, probably something heroic, like helping him save the missing boy. He would be very romantic about it, as if he would die if

270

we didn't consummate our relationship. She said that's how I'd know he was going to kill me, but that now it was the lambs who did the slaughtering.

I didn't believe her, but I was glad she followed me to his room. I didn't see her there, but she had this smell like rain, like an open window. It made me feel safer, maybe even courageous. And when Kestrel did say that he needed me to help save Owen Panzera, and we'd disappear together after it was done—word for word as she'd predicted—I wondered why I'd never seen him at school, or why I came here only at night. I wondered why he couldn't run these fact-finding errands himself—I wondered what he contributed to the "investigation" at all.

I followed him toward the door. I paused at the top of the steps, and when he turned back to hurry me along, I told him I was afraid. She said he would like that, and it would make him vulnerable. And when he swept back toward me with his arms out for an embrace, I made myself really look at his face. Really see him, without hearing his romantic language or condescending praise. His face was horrible, eyes full of malice, salivating mouth, cartoonishly false smile.

I sliced him from his navel to his throat with his own blade.

He fell backwards, down the stairs, and landed on the sidewalk that would, at this hour, be empty until the sun rises and bakes his carcass.

She seemed really proud of me. I felt pretty proud of myself, actually.

~Robin

Sieg

These pages had been torn out of a notepad, and folded as if they'd been placed in an envelope, perhaps to be mailed. They are believed to be part of a records cache from the American vampire hunting collective known as "The Fold." The Fold is only loosely organized, and their documentation is known to be sloppy. These entries are believed to have been written by a veteran vampire hunter known as "Doc", while he was on the payroll of the Catholic Church.

22. 19 NIGHTS IN KIRIBATI - D.C. Kugtima

3/1/25 Afternoon? Tarawa Atoll. Kiribati.

Just got in. Long fucking flight. I've got no idea where my gear is. I'm expecting my contact to find me tonight. I've got no files, no phone. But it's gorgeous out here, and I'm sure they've got good fish and beer. I wish this was a vacation. This whole place seems to be one giant beach.

3/1/25 10:17pm, I think. Not sure if I've got the time zone figured out yet.

It's pronounced "Keer-I-Bahs". Everyone here seems to speak English, and they're friendly enough. They speak some indigenous language when they don't want us to know what they're saying. I'm being treated with a lot of respect. I think they know I'm here to deal with a problem.

The fish was amazing by the way.

This place is insanely isolated. I'm having a hard time figuring how a vamp ended up here. Hoping it's not something else, like a revenant. Not sure what the local necrofauna situation is. If it wasn't some sort of spontaneous event, it would have to be a creep that came over on a freighter, but I'm having trouble believing a vamp could make a trip this long, undiscovered, on a small ship. Hopefully, details tomorrow.

3/2/25 11:00 pm.

This was a busy day. I met my contact, claimed to be an ex-USAID guy, pretty sure he works for the company, Malcom. Muscular, mid-thirties white guy with longish blond hair and a Hawaiian shirt. He had a local cop with him, Tataro. Tataro explained there's been 2 exsanguinations recently, both by the shore. One was a fisherman who'd (apparently) been sleeping by his beached boat, killed last week, and the other was a young widow who'd been drained at her home three nights ago.

The victims were found several miles apart, and didn't seem to know each other. Both bodies showed signs of violence—neck bruising and bloody fingernails on the fisherman, and shoulder bruises and torn hair on the woman. I think she was jumped in bed, while sleeping on her stomach.

Seems like a fresh vamp. The suck wounds were pretty ragged, no sign of fangs yet, and the violence seems to indicate a lack of charm powers. The really odd thing is the tracks I found in the sand—looks more like the vamp was crawling on its knees. If it's not flying yet, great, should be an easy kill, but why is it crawling?

Most of the tracks had been erased by the tide, so the vamp, if that's what it was, had been hugging the shore. We walked over a mile, but I couldn't pick up the trail. Not too many places to hide here, it's just an atoll with a few thousand people living here. I'm sure someone is going to see it soon.

We dropped by the hospital, and I took a look at the bodies. Tataro seems to know the deal, and he didn't ask questions when I asked to have the hearts removed. I didn't feel that cold around them, so I'm pretty sure they weren't going to turn, but I stuck around while the pathologist did her work. Bonus: windows in the morgue, and direct sunlight on the bodies as she cut.

I'm thinking this is a standard type 1 vamp. I ran into a manananggal once, in Manilla, and, seriously, fuck that. These subspecies can get positively nightmarish.

I still don't have my gear. I bugged Malcom about it, he said he'd look into it.

3/3/25

We got it. I mean, an old man took it out last night. I think his name was Karau. Lived with his extended family in a cinderblock house by the lagoon. He apparently found something killing one of his pigs, and he ran back into his house and got a...sword? It was made of bamboo and shark teeth, and, wow, I've never felt sorry for a vamp before. Pieces. He might as well have been using a chainsaw. I think the weapon was some kind of family heirloom.

I don't think Karau killed it though, no true decapitation. But he disabled it enough for the sun to kill it. The skin and flesh were black but not ashy, so I'm sticking with my fresh vamp theory.

But here's the odd part: both of the vampire's legs were severed below the calves. These injuries had been partially healed, but given the condition of the body, I'm not sure if he (30ish male, swollen features, black hair, fangs just starting) had lost his legs before turning, or if he was growing them back. That explains the weird tracks.

No clothes by the way. Not my first naked vamp, but one more oddity.

We did an "autopsy," and I had the heart burned. The pathologist seems to believe whatever Tataro tells her (in "Gilbertese") so I didn't get any pushback. The corpse doesn't seem to be local. Features might be Fillipino. (A sailor?) I took fingerprints and gave them to Malcom to see if he can ID them. If the vamp isn't from here, they're just going to burn the body and sweep the whole thing under the rug.

I'm going to stay for an extra week. Malcom suggested I stay on, said he'd talk to the church guys about paying for it. I like it here, it's peaceful, though a bit sad, because apparently this entire country is going to disappear as the sea levels rise because of global warming. I'm having the Order pay for my vacation, because, what if our vamp turned someone? I ought to know in a week.

3/7/25

This is seriously fucked up. I really thought I was done here. But this afternoon, a pair of fishermen caught something in their nets. It got all tangled up. They said it was moving, and they're really spooked about the entire episode, though I think Tataro has got them calmed down a bit.

The vamp—if it was a vamp—was apparently pretty weak, as I'd expect from any vampire in a body of water. Water seems to disrupt their link to the earth. Couldn't rip its way out of a hemp net. It got burnt by the sun, and died, just like our previous vamp.

Here's the scary part—and when a vampire hunter tells you something is scary, you better fucking listen: this vamp is also missing his lower legs, at roughly the same spot. I've got no idea what any of this means. Vampires swimming in the ocean? This just isn't a thing. And all amputees? I can see where someone might think it was sharks, but I've never heard of any animal that wanted to eat undead flesh. These wounds weren't healed at all, just ragged and torn. I've chopped up a lot of bodies in my day, and this was some seriously sloppy work. The leg bones looked like they'd been broken with a hammer. The flesh was blackened, but that just looked like typical sunkill damage.

I'm wondering if this is some unrecorded subspecies? Swimming vamps? But I'd expect some kind of adaptations, like in the tree vamps (Vetalas?) or the diggers. No webbed fingers, though the flesh is bloated and waterlogged.

I examined the body before I burnt it. No typical turning wounds in the neck or wrists. Once again, black hair, doesn't look Polynesian. These vamps seem to be real pushovers, but I really think I need to stay and get to the bottom of this. I took fingerprints again, and gave them to Malcom. If we can find out where these guys came from, maybe we can figure out what's turning them. And I'm not going to sleep well until we figure out the amputation thing.

Malcom is getting me another extension. I wish I could enjoy it, this place is beautiful. Shame I'm alone.

3/9/25

I think we've got some kind of infestation. Kiribati is made up of a couple of dozen islands, and, while I haven't heard of any more human fatalities, Tatoro has heard rumors of dead animals on one of the other islands.

Malcom said he hasn't got any hits on the fingerprints. Maybe I should have taken some genetic samples? I know vamp blood doesn't test, but I'm wondering if skin samples have any useful DNA? I should ask Rossini when I get back.

Tatoro and I are going to Makin Island tomorrow. Malcom finally brought my kit, so I'm properly armed. Honestly, I feel like I could take one of these guys out with a pocket knife, but I know not to get cocky. A cocky hunter is a dead hunter. I haven't forgotten Alabama.

3/10/25

Turns out it was just one dead goat, and it's pretty badly torn up, might have been a pack of dogs that got it. It seems pretty low on blood, but there's two possible scenarios.

A: A vamp drained it, and the dogs found it and ate the flesh. An older vamp would usually taint the meat beyond eating, but if this is a freshie, the meat might still be ok enough for a dog.

B: A local pack of feral dogs (yeah, it's a thing) killed the goat, and it bled out elsewhere, then they dragged it to the beach. Plausible.

Honestly, I'd be ready to let the whole thing go if it wasn't for the amputations. I was thinking, maybe some Filipino pirates found an infested ship, chopped up the vamps and threw them overboard. It could happen out here. But why not chop the heads off? And why such awful, saw and hammer style amputations? How did they not have a knife?

And why the legs?

3/11/25

Marakei atoll is very lightly populated and we're camping out in an abandoned thatched hut. We've got beer, fish and spam, cooking over a fire. The beach is great, and I kind of wish I knew how to surf. Honestly, I can't even really swim, so these boat trips make me a bit nervous. And these boats are old.

Funny that I never thought about retiring until I came here. With a career like mine, never really expected to live long enough to retire. But how am I going to retire? I've been paycheck to paycheck for over 30 years now. Not even paychecks—envelopes of cash from my clients. Never made enough to put away anything. Didn't seem to matter.

The church guys probably got bennies, probably listed as monks on paper. Or I could have got a job with my brother. Why did this seem like a better idea?

3/13/25

Malcom radioed and said they haven't heard anymore reports, but he still wants me to stay. As long as the money's coming in, it's a gig.

Tatoro has been teaching me boat stuff. I'm still afraid of open water, but I can now go from atoll to atoll without much trouble. We've been listening for rumors and police reports. I walk different beaches every morning, looking for dead animals and weird tracks in the sand.

Tatoro has to get back to work. They got me a little motorboat and a radio. I'm on my own.

3/15/25

I've been running out of islands. I think I hit 20 different beaches. This island is empty except for the remnants of an airfield and some gutted planes. There's a cinderblock hut that ought to be good for camping. I'm going to drag the boat inland a bit.

I'm tan now, and I lost my beer gut. The guys back home are going to be seriously jealous. Right now Frankie's probably doing a stakeout in Detroit, dodging gangbangers while hiding out in a crackhouse. I heard sometimes the gangs hire him to clear out buildings.

But I think I may have found something. At the shoreline, I found some weird tracks. Dents in the sand, smoothed over by the waves. Maybe someone was just digging clams, I'm assuming they do that here. But, maybe it was an amputated vamp crawling over the sand on hands and stumps.

I found a dead gull covered in crabs. Doesn't mean anything, gulls die. Everything dies.

I'm going to wait here tonight. The amputee thing is still driving me crazy.

3/16/25

I saw it last night! I was on the roof of the hut with night vision binoculars, and I saw someone by the shore, walking really slow. It didn't seem to notice me, I was downwind, and I stayed quiet. It wandered around a bit, then picked up something, and walked into the water.

If I just discovered a new species of vamp, I'm going to be the most famous member of the most obscure profession on the planet.

I checked out the shore in the morning. I found another dead gull, also covered with crabs. And more footprints. And they are footprints, kind of. I'm seeing toe prints, little toes, on weird, deep round dents. Weird little feet on what? The others looked mostly human. Maybe they've got weird feet and the locals cut them off? I'd buy that as a theory, but I'm sure Tataro would have told me.

I was going to call Malcom, but I don't want anyone else showing up. I don't want to spook it.

I'm going to get a lot of rest today. Tonight is going to be a big night.

3/17/25

In thirty years, I've never had a night like last night.

I was on top of the hut again, with the "binoculars," NVGs, a flare gun, a couple of flashlights, a panga and Bobby's old .44 magnum revolver with those bullets. I know, I know, never, ever hunt alone. It was stupid, but it made sense at the time. And I was wearing my kevlar pants and jacket, so I felt ready for it.

I was looking around, but mostly focussed on the same stretch of beach, and that's where it showed up. It slowly walked out of the ocean, carrying what later turned out to be a big rock. That's how it anchored itself to the seafloor, so it didn't float away and get weak.

I watched it stare at a tree and a gull flew down to the beach in front of it. We've seen this before. So, I knew it had the gaze. No problem, I can shrug that stuff off. I don't even need the mirror shades anymore.

I was waiting for it to start feeding, and I was going to run up and blast it. I hadn't noticed the wind shifting. Before it went after the bird, it suddenly turned and looked right at me.

I was a quarter mile away, but I'm sure it saw me. It was creepy as hell.

So, I was alone with this vamp, and I had no idea what it was capable of. I didn't think it could fly, but if this was a new species, I was in danger. And having the damned thing looking directly at me meant I'd lost my main advantage. I was thinking about just retreating into the hut. That much concrete and cinderblock would keep me safe. The door was steel, rusty but still solid, and the latch still worked.

I figured I could make it to safety before it got to me, so I just sat there for a while. We were both staring at each other. Finally, it started moving. I thought it would run to the sea, but it just slowly walked towards me. This freaked me out. This just doesn't happen. I've been sneaked up on, I've been stalked, I've been charged, but I've never just been approached. It walked slowly, awkwardly.

It seemed—you're going to laugh when I say this—it seemed rude to just wait up there. So I got down, checked my loads and waited. It took a while—she was slow—but eventually she made it to my camp. She walked up to within twenty feet of me, and she stopped. Yes, she.

She looked mostly human, except bloated. She was naked, like the others. She didn't really have feet, just toes growing out of some partially healed stumps. So, she'd had legs when she turned. She was regrowing her severed legs, nothing I hadn't seen before. She seemed to be a typical type 1 bloodsucker, not too old, but old enough to have the gaze.

With her swollen face, it was hard to tell her age. She was really short, but she'd get taller when her legs grew back. Black hair, fairly dark skin.

I noticed she wasn't making eye contact. That was really odd, because the first thing most vamps do is the gaze. I felt that she was trying not to use any power on me. This was, by far, the least threatening encounter I've ever had with a vampire that was aware of my presence.

She started making noises, almost like hisses and growls, then I heard the words. She was still verbal. Rare, but not unknown in a type 1. She pointed at me and asked "Supami? Supami?" When I held up my hands, I don't know what you're saying, she seemed to relax.

Then she started speaking in Spanish. My Spanish isn't great, but it was just enough. She asked me "Can you help me or can you kill me?"

That took a while, and much repeating, to get across. We were both getting frustrated, and I could see that dawn was approaching. I think she might have just stood there and dawned herself, but I needed to know more about her. Where she came from, how she got here, the thing with the legs.

I gestured for her to get inside the hut. She hesitated for a bit, then nodded and went inside. She saw my sleeping pad, and I pointed at it, and she laid down on it. She just looked at me, and stayed perfectly still, until the sun came up. Her eyes slowly closed, and she was dead again.

I knew I was safe now. The sunlight was as good as any wall. As tired as I was after an all-nighter, I cooked breakfast and thought. Malcom must have had church connections or US government connections, or maybe CIA connections. I wasn't really sure who he worked for, but I figure he needed to know this.

So, I was already planning on keeping her "alive" for a while. Actual communication with type 1 vamps was incredibly rare, though we've all heard the rumors that the church talks to elders.

I got on the radio, and got someone to wake Malcom up. He was still groggy when he answered. I told him, "I found a third one."

He cheered up immediately. "Fantastic. Did you kill her?" That's exactly what he said, and I'm glad I was paying attention. I got it so quickly that I only paused a moment before answering.

I lied. I told him "Yeah, I burned her up."

A second later he replied "All right. I'll come by in a couple of hours, we can recover the body and dispose of it."

The conversation was only making me more uncomfortable. I lied to him again. "No need, I used the thermite gun. She's dust. Just ashes."

He sounded a bit surprised. If he bought that, he clearly wasn't too familiar with vamps or blasters. He just said "Oh...Copy that."

I knew I needed to keep him away from her for now, so I told him I'd be coming in in a few hours. I needed time to think.

He had said "Did you kill her." Her. That meant he knew how many vampires were in the area, and he knew their genders. So, apparently, there were only two male vamps, who were already dead. How many females? I doubted it was that many, or they'd have called in additional hunters.

A scenario immediately came together in my head. I guessed there was a CIA lab on one of the nearby islands, or maybe on a ship. They were doing some kind of experiments on vamps, maybe weaponizing them again, like that thing we heard about in Guatemala. I was guessing that they cut off their legs to make them easier to manage, though I'm not sure why they just wouldn't use chains and cages.

I'm as patriotic as the next guy, but if the CIA or the military was weaponizing vamps, that shit needed to end right now. I've seen the kind of damage an infestation can do. That's not something to fuck around with. But, before I could do anything, I needed to talk to her at length. Which wasn't going to happen if the CIA or the military took her back or burned her.

So, I'm going back to Tarawa in a few hours, and I'll figure out my next move there.

Before I leave I'm going to leave a note that says "No Vamos." I think that means "Don't go."

3/19/25

Total shit show. Malcom is dead, and I might be next.

I went back to Tarawa and drank a beer with Malcom. He asked me what happened, and I told him I found her tangled up in some seaweed on the beach, and I dawned her then blasted what was left. "No remains?" he asked.

I told him that a blaster doesn't leave much. I thought he bought it.

He immediately suggested the job was probably done, it was clear he wanted to ship me home ASAP, but I told him I needed to stay another week, just to make sure this wasn't some kind of infestation. He didn't really have a good counter argument, so he agreed to get me paid and supplied for another week. I think his plan was to let me get bored and just go home.

The fact that he already wanted me home meant that there had only been three escapees. We'd found them all.

I went back to the airport, and I found what I needed.

I slept a bit, then returned to the island. I got there after dark. I found her waiting by the hut, feeding on a gull. She'd dried out quite a bit. Her flesh wasn't as swollen, and I could see that she was probably in her forties, with a trim build and long hair. She looked like she'd been really pretty once. She'd put on some of my extra clothes, and she looked almost human, if I ignored her feet.

I took out my new digital two way translator and started talking to her. It didn't work at first—the vamp thing with video cameras blurring out, it works with microphones and any digital technology as well. The translator couldn't hear her, so I'd repeat whatever she said, and write down the translation. She knew a smattering of English as well, so we managed to communicate.

WHAT THE ACTUAL FUCK. What she said was so much worse than my CIA lab theory. She was Mexican. She'd been an undocumented farmworker in Texas. She was busted by ICE and sent somewhere on a plane. I think she may have been describing Guantanamo Bay.

THEY MADE HER INTO A VAMPIRE. That's what she said. They strapped dozens of them down and ran blood into them. Clearly, they had a captive elder. This is so much worse than just killing them. She woke up on a submarine, and they were transported to some kind of underwater facility. Their job was to wander around on the seafloor and put rocks in baskets.

I've read about this. Some kind of metallic nodules collect on the ocean floor. They're really valuable. There's millions of tons of the stuff. A number of countries and companies have been trying to develop submersible robot tech to collect these rocks. Somebody who knew about the undead had a brilliant, cruel, insane idea. Vampires don't need air. You don't have to pay them. Apparently deep ocean pressures don't kill them.

You just need to make them, and keep them fed on animal blood to keep them docile. They bolted heavy steel boots to their legs, directly through the bones. This was to keep them from running or floating away. Underwater, they'd live, maybe, forever.

My soul felt sick hearing about this. What kind of fucking monsters could do this to human beings? Weren't their lives hard enough as migrant workers? To keep them in the cold and the dark, effectively forever, just to make a few bucks. With no sunlight, they'd work endlessly, denied even the dormancy they usually get in the day. Hell. It was hell.

Marisol, that was her name, she and a few others had decided to escape. Knowing what they were, and guessing that they'd heal, they found a piece of rusty metal and had the others cut their legs off. Then, in pain, helplessly, they just drifted with the currents.

All that time, going hungry. The first vamp, the man, clearly hadn't been strong enough to resist the hunger. Marisol, though, she was tough. Extremely religious, she was devastated in knowing what she'd become. She would have just dawned herself, and ended it, but there was a righteous fury in her, and she wanted to make things right. She wanted to rescue the rest of her comrades on the seafloor.

She drew a symbol for me. It looked like a fish, with SUPAMI written on it. It looked like a corporate logo.

By dawn, we'd spoken enough. She laid down and died again.

I still didn't know what to do, or how to fix this, but at least I knew what was going on.

So did Malcom. I figured that out when I turned around and saw him standing there, with a gun in his hand.

He just shook his head and said, "Doc, I thought you burned her."

I didn't say anything. What was there to say? He knew I'd lied, he'd find the translator and my notes. I didn't imagine that he'd let me live. Not when billions were at stake.

He was too smart to get within twenty feet of me. He was muscular, well trained, probably ex-military, heartless. He was also an idiot. He was trained to fight people. Humans. Anyone can fight a human.

I'd been fighting insanely fast vampires for thirty years. And I'd survived. And I had one more advantage: He didn't know what a blaster looked like.

My favorite anti-vamp weapon is made of two steel pipes, side by side. One pipe contains pressurized air, and the other is packed full of thermite and various pyrotechnics, with an igniter. It's a bad thing to be caught with a weapon like that, so the compact side by side model is designed to look just like a pair of binoculars. And, of course I was wearing it around my neck the entire time I was interviewing a vampire.

I'd like to think that Malcom knew everything, that he was completely onboard with all of it, because I've never killed a human before, and that asshole suffered as his face burned off.

I was in a mood, and I might have just let him scream, but I needed his blood, so I smashed his head and drained him into a rusty bucket.

It took a while to wake Marisol up. I wasn't comfortable having her drink human blood, that usually led to feral behavior, but at least she wasn't killing for it. I needed her feet to grow back, we had places to go and only human blood was going to fix that.

5/22/25

This is going to be one of the worst nights of my life, but I'm fine with it. I have to be.

It wasn't hard to track down Sub Pacific Mineralogical, LTD. SuPaMi. A fairly small startup, owned by ex-spooks, poised to become multibillionaires. I know they're having their major executive conference at their main office in Hawaii tonight.

Marisol is dressed like a caterer, and, with her use of the gaze, I don't think she'll have any problem getting in. I'm going to shoot up the place from the outside, and I'm sure they'll abandon the riffraff and all run to the panic room, where Marisol will be waiting, with a suicide vest.

I tried to talk her out of it, but she's ready. She knows what happens to her if she continues to live. I want her as my hound, as my friend, but not at the cost of her soul.

I'm going to miss her. If I survive this night, I'm done. I'm out of the game, and I'm going to find a quiet place, maybe find someone like Marisol, and we'll see what happens.

I'll mail this to you assholes before the fun starts tonight. Keep an eye on the spooks and the tech bros, I think they're ready to undo all our work. Make me proud. Gotta go. Bye.

HARUTO'S NOTES 7/24/2023

TO DO:

    REVIEW UNTYPED DOCUMENTS
    ORGANIZE NEW RECORDS
    EMAIL VAMPA MUSEUM ABOUT 17TH CENTURY STAKES
    CALL KAY AGAIN
    NEW CYNTHIA BLEDSOE FILES
    TRANSFER FUNDS
    TALK TO MAI ABOUT NEW BREED

*I'M NOT SURE WHAT'S COMING, BUT THE HUNTERS ARE CALLING EVERY DAY. I THINK WE'RE IN FOR SOMETHING REALLY BIG.

Acknowledgments

Thanks are due, and as we release our eighth anthology under the Spec Pub imprint, we would like to acknowledge the following for their support and contributions. First, the authors for trusting us with their exquisite stories.

Our never-ending appreciation to Susan Tulio, proofreader extraordinaire and support dynamo. We're thankful for her sharp eyes and her friendship. Thank you to Chris Bauer for always keeping us informed on the local haps, and to Ef Deal for being our most vocal encouragement. To Mel Sullivan for pushing local indie authors, and to the Doylestown Bookstore for making Bucks a great place for the arts.

Thanks to Alan, Dave, Antonia, Mike, Claire, L.C., and the gang from the SW publishing group for navigating the thorny tree that is indie publishing and offering help and support. The Philadelphia Writers Group and Eric Smith for his tireless dedication in supporting Philly authors. And for the support of the HWA PA Chapter, and its amazing leaders, Ken, Amanda and Jacque.

Thanks to Nancy Holder and Vaughn A. Jackson for being the best vampire blurbers there are and all around cool people.

Thank you, Ed Crimi and Megan Flannery at the Vampa museum in Doylestown. You have done amazing things in the last year, and we are so honored for your help and support. Bring on the Vampires!

A great thanks to all the friends and colleagues we've met over the past year at conventions and events, from Bucks County Paracon to the World Fantasy Convention in Niagara. We've been blessed to meet, hang out with and work with terrific writers, editors, publishers and artists and have learned something new at each event to keep us moving toward our writing and publishing ambitions.

And as always, to our readers. We at Spec Pub create and produce a special kind of terror and fantasy, and we're so pleased you keep coming along for the ride.

For more information on Vampa, the Vampire and Paranormal Museum, go to:
https://www.vampamuseum.com/

(We highly recommend this place if you are a paranormal fan, a history fan, an antiques fan, or an amazing architecture fan)

About the Authors

LCW Allingham is an award-winning Philadelphia area author, artist, and editor, and a former dive bar rock star.

George K. Angelou is a published author of short speculative fiction. He's currently putting the finishing touches on his first science fiction novel, and also runs the YouTube channel Write Like a Legend, where he analyses the literary techniques used by his favourite authors.

Juno Crew is a college student studying to be an English middle or high school teacher. He writes horror, fantasy, and romance, using these genres to explore queerness, mental illness, and other social issues. Juno believes writing and language have the power to help others find themselves and feel seen. When not writing, Juno can be found with his nose buried in a book, working on several different sewing projects, or playing D&D.

Artist **Sarah Doebereiner** is from central Ohio. Macabre themes fascinate her because of their tendency to stay with readers long after the book has closed, but the joy in short fiction and artwork is the opportunity to try out all kinds of genres.

William J. Donahue's published works include the novels Find Your Way Back to Me (October 2025), Only Monsters Remain, Crawl on Your Belly All the Days of Your Life, and Burn Beautiful Soul. His short fiction has appeared in The Horror Zine, as well as in the horror anthologies Cry Baby Bridge, Heavy Metal Nightmares, and House of Haunts. He lives in a small but well-guarded fortress somewhere on the map between Philadelphia and Bethlehem, Pennsylvania. Although his home lacks a proper moat, it does have plenty of snakes.

River Eno is managing copy editor and co-owner of Speculation Publications. She writes dark-erotic fantasy novels—The Anastasia Evolution Series—and horror-adjacent short stories—usually with a bend toward paganism or pagan archetypes. Residing on the east coast with rescue dogs, old turtles and family; River is vegan, a practicing solitary witch, and an herbalism enthusiast with polyglottal aspirations.

Henry Herz has written for Daily Science Fiction, Weird Tales, Pseudopod, Metastellar, Titan Books, Highlights for Children, Ladybug Magazine, and anthologies from Penguin-Random House, Albert Whitman, Blackstone Publishing, Third Flatiron, Brigids Gate Press, Air and Nothingness Press, Baen Books, and elsewhere. He's edited nine anthologies and written fourteen picture books.

Mina Humiston was born and raised in Southern California. She loves historical fiction, historical nonfiction, and ghost stories. After reading Dracula in high school, she became especially enamored with gothic horror. She has previously published poetry in Sylvia Magazine.

Gwendolyn Kiste is the three-time Bram Stoker Award-winning author of The Rust Maidens, Reluctant Immortals, Boneset & Feathers, Pretty Marys All in a Row, and The Haunting of Velkwood. Her short fiction and nonfiction have appeared in outlets including Lit Hub, Nightmare, Best American Science Fiction and Fantasy, CrimeReads, Tor Nightfire, The Lineup, and The Dark. She's a Lambda Literary Award winner, and her fiction has also received the This Is Horror award for Novel of the Year as well as nominations for the Premios Kelvin, Ignotus, and Dragon Awards. Originally from Ohio, she now resides on an abandoned horse farm outside of Pittsburgh with her husband, their excitable calico cat, and not nearly enough ghosts.

D.C. Kugtima is a highschool dropout, Hollywood technician, patented inventor, ski-biker and medievalist who's recently been published in a few other anthologies. He lives in Long Beach, California with his lovely (and patient) fiancee and a pair of lovable but disobedient maltipoos.

Camellia Landman is a freelance editor and writer from Michigan. After earning a Master's in Publishing at New York University, she has been focusing more on her own work and is set to have her first short story published in the Madame, Don't Forget Your Sword anthology in May 2025. She can usually be found typing away at the coffee shop or pitching ideas to her husky, Zeus. When she's not writing, she's creating elaborate Dungeons and Dragons campaigns to excite and enrage her friends.

Carter Lappin is a Californian author. Her works of fiction have appeared in publications such as Brigids Gate Press, Manawaker Studio, Air and Nothingness Press, and Sunlight Press.

Caolán Mac an Aircinn is a translator, classicist and writer from Dublin, Ireland who publishes both in English and in his native Irish. When he is not working or writing, he enjoys playing the Irish fiddle and bothering his cats.

Hope Madden is an award-winning writer, filmmaker, and film critic based in Columbus, Ohio. Her first novella, Roost, published in March of 2022 with Off Limits Press. Her short story "Aggrieved" is featured in the 2022 feminist horror anthology Incubate, from Speculation Publications. She's had three shorts published in 2024 and 2025 by Wicked Shadow Press: "Meat" in the anthology Flash of the Dead: Requiem; "Clown Wanted" in their seasonal anthology, Flash of the Dead: Halloween; and "Customer Service" in their 2025 anthology, Petting Boo. Also in 2025, her short story "Consumed" will appear in the Arbutus Studios anthology Consumed, and "Birds and Beasts" is featured in the Speculation Publications anthology Vampire Hunters: An Incomplete Record of Personal Accounts. Her second novella, Killer Pictures, is out in 2025 from World Castle Publishing. Her first feature film, Obstacle Corpse, is now streaming on Amazon Prime.

TT Madden (they/them) is the genderfluid, mixed-race author of The Familialists and The Cosmic Color, who refuses to keep "politics" out of their writing. Their work in scifi, fantasy, and horror often deals with the intersections of their various identities. Their forthcoming novellas include the queer body swap horror Student Bodies with Little Ghost Books, the YA horror Gorman's House, with Mad Axe Media, and the queer, religious horror The Neon Revelation, with Timber Ghost Press.

Lee Meeder retired from the practice of medicine specializing in Anesthesiology in 2022. He immediately increased his time spent on exploring his creative side, including story-writing, screenplay writing/modification, acting, improvisation, music, and standup.

A.R.C. Mitra writes gothic horror, ghost stories and retold fairy tales and folklore. She is currently based in New York City. Her work has been published in anthologies by Hear Us Scream Press, Morian Press, Love Letters to Poe and Quill and Crow Publishing House, as well as in Speculation Publications' Incubate: A Horror Collection of Feminine Power.

She has also been published in Dark Moon Digest, The Fabulist and Allegory.

Bill Mulligan has taught high school science for over 25 years. Outside of school, he makes indie films and podcasts with his friends. He wrote the screenplays for such award winning short films as 400 Ways to Kill a Vampire, Emotional Support Demon, and Belladonna. His first novel, Raum, was published by Falstaff Books in 2023.

Nico Martinez Nocito (they/them) writes speculative fiction and poetry with a queer, feminist bent. Their work can be found in Strange Horizons, Utopia Science Fiction, and Flame Tree Press, and has been nominated for the Rhysling Award.

Dale Parnell lives in Staffordshire, England, with his wife and their imaginary dog, Moriarty. He writes fiction, mainly fantasy, sci-fi and horror, along with the occasional poem, and is featured in over sixty excellent anthologies from a variety of independent publishers. Dale has self-published three collections of short stories, and his debut novel PYR, a science-fiction space opera, is available now. Dale is currently working on a follow-up to PYR, and his strangest wish is to find a copy of one his books for sale in a second-hand bookshop.

Toni Owen-Blue is a writer and artist who lives in the UK. She is best known for her interactive fiction apps, which include "Halfling Dale" and "Waytales – Steps Unlock Story".

Johan Robertsson writes spooky, twist-filled fiction with an inky drop of magic. He left marketing behind, sold off years of curious collections, and now lives in historical Lund, Sweden—where he gets mauled in BJJ, slowly loses his hearing to audiobooks, and bikes around looking for lights in the sky.

A.C. Wise is the author of the novels Wendy, Darling, Hooked, and the forthcoming Ballad of the Bone Road (January 2026), along with various collections, novellas, and short stories. Her work has won the Sunburst Award, and been a finalist for the Nebula, Stoker, World Fantasy, Shirley Jackson, Locus, British Fantasy, Aurora, Igynte, and Lamba Literary Awards. In addition to her fiction, she contributes regular review columns to Locus and Apex Magazine.

For more information go to
www.speculationpub.com/authors

The Collections of Utter Speculation
The Lost Colony of Roanoke
The Jersey Devil
Lady in White
The Dancing Plague
Cry Baby Bridge
Novellas of Utter Speculation
Pay the Piper by Sarah Connell

Winter Lore Series
Yule : Tales of Winter Solstice
Evergreen : Tales of Winter Shadows
Aurora : Tales of Winter Dreams

Our other Anthologies
Incubate: a horror collection of feminine power
Beach Shorts
Grimm Retold

And our other books
Work in Progress: Story Crafting Notebook
Muse
Love, War and Eternally Damning Prophesies
The Hollow

www.speculationpub.com

www.ingramcontent.com/pod-product-compliance
Lightning Source LLC
Chambersburg PA
CBHW032343310726
48973CB00007B/1837